3.50

**Dangerous new ideas
from a gifted child . . .**

. . . cleverly concealed in
a flash-flood of action, emotion
and innocent excitement !

Dangerous new ideas:

About humanity, aliens
and technology !

About war, weapons
and tactics !

And ultimately, about the effect
violence has on children,
as seen from the eyes of a child.

Cover photo by
JonnicTee

Cover sculpture by
Neil Lee Thompsett

Becoming Human

by
Neil Lee Thompsett

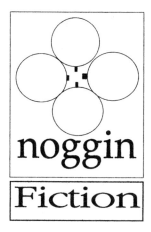

noggin

Fiction

Becoming Human

ISBN 1-892412-05-5

FIRST EDITION
MAY 1998

Published by
noggin
Galactic Headquarters
289 South Robertson Blvd, Penthouse Suite 880
Beverly Hills California, CA 90211

To order

Copies of this book are available for US$5.00 plus US$2.00 for shipping and handling. Write to the above address and include payment in full. (Don't forget this last part).
Make out cheques to: Neil Lee Thompsett
(Prices subject to change without warning)

Warning

Weasel words

This is a work of fiction.
Any resemblance to any person, living, dead or unborn, or any locale or event in the past, present or future is entirely coincidental.

And any attempt to claim otherwise is just plain stupid.

To my mom,
who is responsible
for me becoming human
in the first place.

And who is
the most beautiful alien
in all the world.

Introduction

Humanity is like a bacteria colony in a petri dish. It will grow madly, without thought of consequence, until all of its resources are exhausted. Then it will die . . . or escape the petri dish.

For the careful scientist, one thing to always keep in mind in the last stages of bacterial growth is this: never uncover the bloody petri dish.

Once upon a time, down a far dead-end alley of the universe , an insignificant solar system with only one fertile planet began to erupt with life. Timid creatures, curiously well evolved for this planet, peeked out from their homes high in the trees. They spoke a complex language and had legends of other times and other places but for now they had a more pressing need: they were hungry; they were naked; the trees were full of different but similar creatures, covered with fur and the fruit was scarce. A few of them, over time, cautiously went down and stood on the ground, then naturally rose to balance on two feet. There was food aplenty for those who could run and think. And they multiplied.

This lifeform called themselves the Human Race, and when food was good, they multiplied. And when it wasn't, they changed their way of living to make it good. Or changed the world to suit their way of living. And nothing - not even heaven itself - could stand in their way.

Over time their environment was thoroughly infected. Even they, in their arrogance, began to fear that they might have reached the limit of their part of the petri dish. So they had to go and live on other parts of the dish - parts they had never been able to reach before - the planets and moons closest to their home.

The moon was first, but it was only a stepping stone. They trod on it briefly to make their large leaps to other stones in the great petri dish of space.

The Planet Mars was the first true planet to be colonized by humans. The closest planet to Earth both in distance and in environment, Mars was the easiest leap to make. Although it wasn't particularly hospitable to humanity, it wasn't totally hostile, either. It presented not much more trouble than living at the South Pole or at the bottom of the sea. The only troublesome part was in getting there, but it took no more than a bit of hardship, a bit of money, a bit of time. The usual story.

Soon the Martian Colonists became adolescents and, like many growing colonies before them in human history, claimed their independence over a long war. The same happened on the moon. Suddenly there were three separate sections of the petri dish growing like mad and competing for the same resources in the Solar System.

Over hundreds of years the many countries that had existed on Earth became taken over by three major nations. Japan owned all of Asia. The British Empire took over all of Europe and Africa, and America took over Canada, Mexico and South America. Each became more isolated, more corrupt and more paranoid. The Earth factions, as well as the independent colonies, fought over and fed on the resources of the remaining planets to save their particular way of life. Settlements on the moons of Saturn and Jupiter and even the lonely planet of Pluto were ravaged and destroyed in terrible wars and environmental rapes. Some planets, like Jupiter, Saturn and even Venus defied their technology, but everything else was fair game.

After they took all the resources that they could get, they were left with a dying solar system. The limits of the petri dish had been reached. Then, just when they needed it most, the lid came off.

Mercury was the only unmined place left that they had the technology to exploit. The Colonies and the main players on Earth all arrived at the same time. As usual, with this form of life, war broke out. In the struggle, for supremacy, planet-busting mining explosives were combined with nuclear technology and Mercury was hit such a whack, that it was driven right into the sun.

Much to the surprise of all, it went right through and left a clearly visible hole right in the middle - leading to who knows where.

True to their monkey nature, humans couldn't resist it. They toyed with it for years. They came close, and jumped away. They sent probes at it. They sent people at it. They sent bombs at it. But none even got close for decades without being burned by the sun's tremendous heat.

Suddenly a new technology was developed. A heat superconductor. The hotter it got, the more it funneled the heat into the engines, so the faster the ship went. By the time a HotSoup craft neared the Sun, it was going faster than the speed limit some said. No-one knew. Like much of human technology, it wasn't perfectly understood - but it did work. The Humans saw this as another gateway to a new universe of resources. They observed it for months at a time sending more Hotsoup probes and waiting to see if the hole would disappear.

But not one probe ever came back nor was one even heard from. Theories abounded. Then, suddenly, years after the first HotSoup probe went in, pictures started coming back from the probe. It had travelled so far that, even at lightspeed, it took years to send the signal back through normal space. The humans theory was correct. It was a way out to a universe full of lands and resources.

The lab was about to be infected.

After the news spread through the Moon, Mars and Earth, giant HotSoup ships were built and sent into the wormhole. Since there were no resources left, virtually everything on the planets were recycled to build ships in their millions. Like a disturbed anthill in space billions tried to leave a dying solar system. Thousands of ships left every day not knowing if they would ever return to Earth - either the journey would be too far, or the wormhole only worked one way or might collapse as easily as it opened. For whatever reason, no ship ever counted on returning - and there was very little to return to.

Some ships were carrying colonists but most were carrying the common cargo of conquest - military weapons, land vehicles , troops , space fighters, air planes and all the other building blocks of war.

This was the paradise that the Humans hoped for, an endless petri dish - and an eternal expanse of nutrient - infinite universes of it - to restart a new life, and to stop worrying about overpopulation. The only problem they faced were the aliens that lived on these new planets. The Humans didn't know if the Aliens were hostile or peaceful. If they would be welcoming or warlike. Friends or enemies.

But it was not a serious problem. Humans have always had the perfect solution for these kinds of situations. It was a strategy arrived at by all the human factions, almost at the same time, without any consultation at all.

It was a simple and elegant strategy: and only required two words that are common in every human language:

"Kill everything."

Chapter **1**

The Invasion

*"What we fear are the things
that we do not understand... "*

Dear diary, I wish monsters would invade or something - I'm sooooooo bored . . .

It was a common day like any other; the three moons
were showing in the reflection of the sun; the population
in the colony of the Degos system were as happy as ever.
Tonight was to be the anniversary of the Treaty of Degos
- 4000 years of blissful peace.

Ah-ztes , the young one recording in the diary was
the son of the Planet Ambassador, Ah-Denos. Lately Ah-
Denos had been spending a lot of time on Congress Moon,
helping to organize the treaty renewal service and Ah-
ztes was bored.

He quit recording and began thinking about the big
celebration that would start tonight. He hoped that the
old classic saucer-fighters would drop celebration plasma
bombs, they were so exciting to watch! Maybe they'd let

a few off early just to practice and Ah-ztes would have something to watch, instead of being stuck recording stupid stuff in some lame dairy. His friends all had jobs to do for the celebration but not him. The son of the Ambassador couldn't do ordinary work. He had to do extraordinary work - but unfortunately there was none of that available - at least none that Ah-ztes was qualified for. Well, maybe putting it all down and making a permanent record in his diary - for the billions who couldn't be here. He'd taken pills that had rearranged his molecular structure so he was in direct contact with the Recorder, the biggest database in the world. The diary was remotely connected right to his brain and not only recorded sights and sounds, but smells and the emotions he felt during each part of the celebration - he hoped he wasn't bored by his father's speech - billions would be yawning. He sighed and went back to work, just thinking of recording again made it so. He felt, in his mind, that the machine was working and tried to spice up his report.

"Last night I had a dream; "he thought - recalling it for the recording; " I was in my bedroom and I heard a big rumbling and then the outside went from darkness to brightness I felt my body being risen out of my window and into a strange little room where I became a monster."

"Being risen" is not grammatically correct" flashed a thought in his mind from the Recorder - which was buried somewhere in the capital city. "Shall I correct this segment ?"

"No" Ah-ztes thought, stubbornly. "What do you

know - you're buried under a mountain - you don't get out much. People talk differently than they did in the Dark Ages."

"Young Ah-ztes" said the voice of the recorder in his mind; "I have been conscious for all of the 4000 years of the peace - and for 16,000 years before that. I am aware of the uses of the language, both in the past and in the present and, by extrapolation, some ways into the future. So my advice . . ."

"Wow- that long" said Ah-ztes. "Did you ever run into the humans ?"

"I did"

" Today in class I learned about humans, their nature, what they look like, their civilization and thinking possibilities." Said Ah-ztes. "I learned that they are the most dangerous types of animals alive ! I heard that they were quarantined behind the Ultimate Wormhole in a solar system so far away that they could never travel to civilization again. I also learned that if you run into one than you must act afraid and no matter what they do, you don't fight back. Then they will realize you are a civilized being and let you be."

"Rubbish" said the Recorder

"Schoolcast " insisted Ah-ztes

"Still rubbish" said the Recorder. "The humans are carriers. The disease they carry is called violence. It is unknown among the civilized worlds today, but I have seen it first-hand. It cannot be described. But I tell you the schoolcast was right in one thing: you must be afraid. Be very afraid. For if you should ever run into a human, it will mean the end of life as we know it."

"Are they so very different from us ? They're intelligent aren't they ? They build civilizations and have technology don't they ? They even look like us - isn't that right ?

"All the races of the civilized world look similar. Some are grey. Some are green. Some are white. Some are short, some tall and some middle sized. But all are totally hairless and have the beautiful big teardrop eyes that you have."

"Humans are not like that ? I thought they were bilateral bipeds. . ."

"They have hair. Pelts. Like animals. Small eyes."

"Ewwww. Really "

" Loud voices. They need them because they can't link - they can't think and have that thought communicated to another being without saying it out loud - like children or handicapped people , and, if they have no-one to kill or maim, they will actually kill and maim each other."

"Why"

"They need no reason. It is the disease they carry."

"That can't be. It defies all reason. You're just too old, Recorder. Everything scares you"

"Everything about humans does . . ."

He disconnected his mind from the Recorder in midsentence. He went over what he had recorded - viewing it on a hand-held machine rather than in his mind and checked for mistakes other than grammar. Then he put the contraption down.

"Ah-ztes ? Go to the replication box and get some

tampa eggs, we're fresh out." said a musical voice.

He looked at his mother from head to toe and smiled. She was so pretty in his mind. He wanted to add her to the diary, so he connected his mind to the Recorder.

Just then the sky lit up.

"Ohhhh " thought both he and his mother at the same time.

"It must be the plasma bombs. The celebration has begun."

After he had recorded her, he nodded his head to shut off the Recording and went outside the dwelling place to the large community replication box. He watched the sky and saw huge blasts of light all around. He was happy.

He opened the decompressent doors on walk-in box and went inside, thinking about the dullness in the color. He recorded some ideas to improve the color of Replicators, so going in wouldn't be so boring. He thought of tampa eggs and, when the box created them from random molecules, made sure his hands were underneath them, ready to catch. He had dropped too many in the past to make a mistake now. He recorded his pleasure at catching all of them. He walked out of the box and, hands full, kicked the closure on the decompressent doors. They shut with a hiss.

Suddenly, the most frightful thing came directly at his leg - a beam of pure pain. He instantly tripped over something and fell to the ground in agony, throwing the eggs all over the place.

He knew there was something wrong with his right leg and something sharp was sticking out of it. He had rolled behind the replicator and lay in the bushes, trying to see the damage to his leg, but it was too dark in his little hidey hole. He looked back to see what he had tripped over - it was a body. Dead and mangled.

He looked to his left and saw some sort of beings grouped together like they were an animal pack. They were tall with fur on their heads - hair -and their head size was quite small. Small eyes too. Mean eyes. And they all carried machines in their hands. Humans! Right here!

"Be very afraid" the Recorder said in his mind. "Don't move"

Ah-ztes wasn't afraid. He was fascinated. They had killed, with no reason. And would have killed him to but for a lucky break.

"They likely thought that other one was me - they didn't realize they had hit two separate people" he thought on the Record.

They came up to the body - it was a female from a nearby dwelling, Ah-ztes realized. He could not think of her name.

The humans came and grinned, they laughed then spat on the female - her name was Ah-wy, he now remembered and said a prayer for her.

The humans left the poor body of Ah-wy and ran to Ah-ztes dwelling. He heard three loud noises then his mother screamed.

"Could they actually have hurt her?" he wondered to the Recorder.

"They have killed her" the Recorder said in his mind.

It was like a physical blow. Ah-ztes couldn't breathe. "Why would they do such a thing"

"They are human. It is their nature"

The humans ran out of the house. The house exploded , They left, laughing and one, dressed all in bright yellow, said something that the others found very funny.

"Do you know what they say ?" he thought at the Recorder

"I know their languages. I know their thoughts. They said "The only good alien is a dead alien."

Ah-ztes could not speak or even think. He felt a strange emotion. He looked upwards to the sky and saw two giant bird-like flying machines dropping some sort of flaming fluid on the colony. As soon as it touched the ground the fluid exploded.

He heard screams from the colony and bangs in the air. They were all murderers and showed no emotion whatsoever !

He thought; "Why ever would they hate us so much? Why kill us for no reason ?"

"That is their way"

"I have seen it" thought Ah-ztes, "and still I cannot believe it"

"No civilized person can" came the thoughts of the Recorder. "It was the same before."

"They did this before ?"

"And before and before. Every few thousand years they break out like mad dogs and are smashed back into the stone age and a few survivors are put in some impossible-to-get-out-of place so they can mature. We build their prisons to include everything we know that will lead to intelligent growth. They are given everything necessary to attain civilization - they have everything we have, fresh air, water, flowers, birds, bees, predators, prey - even their day and night is engineered to be a standard day and night. Yet they always break out early. They invent some kind of technology long before they are old enough to handle it. They smash out of containment and come back home, like some mad and murderous nightmare child. Relentless. Unrepentant. Infecting everyone they come into contact with."

"I don't understand. What is this disease that they pass on to us?"

"Do you not have a strange feeling in your mind?"

"I do"

"Do you know what it is?"

"No. It is entirely new to me "

"It is the desire . . ."

"Desire?"

"The desire for revenge"

*   *   *

It was nighttime and he was starving, His neck was hurting and his leg was hurting and it was now swollen, with a jagged piece of bone sticking out of it.

The Recorder broadcast painkillers to him, but they were becoming less and less effective. He felt death coming towards him. He cried out in fear, then fell silent, even more fearful that they would hear him.

He thought, over and over, of the attack the humans did to his home and the settlement.

They wanted the land more than he or his people did. They would kill for it. His people would not kill to defend it. So there was no question of the outcome.

He kept hearing the screams from the babies , the burning of the houses and the humans laughing. He heard howling and imagined even more of them coming towards him. He felt like they were going to dissolve him and all his people into nothing.

He saw them feed on his dignity and his intellect, trying to break him and, in the end, he was broken. He let this new disease, this raw, red feeling, run right through him. It washed over his dignity. It ran through his brain like electricity gone wild.

His dream of being turned into a monster was coming true. He was fully infected now.

He lived only for revenge.

Chapter 2

The Great Alert

Through the sky came a ten-meter oval craft with propellers on the top of it. It came, landed on one of the landing ports then its engines turned off. The doors opened revealing red lights inside the vehicle.

A human dressed all in bright yellow - boots, pants , a supply jacket and a beret - stepped out of the strange craft and stood outside the Headquarters of the United Worlds. He looked up at the building than went into it. His metal-plated bootsteps were heard coming down the stairs and into the halls. A thousand bureaucrats stopped their work to listen and speculate among themselves in MindTalk. They all agreed: the urgent being was going to the main gathering room where the ambassadors from all the other worlds were waiting for the Degos congress to arrive.

"Where are the congressmen ? They never miss a meeting." was the thought that leapt among the minds of the Ambassadors of the Universe.

"What can they be thinking!" came another thought.

"Do they feel they can keep us waiting like Altrossian Warrets?" complained yet another.

The huge doors to the Gathering Room opened up and the ringing bootsteps were heard once more - this time coming right into the Gathering Room and down to the center - the Speakers Circle.

It was a strange being with a strongly built body, small head and fur on the top of it.

"@#^$#^&% $#@ ^&%$#" he said.

No one understood the being. "Give him a translator." thought one of the Ambassadors.

One of the servants came up behind the strange creature in yellow with a translator device. It turned, saw the servant and was startled, falling to the ground clumsily.

The Ambassadors were quite amused at the action.

The being was furious and pulled out a weapon. He pointed it at the confused servant and shot him. He picked up the translator roughly then started to talk into it; "Attention all you non-Human garbage! I am here as a messenger from the battleships right now that orbit your fertile planets! Since my people are a reasonable race I plan to make you a reasonable offer. We are here for your planets and we will kill for them. We have already taken out the colonies in your least populated planets and we are ready to attack any force that tries to go against us! Now we will let you evacuate to other planets but if you try to challenge us we will destroy your major cities."

The creature started to walk away, then turned and

spoke into the translator again. "Oh by the way , is there an Ambassador from the system you call Degos."

Ah-Denos, the father of Ah-ztes, stepped forward. He spoke aloud so the creature could hear. "I am the Degosian Ambassador" he said. "The members of my congress are not here, they've been delayed for some reason, but I can answer any questions you may have."

"Your team will not be arriving. "said the creature. "They were unfortunately vaporized during the discussions we had with Degos. And the only question I have for you is this - with no Degos, why do we need a Degosian Ambassador ?"

Ah-ztes' father shook his head in confusion.

"I feel the same" said the creature in yellow, pulling his weapon once more and pointing it at the shocked Ambassador. The creature looked a moment, but saw no fear in the huge eyes of the Ambassador. "An Ambassador without a country has no reason to live." The human grinned, then pulled the trigger.

A loud bang shot through the room. The Ambassadors all jumped in fright. The humans' grin turned into a loud laugh, then he walked out of the room.

The other Ambassadors looked at the dead one. They called for a paramedic but it was no use. The Ambassador Ah-Denos had died instantly after the shot.

Giant arguments started to fly throughout the minds of the Congress.

"The creature is insane !"

"How can a race like that be intelligent ?"

"It's not - it only speaks - it can't think."

"Is this the disease they call violence ?"

"What can we do to inoculate against it ?"

"Was that a human ?"

"No, they were exterminated 4,000 years ago."

"Could they have survived "

"Never."

"Could any race build a space-faring technology in 4,000 years ?"

"Impossible."

"There were survivors - but kept in quarantine for study purposes at the far end of the galaxy. "

"I remember - wasn't the wormhole closed. It would take ten thousand years to travel from here to there."

"Maybe these are survivors, kept in stasis."

"It spoke the current language as registered in the translator. The language of 4,000 years ago doesn't exist anywhere. If they were survivors, the translator would not have functioned."

"We must take affirmative action towards this massacre!"

"We can't let them have their demands. We can't just leave. Where would we go ?" came the thoughts of an Ambassador.

" SILENCE ! ALL OF YOU , STOP ARGUING." a powerful thought-voice drowned them all out instantly.

"Who thinks with such authority" came a timid thought from the group.

"I am your Recorder" said the voice, much less loudly now.

A chorus of mental "Ahhhhhs" swept around the

room. The Recorder was the personal name of the mythical Source - the huge living database that had become self-conscious 20,000 years ago and was said to be responsible for organizing the United Worlds and for keeping the many civilized worlds of the galaxy in touch and on track. It was the closest thing to God that the universe was aware of.

Although it seldom touched the lives of individuals at all, it was the reference guide for everything, from technology to play theory and was always directly in touch with a few select individuals out of the hundreds of billions in the galaxy. Most people - and even most of the high powered Ambassadors in the Gathering Room - had never had any contact directly, but all knew of this powerful Infobeing from story, legend and rumour.

"I am here in this troubled time to help."

"Are these really humans ? If it's really humans, we will have to unite to crush them. Again." came from the mind of one Ambassador.

"Is that a true story - I thought it was a myth"

"No, it was true. 10 thousand years ago we really did defeat the humans - and now, that they threaten us again, we must do it again - or be exterminated."

"How. We know nothing of war. Or violence." thought another.

"It is not war. We must be careful of this. War is very addictive. Consider it more medicine. This is a deadly outbreak of an almost unstoppable virus. We must find a cure. I am in direct contact with one of you - and, to make things easier, I command you to work with and through her for the duration of this outbreak."

"The Recorder means me." came a thought from behind them. The ambassadors turned around as one. They saw a stately old woman in some kind of battledress who came through the back exit door accompanied by two Degosians. The Ambassadors all stood in respect. It was Chairman Ah-Xento - one of the most respected minds in the galaxy, retired now, but still well connected among the centers of power and government.

She was holding something squat and dangerous looking.

"What is this device ?" came a random thought.

" A biogenic plasma gun - and one which has been recently fired. " she answered, sitting down in an unoccupied chair.

She put her plasma gun down slowly on a table and took off her cloak. The Degosians started to leave the rooms holding their plasma guns firmly.

"Chairman Ah-Xento, the Humans destroyed Degos. Your ship was there. How did you survive ?" thought one of the shocked Ambassadors.

" They opened fire on our ship, I lost my ship and most of my crew. We three survived in a pod. The Recorder helped us and showed us how to build these weapons to fight the humans.

They have now invaded my home Degos, they have taken over three of the settlements there and they move toward other planets every day. Thousands of their ships pour through the wormhole daily. They are taking hsotages and demanding land in return."

"Chairman - they have done more than that. According to the one who was here, they have totally destroyed all life on Degos. There is nothing left now"

"Gods. Really ? I had many good friends there."

" What will we do now ?"

"I am in constant contact with the Recorder." thought the Chairman. "We will have the ultimate reference in building a military technology quickly. We can be ready almost immediately and strike with weapons of destruction such as the universe has never seen - and be rid of these humans for all time. I only need your approval."

"We will show them not to pick a fight with us any longer." thought an ambassador.

"We must not be hasty. Surely we can reason with them. Violence, like that done on the floor this very day , is not something we can agree with or do ourselves."

"We all need you to decide now. As we speak, our people are suffering and dying. The only defence against force is a greater force. Do we go ahead now or not ?" thought the Chairman.

"YESSSSSS !" came the thoughtvote, but it was only slightly greater than the great chorus of "Noooo !" and this division would cause trouble for years to come.

"The YES vote takes it." declared the Chairman. "Now let me show you how we will defeat them . . .

. . . again."

Chapter 3

From a free boy to a slave

The morning came as fast as Ah-ztes could open his eyes. He felt terrible, his hope was gone and he couldn't see well. He looked up and saw two creatures standing over him. They cut him loose from his tangled, bloody clothing, then picked him up,

They were much taller than he was , they were even possibly human but he was too weak to run away and too groggy to care. Confusion and depression had hold of him fully.

The humans carried him into some land vehicle. and another human, sitting in front of him, aggressively grabbed his head and strapped him down.

The human took out a needle and injected something into Ah-ztes' arm.

"What is it ?" Ah-ztes asked in his mind.

"Relax" came the voice of the Recorder, "They mean you no harm now"

Ah-ztes felt drowsy once more then blacked out. He regained consciousness around 3 hours later. This time he was in a different room where a bright light was flashing at him. A man appeared in white dressings with a mask over his face. Ah-ztes watched him carefully, recording everything.

The Human put some lenses on Ah-ztes' eyes then injected him in the leg. Ah-ztes felt a pull from his leg but he felt no pain. He felt a cold piece of metal being placed into his leg.

Suddenly the lights turned off and he was carried away. He was put on to a wheelchair and rolled off to the hallway area. The lights in the hall were dim so he couldn't tell if it was a human habitat or not.

The doors crashed open to the outside of the hall. He saw the sunlight shine outside the doors, but the chair stopped suddenly, just inside, and the human, who had been pushing him walked in front of him.

The Human's face went into the light and Ah-ztes saw his thick eye brows, his fur on his head then the body build. Ah-ztes finally knew for sure that the creature was a human and Ah-ztes was shocked.

The human took Ah-ztes' hand and shouted in some sort of spoken language. "!@#@@!^^%#&** ()^%$#<^ @%&%#%&" the human said.

"We've fixed your leg, alien scum - now you can work for us." translated the Recorder.

The human looked down to Ah-ztes' legs and back up to his eyes not knowing that the alien boy was in contact with anyone. He looked into Ah-ztes' face then grinned Ah-ztes looked at his own leg to see what the human was looking at. He saw his leg and let out a shocked cry. He had no leg. It was now artificial, The human dumped Ah-ztes out of the wheel chair and threw him out the doors. Ah-ztes hopped out, fell down the steps and saw the outside.

He was still in the settlement.

The buildings were partly destroyed, and there were humans everywhere he looked. They were all dressed the same and all had weapons. A few of the residents, under Human supervision, were working. Others were lying beaten or even dead.

Ah-ztes let his head drop to the ground in shame. He couldn't believe that the primitive race called the Humans could take over a civilized planet within an hour or two.

"Why not " asked the Recorder in his mind. "You have no defenses, you don't know how to fight. You abhor violence. I'm surprised it took that long."

A Human came up to Ah-ztes and helped him up then began pushing him toward an old manufacturing chamber. When the door opened he saw the residents in chains, pulling broken tanks around and making things.

The human took Ah-ztes down to the basement. The decompressent doors opened up and there were other children his age sitting about, listlessly. The human threw Ah-ztes onto the floor then went back upstairs.

"Where did you come from ?" said a voice in Ah-ztes' head

" Are there any more survivors?" thought another.

" I don't know" Ah-ztes thought to the group. "I was wounded and knocked out. They cut off my leg."

A girl walked forwards towards the light. She was small, gaunt and beautiful. Her eyes were quite large and dark, and her skin was frail and smooth looking.

"I am Ah-Quasaferu, I am from the settlement on the other side of the Eclipse mountains." she thought at him, shyly. "My family have all been killed. All of us, here in this prison, share the same story about being wounded and captured."

Ah-ztes was shocked and walked forward. He saw other children, some crying and others having no limbs.

"They want us to work for them" Ah-ztes groupthought

"How do you know?" thought someone

"One spoke to me"

"You understand their howling?"

"No - I . . ."

"Do not tell them of your contact with me" thought the Recorder on Ah-ztes' private wavelength.

"Yes, I do understand them" He completed his groupthought. "I was studying it in ancient history when the attack came"

"Are these the same boogiemen humans of legends and tall tales?"

"Yes. The same - 10,000 years older - but I guess not 10,000 years wiser." thought Ah-ztes.

The group turned toward him, looking for answers. With his aristocratic bearing and his knowledge, he had become the natural leader for these confused children. It was a position he assumed without question.

The lights were dim and the air was stuffy. The

start of a new day led to another child dying of inatten-
tion. All the children, even Ah-ztes, wept openly at the
sadness and the unnecessity of it.

Three days passed for Ah-ztes. He had no water and
no food but what kept him going was his new friend, Ah-
Quasaferu, the girl from the Eclipse Hill Settlement. They
became such good friends that they didn't have to speak
much.

Ah-ztes was sitting down on a stool, looking at the
floor. Ah-Quasaferu was lying on the floor , trying to sleep.
She turned her head around and saw Ah-ztes and moved
towards him. When she was close, she knelt down and
talked to Ah-ztes silently.

" Ah-ztes ? Are you all right ?" she thought.

" No. I am the leader here, yet there is no place I
can lead these poor souls to. I cannot save you, either,
girl. What are you doing up anyway. Tomorrow might
be the day where the humans send us up to work. And
that can bevery bad. You need all the rest you can get"

"Tomorrow the humans are going to put us to work,
are you scared of what they might put you to do?" asked
Ah-Quasaferu.

" Yes - I guess."

Ah-Quasaferu smiled and patted him on the shoulder. she walked back to her side of the floor and went
back to sleep.

*   *   *

The morning suns rose and pushed back the dark

shadows of the three moons, the eclipse disappeared for another day and the labor day started.

" !#@#?" said a voice. "Get up Hoppy" the Recorder translated the human speech.

Ah-ztes felt a jerk on his shoulder. He opened his eyes and saw a human. The human grabbed him, pulled him to his feet and began taking him upstairs.

The basement doors opened and the human wanted Ah-ztes to go further up the stairs under his own power. The human kept poking him with an assault gun almost the size of Ah-ztes. Ah-ztes did not want to make any vital signs of aggression, he was afraid of dying here, for nothing, so he did what the human told him to do.

As he climbed the stairs, the first signs of the surface started to show up, the sunlight glared on the stairs and the railings. The human pushed Ah-ztes forward to the outside door. Ah-ztes stood still at the top and waited. He was too afraid of the consequences if he ran away.

The human came into the light. He grabbed Ah-ztes' hand and stormed off pulling Ah-ztes alongside of him.

" Where are we going ? Are you going to tell me where I will be working ? Speak up !" said Ah-ztes out loud - the words supplied by the Recorder.

He received no answer. The human stopped at the old factory which once created biogenetic machines and materials .

" What are we doing here ?" asked Ah-ztes.

The front doors opened up and Ah-ztes saw many children working on the pressing molds and moving large containers around. Another human came up to him. He looked at Ah-ztes and then talked to the other human quietly so Ah-ztes could not hear. The human that took Ah-ztes from the basement of the children, let go of him and left. The other human grabbed Ah-ztes by the shoulder and took him to a seat and firmly pushed him down into it. As Ah-ztes turned around to look at him, he attached some kind of badge on to Ah-ztes' over-shirt.

" The soldier that brought you here said you speak some Fanigalo. I don't, but with this translator I can talk to you and you can talk to me. I want you to separate the powder from the metal, After you are done call me and I shall give you your next task." the human grabbed Ah-ztes and put a thick tight chain around his neck. Then the human pushed him to the wall and took out a small box with a button on the top of it. The human reached out his hand, holding the small box near Ah-ztes' neck , and then pushed the button .

A buzzing sound started to vibrate Ah-ztes' neck , then a sharp painful electric pulse went through his body, paralyzing his artificial leg.

" This is just a sample of my power. Don't think that I am getting soft . The truth is that I don't give a damn if I kill you. Your leg should become functional within an hour."

He dropped Ah-ztes onto the floor and started to walk away.

Ah-ztes limped over to the chair and sat down. He was numb all around his body and his eye coordination began to become dark and weak. He saw burned cylinder containers with black powder around their outer rims.

His hands were shaky and he couldn't pick anything up. He got a hold of himself and started to work, cleaning out the capsules.

" Hey you , Give me some of your cartridges, and drop your drill at three o'clock."whispered a thought in his head. Ah-ztes looked down under the table and saw one of the residents crawling on his hands and knees.

" Who are you?" thought Ah-ztes.

The person gave him no answer -just held out his hand. So Ah-ztes took four cartridges and handed them over to the stranger. The stranger crawled away and ran into the shadows.

All of a sudden five residents ran out of the shadows. They started shooting the human overseers and ran after the few humans who escaped their surprise attack. The person who asked Ah-ztes for the cartridges ran to a fire pot of boiling oil. He put his hand up and threw the cartridges in.

A loud bang came after that and the person ran off.

The doors started to open, and seven humans ran into the factory carrying guns and wearing helmets. They pushed buttons on their cuffs.

Ah-ztes hid under the table thinking that he would get hurt in the cross fire. His neck started to tingle under the chain, but the tingle went away before it began to hurt. The control chains must have been damaged in the explosion or the one pushing the button was killed.

A resident stood up on the table and started to groupthink and gesture.

" We can't be pushed around by this inferior race !

It is time to call a rebellion. All of you could stay and join us or you could run away right now. Either way, we will not be pushed around by them. We have caught their violent disease and know the answer - you must become violent to fight violence - it is the only vaccine."

The humans ran into the backroom, pointing their guns at the person on the table.

Bang !

The table talker fired and a human fell to the ground with a bullethole in his chest. The humans looked to the right and saw the other band of aliens shooting at them. No strangers to violence and combat, they all immediately fell to the floor and pushed a table over for cover.

Without even conversing, they began to return a merciless fire at the armed residents. The table-talker was the first to fall. Soon most of the others were dead and those who weren't, were madly trying to reload.

" On the count of three we tear gas the bastards" said one of the humans. They all put on a mouth piece and one threw a giant grenade.

Clouds of smoke filled the room, More armed humans started to race in to the Factory. They dragged out the aliens that were forced to work there. They took the ones remaining who had had the the guns and tied them to posts.

A human walked in front of them and started to dictate. " You tried to form a rebellion against us and you lost. Because of their mistake, you all will suffer. But they will suffer most."

The human walked backwards, he rose his hand and

the other humans rose their guns, He chopped the air and the guns went off.

The residents tied to the posts now hung lifeless, their bodies filled with bullet holes and blood dripping out of every cut.

The humans backed away and started to lead the residents back to their cells and bunkers. They threw Ah-ztes into his basement, with the other children.

Ah-ztes crawled to the girl, who was sound asleep, and lay next to her. He looked at her, staring at her face. He kissed her softly on the cheek then went to sleep.

Chapter 4

The beginning of war

In the depths of the space close to the Shasta system, in the middle of nowhere was a small starship. It was half a mile wide and three miles long. There were bio genetic telescopes and scanners on each side. There were no weapons. The lights were red all around throughout the survey ship Shama.

The restless souls on the surveyship were homesick and tired. They were coming back from charting a new vortex worm hole which had opened up near the planet of Sivil and went through to a remote star. They had spent years exploring the system beyond the wormhole. They had seen the humans probing the gateway from the other side and they had takent he long way home rather than show the humans how to go through the wormhole.

" Hey Ah-Nawo? , who are you waiting to see when you reach Degos?" thought the room mate.

"Well I plan to see my brother Ah-ztes and my parents. Its been six years since I saw them you know." Ah-

Nawo replied.

" Oh , I hope to see my wife Ah-Seskem again. My son was just born about the time I left. I want to know how much he has grown and how much the settlement has changed."

Suddenly there was a giant rumble near their room. The ship shuddered and shook. The siren screamed on, the sound that all feared for it meant that this was not a drill .

All of a sudden both of them began to float.

"Oh my gods, the gravity went off " thought the room mate

"Don't worry. we can still make it to the escape pods," mind-shouted Ah-Nawo. Ah-Nawo grabbed the hand of the room mate, stepped on to the wall and jumped. Within a few seconds he reached the door leading to the outside hall from his room.

Ah-Nawo grabbed onto the handle of the door and to his room mate. "Now hold on to me" he said.

Another rumble happened . this time it came from the left side of his room. A giant explosion was heard followed by a couple more loud shots. All of a sudden there was a tearing sound, then the most unbelievable thing started to happen; the wall snapped in two. The air became colder and the oxygen became thinner.

"I can't hold on any longer" said the room mate .

" Don't give up on me soldier, we still have a chance to open the door." Ah-Nawo tried to pull the room mate up to him.

"Grab on to my shoulder, Try to reach the open

button for the door."

The room-mate climbed up Ah-Nawos arm and reached for the button and pushed it. The room-mate grabbed on to the outside handle of the door.

"Ah-Nawo, tell my wife I love her. That my last thought was of her." The room-mate looked in his eyes and let go - flying across the room in the suction.

"Don't do this." mind-screamed Ah-Nawos. "We can save ourselves."

Too late. There was no reply. The room-mates' mind was completely shut off. The vacuum of the room was becoming more powerful. It sucked the room-mate right across their former room, turning him into a frozen piece of ice before pulling him right out into space through the crack in the hull.

"Gods, I hope he was dead " thought Ah-Nawos. He was still in vacuum and his own skin turned from dark grey to pale, white as a ghost.

Ah-Nawos opened the door and pulled himself up. The vacuum became even stronger. Ah-Nawos quickly pushed the close button outside.

The vacuum became weaker and weaker, until it stopped.

Ah-Nawos fell to the floor. He looked around and saw fire coming out of the room bunker next to him. the hall was a mess, there were dead bodies in pieces every-where, the air was dangerously thin and the gravity was non-existent. He crawled up the wall until he could get his feet under him, then pushed off toward the escape pods. The air was terribly low in oxygen and extremely cold.

"Which pod is functional ?" he thought at the computer.

The computer flashed "None of the remaining pods are functional !"

Ah-Nawo panted and was losing all possible hope. He took a deep breath and found very little air. He began panting. Then he remembered the number one rule when dealing with computers - ask the right question.

"Any craft functional ?" he thought at it.

The computer started to quote another sentence in his mind - painfully slowly for Ah-Nawo, who was now holding his breath and starting to black out.

"One saucer fully functional."

"Where ?"

"Flight deck."

Ah-Nawo gained hope again then tried to fly down the ladder. It was clogged with bodies. He started to pull them out of the way. He struggled to breathe in the thinning atmosphere and started to feel dizzy.

"Warning!, oxygen exhausted." said the message computer .

The lights started to flash faster before his eyes as he pulled and ripped at the bodies of his friends. A scene from hell. His heart started to race. His dead friends were killing him. He cursed his friends, then started to climb down faster. Finally, the last body drifted away. He opened the decompressant doors to the docking bay.

There was the shuttle in perfect condition.

He bounced himself off the doorframe and flew

across the huge bay. He turned to hit the opening button for the outer gates in full flight and kept going.

"Open the shuttle air-lock" he thought, seconds before impact. It opened and he flew in, crashing against the inside wall.

"Shut and recycle" he thought, in a panic, before he could bounce right back out again.

"Warning! fifteen seconds till bay gates open." said the computer.

Ah-Nawo, floating in the air-lock and still holding his breath, started to feel even more dizzy. He couldn't see straight. Big blots of color were flashing before his eyes. He started to black out. He couldn't control himself - he had to breath. He gasped. Thank the Gods - there was air. The air became thicker. He started to be able to breathe more than pant.

He opened the inner doors of the lock and climbed into Command Position, strapping himself down so he wouldn't float away. He could see the outer gates had started to open. The vacuum suction started up again and loose objects on the flight deck began inching, then flying out into deep space.

Ah-Nawo started the engines up and the shuttle started to hover. A sudden jerk forwards reminded him that he was subject to vacuum suction too. He took control.

The gates were fully opened up now. He put the engines on full throttle and flew out of the docking bay. As he arced out of the bay and into space, the starship Shama - his home for the past 6 years - started to explode into little pieces. The outside was filled with debris and bodies.

A bright beam of light shot towards Ah-Nawos in his tiny shuttle. He wasn't sure if it was a weapon or an accident but decided not to take any chances. The cloud of all the exposed oxygen from the ship was everywhere. Loose debris and bodies were flying out in a huge circle. Ah-Nawo put the engines to full throttle once more and caught up with the leading edge of debris, then throttled back to match speed. He let go of all control and tumbled with the garbage - just another piece of flotsam.

Coming out of the starfield were thousands of starships of a design that he had never seen. They covered his entire field of vision as he tumbled with the remains of his ship.

They were present at every angle. No matter how the shuttle tumbled and turned, there was always a strange ship in his eyes.

All of a sudden , a swarm of small fighters came in from all directions, sniffing through the cloud of debris, looking for survivors. He could see them blasting a few bits of wreckage - perhaps killing more of his friends.

He did nothing, hoping they would not notice him in the great wash of bits and pieces. He realized that they were human and that his survey ship's cautious exit fromt he human system had been a waste of time. The humans had found a way throught he wormhole after all.

He knew now there would be no chance of a space rescue. He was afraid to signal anyone. His only choice was to crash land on one of the planets closest to him.

But it would have to be a barely uncontrolled crash, otherwise he would attract the deadly attention of the wolf pack of fighters.

He decided not to make a plan. Just to react to the moment. That way the fighters would see no logical pattern to pursue.

He crashed into the atmosphere of the desert world of Sivel, totally ignored by the massive force because he was smoking and flaring like just a million other pieces of flying rubble.

The whole shuttle started to rumble. The air became hotter. Without the fine controls needed for entering atmosphere, the shuttle started to burn up.

" Warning , wings lost, wings lost." said the shuttle computer out loud.

The small nose engines started, all of the main engines were shut down and Ah-Nawo dared not ignite them for fear of attracting the attention of the fighters, who were still lancing promising bits of debris with explosive beams of energy .

The gas tanks were burned away, flaring down and away from the shuttle.

Gradually the nose engines made a difference. The falling slowed, then almost stopped. The shuttle came down, nose first, into a sand dune, then the entire craft fell over, upside down.

Ah-Nawo opened the capsule. The door, which was now the floor, pushed open, rolling the entire shuttle over. This pushed it into a further roll which, when the shuttle came around again, ripped the door right off and spit Ah-

Nawo out on the sand. The outside of the shuttle was still on fire and burned brightly, sending black smoke into the sky to join the thousand other plumes which arose from other downed debris.

Ah-Nawo, in gravity now, slogged through the sand and back to the burning shuttle-craft. The whole glass screen was fractured everywhere and pitch black. Nawo looked around the cockpit for supplies and a weapon.

He picked up an acid beast shackle then carefully jumped out of the capsule.

He looked up to the glaring sun. Aboard a ship for 6 years, he was not used to the hot dry air. He took off his jacket and took a pill from the jacket pocket and placed it in his mouth. All of a sudden his eyes became darker and his skin changed to a bluish green.

Nawo started to walk in the direction of the sun.

*   *   *

High above, in that strange border between space and atmosphere, a fighter hovered, spewing gas from its nose to counteract the pull of the gravity well. "The target starship is no longer threat. Sir." said the pilot. "There are no survivors. Target practice is over lads. Cedi master returning to mother ship."

"Permission granted" said the radio.

The report was sent to the flagship of the human Pirate Patriots. It was named " Mayflower". On one side of the ship was a huge painted flag , showing sixty three stars printed on a blue square; on the other side was a picture of a skull and cross bones on sixteen red and white stripes.

This Mayflower, in contrast to its original 90 foot long namesake, was around three miles wide and twelve miles long. It was heavily armored with thick deposits of alloy. Giant cannons were all over each side of the ship, and there were six engines that were as big as towers. The ship was all machine with no color and no spirit of life except for the bright flags on its sides. The life inside was all dark, there was no gravity through out the ship. The cockpit lights were shining red, the crew were a mere ten live people. Hundreds of thousands, however, were in stasis, waiting to be called into action.

"Sir we destroyed a starship, most likely an alien battle ship." said the radio monitor.

" Damn ! They're trying to cause an attack towards us. They are insane. They have broken the deal that General Nevel Thomas offered. Now they must pay for their mistake."said the commander. "Change course to the planet they call Arotosa. We will take over the entire planet to show that we will not put up with any resistance."

*   *   *

The day was hot; the sun was throwing its most powerful heat wave. There was no wind to cool off and no water for as far as the eye could see. There were only deserted settlements and mountains of bright yellow sand. There was no one in the vast plains, no people, no visible life but that one creature who was walking alone in the desert.

Nothing moved. The area teemed with small scurrying life, but nothing moved now. All waited to see if the large creature would die or move on. All small creatures speculated whether it would be feast or famine for them.

" I've got to keep moving, I've got to keep going, I can make it !" The creature mumbled. He put himself in motion and walked further and further north, until he could walk no further.

He fell to the ground, breathing heavily and exhaustedly. Dozens of small, unnoticed things took a cautious step toward the fallen figure.

" I can't stop, I can't stop, I have to get up and go further!"

He closed his eyes to moisten them, then fell asleep.

One small creature, hungry and impatient, ran up to the fallen animal and prepared to take a bite. Suddenly a sandy boot descended and crushed the small predator with a sharp crackle. Other small creatures stayed motionless in the hot sun, waiting.

" Is he dead ?"said a voice out loud.

" He shouldn't be !"said another.

Then he heard no more.

The fallen one awoke, He saw no burning sunlight and noticed that the air was cool. He stood up and looked around. He was in some sort of cave. He noticed two people, strangely dressed, who started to back off as soon as he directed his gaze their way. They ran towards a door and went out .The doors closed and, as they did so, the lights went off. He was left in darkness.

" Who are you people?" he shouted out loud.

" Don't shout so loud, fool, you'll cause a cave in !" came a calm thought.

He turned around and saw a person sitting in the shadowy corner of the room, lit up by a small spotlight on the ceiling.

" Who are you ?" He sent a thought back

" I am called Ah-Drake, of the desert people, and you ?"

" I am Ah-Nawo. From the survey ship Shama. There was some kind of accident or attack or something."He sent a full mental picture of the attack and of his escape. "I think it was caused by humans."

" So you are the one crashing into the planet, well don't think that you 'll get any help from the people here, they are much too scared to go back to the surface after the invasion." said Ah-Drake.

"Invasion ?"

"Humans, like you say- an outbreak all across the outer systems.

"I know where they came from. There's a wormhole - one end of it is right here by Sivil. The other end comes out in their system. We found it and explored it and suspected it was humans, but it seemed too strange to be true. Humans ? That's like saying trolls . . . did humans ever exist ? And if they did I thought we killed them all thousands of years ago - in fact weren't we just going to have a big celebration on Degos - 4000 years of peace ?"

"They slagged Degos first, so the celebration is off,

I guess. Then they went on from there. More appeared
here. And we've heard they've appeared in other systems
too. Nothing but ruins and devastation behind them.
Theory is they're now headed for Arotosa . . ."

"My family was on Degos "

"Sorry. We've heard no word from them. We have
to assume there are no survivors "

"Doesn't your thought thrower work ?"

"It does"

"I thought the thought thrower people never left
their posts "

"They don't. That's why we're assuming no survivors"

" Who are these humans ? Why would they attack
us ? Do the joined forces at Congress.Moon know of their
attacks ?" asked Ah-Nawo.

" They do - we've gotten thrown thoughts from them.
Chairman Ah-Xentos is in full contact with the Recorder.
She's sent out thoughts on old weapons and fight-craft so
survivor groups like us can respond to this horrible
plague.

"Humans are here, too ?"

"I think they were here first - if, as you say the wormhole comes out here, then that explains it. They attacked
us without warning. They set up camps everywhere !
They now own the surface here. Only time will tell before they find us and kill us. They almost have control
over all of the United Planets, people are saying. I don't
think it's true, but it's coming if they continue like this.
Perhaps we can give the disease a bit of sickness before

that happens." Ah-Drake said.

" I was part of a crew on a survey ship called the Shama. We were investigating the system beyond the wormhole. Maybe that is only way out of the quarantine area. If we could get back there and close it, it would seal them off forever." thought Ah-Nawo.

"If we can survive the next couple of days " Ah-Drake mindspoke, " We'll think about flying out to space and closing up wormholes. For now, let's concentrate on surviving the night. We've got huge replicator boxes making atmosphere fighters from the thoughts of Chairman Xentos, but the harder they work, the more noticeable we'll be to the human invaders. I'm afraid to try making anything else right now -like space shuttles because the humans may be able to intercept the thought throwing process."

Ah-Nawo walked to the door " Can I get out of here now ?

"Sure. You're not a prisoner. But where do you think you will go ?"

"There must be someone somewhere who can lend me a ship. I know how to plug up the human hordes."

"There isn't a space-capable ship left on -planet or in orbit. Believe me I've checked. Only the human craft and no-one is quite sure how they fly. They are some kind of mechanical wonders. Some people are saying that the human ships are not even alive.

"Gods. Can it be true ?"

"I don't think so, either" thought Ah-Drake, "it goes against all the rules of space-travel that we know - but just a week ago, who could believe violence and war from an intelligent species ?" Ah-Drake looked at Ah-Nawo closely as if this were some kind of test.

"I can believe that part of it" thought Ah-Nawo "I need to talk to someone that can loan me an atmosphere ship!"

"Why, do you want to get away ?"

"Get away ? Hell no. I probably shouldn't tell you this - you'll likely have me sent away and reprogrammed or something, but I have the strangest urge I've ever had."

"To do what ?"

"To kill those bastards !"

Drake started to get up and walk to the door, holding his thoughts to himself.

"I know I shouldn't be feeling this way. Maybe I need a flash-therapy session or a code-yank. But, by all the Gods, I tell you - those bastards killed my family. They slagged my home. They blew my ship out of space and killed all my crewmates, and no matter how uncivilized it sounds - they must die for it !"

Ah-Drake took out a key and placed it into the door.

Ah-Nawo tensed and looked at him nervously.

A gust of steam came out of the door, then there was light shining though the mist. Ah- Nawo saw a man walk into the cell . He was tall and dark skinned with big blue eyes which glowed through the darkness of the room.

" General Drake, is he ready to join our forces ?"The man mindspoke.

" Yes." replied Drake. "He has it ."

"What do I have " queried Ah-Nawo

"The disease."

"No. I'm very healthy. I just had my shipboard meds exam before ..."

"The human disease. Bloodlust. The urge to kill. You have it bad."

Ah-Nawo paused to think about it. "Yes. You're right. I do - Gods help me, I do. I can see nothing in my future but killing those bastards."

" Good. Right now, for us, that's good, not bad. I had to see if you were a hostile person. If not, you were not the type of person we were looking for.

Now that we know, you have a chance to satisfy the urgings of your disease. We can help you to kill - do you want to join us or do you want to be returned to the surface ?" Drake said.

" It's too dangerous to go to the surface, and I guess I will not be returning home for a while. So I will join you - but only until we find a ship that can go out of the atmosphere. I can kill more out there." Ah-Nawo said.

" Welcome to the club, Private!" said Ah-Drake.

Chapter 5

The story of the beginning

The next day came shining through the holes in the ceilings.

The stuffy air in the cold tunnels kept the walls damp and soft. The entrance was jammed up and sealed tight. All of the rotting ropes and cracked panels lay there, covered in cobwebs and dirt.

A loud noise vibrated through the ropes. Dirt started to fall off the rusty cracks and the blistered ropes. The ropes, now revealed as new and strong, started to spin fast pulling hidden weights up into the air. Wind started to fly in , the sunlight hit the floor showing the shadows of three people.

" We caught one of them ! We need help." came an excited thought, zipping through the network of tunnels.

Two tunnel guards came up to the Outsiders and saw the captured prisoner fighting to get away from the Outsider Guards. It was wearing a suit colored red, with a thick helmet which covered most of its head, It had dark eye glasses on it, and its weapon was long and thin car-

rying two small cylinder capsules filled with black powder.

" We caught this one, collapsed near our entrance,
where do we put it ?" asked one of the Outsider Guards.

" Take him to General Ah-Drake's quarters, he will
find something useful for him." thought the tunnel guard.
The guards all marched down the hallway and stopped
half way. They opened a door and threw the prisoner into
a room. They closed the door and went to a mildly damaged thought-thrower machine.

" General Ah-Drake sir, we have captured a human,
He is a classified #345, Quite lethal and dangerous and is
at room section #67" thought the soldier at the machine -
which narrowcast it to the intended recipient, wherever
he might be.

After a while, a door opened up at the end of the
hallway; the General came out fully armed wearing a
translator on the right side of his breast shield. He stopped
in front of the door number #67.

"Is he in there?," he asked.

"Yes sir, I recommend you br-"

The general stopped him from finishing his thought
and said "If anything happens, I want you to seal off this
room until I hold up four fingers , then open the door."

The guard nodded and started to open the door. The
General walked into the room and the door shut closed
behind him.

The room was dark and damp, " Who are you? Let
me go, I will kill you if you don't let me go, you freak!"
said a faint scared voice.

The general looked up and saw the human prisoner. It was a woman, young and small, but fierce. She had curly dark brown hair, green eyes ,and was determined to kill or die trying. She was walking back and holding a knife.

" You are surprisingly brave for someone trapped in a dead end. You can kill me if you want but you won't get out of this room for a long time. I think that if you cooperate with us, we could let you go, back to your friends, back to your family. Now doesn't that sound good ?" said the General.

The human slowly put the knife down, she was trembling down to her knees, but controlled her fears and slowly walked into the shadows, She started to pace around thinking that the alien might attack or possibly kill her.

"There are a couple things I want t know , why does your race want our planets?" General Ah-Drake asked.

" I will not answer any questions that you ask me !" snapped the scared human girl.

" What are you afraid of ? That We will kill you ? We may be the enemy but we still will be respectful." said the General.

The Human girl walked to a corner and sat down. She looked at her legs and started to talk.

" This all started out two years ago, I was living in the Mars colony as a Scientist, I was an astronomer, looking at new worlds and if they were fit for the colonization of people. Our race came from a planet called Earth. We evolved to become smart and broke out to the neighboring planets around our home world.

    We first started to colonize the fourth planet from the sun, Mars, then we moved on to other planets stripping them of their resources and moving to the next planet.

    My name is Debra Sollent, I was born and raised on Mars , I grew up there and joined the army. That's where I started to research other planets, what they had inside them, and how they differed from all the others.

    One day I was observing the sun and the first planet in its rotation around it when a strange thing started to happen. The planet seemed to explode then it went spinning out of it's orbital plane. The orbit decayed, right before my eyes and the planet got pulled into the sun. Instead of just burning up, though, it punched right through the sun and left a big hole there."

    "Gods - Ah Nawo was right"said Ah-Drake.

    "What ?"

    "My colleague told me he believed that the humans came out of an accidentally-opened worm-hole. It appears he was right."

    "Wormhole - is that the name. Are they common ?"

    "That's how everyone travels. Yours was purposely sealed to keep your race there, out of the mainstream. Like a prison, until you matured or got over your disease."

    "We didn't know - we didn't care. This hole was the key to solving our big problem - which was the need for more space and more resources. I was amazed to what I had stumbled upon, a new discovery about the suns and their true meanings in the mysteries of Space. It seemed there were holes in many of them . . ."

"All of them" corrected Ah-Drake, "you just have to be able to find them and use them."

"I put together a quick theory and sent the message to every science lab in the known system. No one thought of my discovery as a lie because the hole in the Sun was now visible to everyone. But no-one knew what to make of it, until I suggested it was a passageway. I saved humanity."

"And possibly killed the rest of civilization. How did you figure it out ?"

" I was the first to find new worlds through the hole, fit for the colonization of Earth and rich in resources. Everyone thought there was another dimension through the hole - or maybe just the other side of the sun. I was the first to actually send a probe through and get a message back. I programmed it to send back through the hole, rather than through ordinary space as usual. So I knew about everything years before everyone else. But no-one could duplicate my results - even I couldn't. I don't why.

"It's quite a feat to send electronic messages through a wormhole - you were very fortunate the first time."

"Once the normal space messages started coming back, everyone agreed with me, but by then I was all set to take advantage of the new Hot Superconductor technology and my ship was one of the first through. Thousands followed. But, because of me , there is a war going on, Since I am part of the army I am meant to help the colonists by clearing the way for them. We are doing all this for your planets and resources. We will have them.

Billions of people are going to risk their lives to get a hold of the planets, they will kill anything that stands in their way and possibly exterminate all things that live on these planets. I tell you this as a warning. I have no personal fight with you - take your people somewhere else. We will not be denied. "

She stopped talking and looked up to the General.

" Well I guess that means that there is no chance of reasoning this problem out , is there ?" said the General.

" No, all of you can, and likely will die - even me , I am expendable and of not much of an importance to anyone. My role is essentially done - I can't top saving humanity, can I ?"said Debra,

"You could save all of civilization" said the General, sadly.

"We don't see it as civilization. Only wild-life." said Debra. "And we've never been very kind to wildlife"

"How did you come to be here"

"My ship was the first through the worm-hole - so it wasn't as sophisticated as the others. The fleet just destroyed a battlecruiser or something."

"Peaceful survey ship."

"Really ? Too bad. Shouldn't have gotten in our way. But a big chunk of that smashed into my ship and took us out. A new ship would have been able to evade it, but not my old piece of junk. Only I survived - and now that you have me, that won't likely be true for long either."

"Quite the opposite, in fact. We are not human, and no such thing would even occur to us - although, now that you mention it, perhaps we should kill you. We have to become as sick as you humans to even enter this contest. What do you think."

"You are dust already. Nothing can stand before us. No animal. No nature. Not heaven itself can survive the human will."

"You may be right. You have been a great help to us, in clarifying what the humans are after. You are free to go. I will have a guard escort you out into the outside." said the general.

" Before I go, let me tell you something you may not know already. There is a way to weaken our defenses. Close up the worm hole and you stop millions of other ships from coming into your solar systems. We will have no reinforcements." said Debra.

"One of my colleagues already suggested that. But why are you telling me this information?" asked the General.

" I created this mess, making people think that we were kept in a far cell called space, having no way of getting out or near to another cell, I made them think that they were put so far away from other life , because we were trapped . Now they are crazy and locked in the thinking of revenge. They fight to prove their existence is meaningful and to make sure they are never put away into a box again. I started this, just as a science project - to see if I could motivate people to follow my idea. It worked like crazy - partly because we were out of resources and had no future - but that wasn't enough for a whole system to jeopardize it's near future and it's present to recycle everything to build ships. Rage did that. Rage that I cre-

ated and rage that I eventually caught myself even though
I thought it was all a lie. Now you tell me it's true. We
were out here before and were beaten back to the stone
age and locked in a place that you thought we could never
get out of. So now I am angrier than ever. And right now,
I say seal off the wormhole for two reasons. One - so that
we can never be sent back to that particular hell. And
second, because there are only Jappos and Brits and Yanks
left. Bloody Earthies. All my Marsfolk are off-system, or
all the important ones. So let the ones who are still there
die. I started the exodus . I plan to end it."she said.

"You would kill your own."

"Without blinking an eye. To me, and to all humans,
other humans, not of our tribe, are as alien to us as you
are."

"And you are the female of the species, the caring,
nurturing sex ?"

"Imagine what the males are like"

He gave them the four-finger signal and the doors
opened. She walked out and down the hall. The guards
gave her a wide berth, and watched her nervously.

" Give that human some water supplies, food, and
her gun back, we are letting her go." said the General.

The guard at the entrance of the caves handed her
the supplies and her weapon. The doors opened, showing the sun setting over the desert dunes.

" Are you sure you want to go back?, Join us and
stop them from winning this war. You can kill many more
out here - and be known as the one who saved civilization." said the General.

" I can kill my own species, but not my own tribe. Not the Marsfolk. That would go against all I believe and all that I was taught. You just don't understand humanity yet. Pity you'll never have the time to do a thorough study." said Debra.

Then the small human female started to walk out. She put her helmet and her dark glasses on again and disappeared into the dusty desert wind, never to be heard or seen from again by anyone on that planet.

But never to be forgotten, either.

Chapter **6**

The story of the human soldiers

A fleet of eight ships left the orbit of the Degos sun and was heading to the third planet from the sun, The name of the planet was Arotosa , the Planet of Mist.

The cargo ships were filled with vehicles and soldiers, ready for action. One by one the ships entered the orbit, then each disappeared into the cloudy atmosphere of the planet.

"Cargo ship 17 , the orders have been given , enter the atmosphere, land on the planet and set up a base." said the transmitter.

" Understood, General. " responded Captain Shon Justin. The outside imperva-glass windows were covered with sheets of flex-metal ,The soldiers left their passenger seats and went into protective plastic capsules leaning on every wall on the ship. The doors and cargo bays were shut tight and the cockpit was now in automatic piloting.

The engines started to accelerate into the planet. The outside of the ship started to light on fire , the inside was extremely warm and shaky. The ship teetered over the edge and fell into the gravity well. Stronger than anticipated gravity got a hold of the ship and pulled it down quickly.

"Warning!, ship hyperdrive gone, ship hyperdrive gone!" the computer said.

The engines started up again and the ship pulled nose-up and slowed down. It came to a final stop a few feet above the planet's surface, then landed.

Inside, the capsules opened up and the soldiers walked out of them and went to the ship's door.

"So we survived this far , now what ?" said Tom.

" I guess we go outside."

The captain came out of the cockpit. "Listen up, there are other teammates out there from the other ships who are expecting you guys. The orders are to clear out the area and set camp. And one more thing, kill anything that is not human."

" Yes sir!" said the troops, all together, like they had been trained to.

The docking bay doors opened, A gust of wind came at them. The outside was beautiful, covered in trees and mist. It all looked like untamed country. The air was humid and hot.

Tom walked outside and saw the other ships had landed and were still slightly flaming because of the atmosphere. He saw the other troops all out and starting to dispatch the cargo of supplies.

" We need more medical supplies on this side!" said the medic.

" Start to dispatch the tanks"said the mechanics.

The cargo doors opened , Three giant vehicles came out. They were shaped quite square with an opening the size of a person. Two planes came out followed by some strange-looking motorcycles.

The beautiful trees were cut down and moved somewhere else, The mechanic shop was created in 15 minutes and the wire fencing was up, slicing through the soft mist.

The base was finally setup and the troops were ready to attack and conquer the area.

A man in his fifties came out of one of the cargo ships and walked up to the working troops. He was dressed in green and smoking a cigar. There were five stripes on each of his shoulders. All of the people saw him and started to stand in formation.

He took out the cigar out of his mouth and started to talk.

" My name is Sergeant Will Fecod and I am here to command you. You maggots are the newest Martian Marines, and your target is to kill anything not human ! Just like our dear captain said. Do we have an understanding ?"

"Yes sir." they responded.

"You, sir, what is your name?" Sgt. Fecod asked.

" Uh, Sir, my name is Private Kim. Sir!"

" Well congratulations, you are the new night man for tonight. I hope you got enough sleep on the way down from space, maggot Kim ! And for the rest of you, at o'five hundred I want a line up for the daily routine of work.

That's right I said work. Until we find something to kill, you have to earn your keep and work. Did you hear me ?" he said.

" Yes sir"

" Did I just hear a pin drop,I said , do you hear me?"

The soldiers became furious and shouted " Yes sir!"

Night fall came fast. It was pitch black and cold. Some camp fires were burning away and becoming dim. In front of the bunkers, there was a man not yet asleep , sitting on his bed. On the side of his bed lay his gun , uniform and a small badge saying David Kim.

Suddenly he heard a creak. Stealthy footsteps came after it. He felt ice run down his back. Kim silently grabbed his gun. Slowly turning around he brought the deadly weapon to point at the area behind him .

" Kim ? Are you all right ?" Kim turned fully around and saw his lover, Linka. She was tall and thin, Her eyes were blue and her hair was dark and thick.

"Oh God - I thought you were an alien! What are you doing up ? I could of shot you!" Kim scolded.

"Maybe some day you will " she teased. "I saw you were chosen for night watchman. I thought that you were not afraid of the dark ?" Linka said."I was trying to see how close I could get to you before you noticed. You're getting better."

" No , I overcame my fear of the dark when I was two ! My fear of you, though, I'll never get over. I'm just a city boy - not a country huntress like you. You've been doing this sneaking around stuff all your life. You're scary. As for me, I'm afraid of the natural animals here - what if they are not domesticated."

" Shh, you're overreacting , there are no animals here and even if there are, you have a gun. Hostile or not they are still practice targets for the invasion tomorrow !" interrupted Linka.

"You're ruthless!" He said .

"I know." Linka responded

"I guess it's time for me to go on duty." Said Kim. "I wish we had time to be together."

He rose from the bed and started to put his uniform on, then picked up his automatic shotgun.

"Come on on rounds with me. You can sense things that I never even notice."

They went out together, both holding guns, and holding hands. The lights were off and the camp fire was dim. Screeches like wolf howls, were heard far away towards the two full grey moons above the tree tops. They walked a short distance away, going around the bunker as they had been taught to when on patrol.

" Wow , there is not so much difference with Earth and here. " said Kim.

"Two moons. Mist. No people." Said Linka.

"Well, other than that"

A gun shot was heard from the bunker he was stationed in.

"Ah!" came a voice, in pain

Bang ! Bang !

Two more shots were fired.

"I have to get to my station" Said Linka, letting go his hand. She ran off silently.

" Linka wait !" He cried , " Linka!" He cried once
more.

Kim started to run back toward the bunker, checking his gun and getting it fire-ready. The fumes of burning gasoline filled the air. The more he came closer the
stronger the fumes got.

Kim stopped running , suddenly.

He saw the bunker burning to the ground. Some
more gun shots were heard. A soldier came out of the
forest and came forward to Kim.

"Kim, where were you ?" said the trooper.

Kim ignored his question and asked "Was there any
survivors when it exploded?"

"Kim, the Sergeant has been killed!"

"How did it happen ?" Kim shouted.

"Alien scouts from the east-west colony, looks like
they knew of our presence." he responded.

Kim turned around, he looked at the burning bunker. He turned towards the scared soldier "Who is in
charge now ?" Kim asked.

" Either Ensign Tom or Lieutenant Bryan is."

Another pair of soldiers came out of the forest.

"Help ! Tom needs some help here" he cried. Kim
and the soldier ran to them. Then stopped.

" Help me!, I am burned all over and I need medical
attendance quick!" screamed the wounded man. Kim bent
down and saw the wound that Tom had. There were burns
all around it, and plasma dripping out of the burns.

"Tom now don't close your eyes and focus on me."
Kim said.

" Don't let the Alien bastards hit you first ! Command and conquer them. - uh..."

"Sir , he's dead." said the soldier.

Kim closed Tom's eyes." I will kill them all !" whispered Kim.

" Privates Log: The next morning came. There were 23 dead bodies from last night's massacre, We couldn't recover the body of my dear Linka. She's missing from the roster but not from my heart. I never knew the powers of loneliness, I feel that the rage has taken control over my spirit. all that I could think about was conquering the alien colonies."

Kim closed his diary , then walked out of his tent. He stared into the sunrise then walked toward the new Sergeant. Bryan was standing and looking at the sun rise, too. Kim came up to him.

"Sarge ? What are you going to do, should we attack now or wait for them?"

" Kim, it's a miracle how a person could come into power over night. I can't believe that the aliens would actually be this hostile. We kept hearing that they were passive and peaceful. I guess that is over. I guess it is time to finish our jobs.

Kim. tell the men to get ready! It's time the aliens really know that we are here. We are trained marines and we will show the power of Earth. We are the superior race and the end product of evolution. The other beings are not going to stop us for one simple reason - because we will kill them all before they get us. I may be new but I can make us win this colony. We will take all the tanks and the planes and head for the alien colony now. "

Kim walked backwards a step or two in shock.

"You have become insane. What about our food supplies ? Ammo lines. Info lines. They are just getting set up now. Get rational." Kim said.

"Rational doesn't win wars. Surprise does. Firepower does. Have we still have any napalm left from that other planet ? At least that should give us some invading time."Bryan said.

Kim started to see how the attack would go. He saw the danger to the aliens of over-power. It would terrorize them. Kim said "Yes Sir !" with new respect and ran to tell the others of the plan.

Burning hot flames came out of the engines of the planes, they started to vibrate faster and faster until they sprang straight up and hovered in the air. The two planes started to disappear into the East.

The surviving soldiers clustered around the radio at the remaining bunker. " Sir we have reached the colony now. Napalm drop in five - four - three -two - one!, Mission success sir"

The flames were heard on the radio.

" Now pilots, land here pilots and stock up , do you read me ? I want you both to start a blitz attack, come back here immediately and load up on everything that flames. More napalm. More fire-bombs. More incendiaries. Use missiles if possible, but your primary mission is to destroy everything with fire. Over and out."

He shut off the radio and stood up, he walked up to the soldiers and shouted "All right ! Move out ! You there

I want the tanks to move first so that we have a protective shield. All motorcyclists start to move east wards now!"

The march started. The soldiers held their guns up in the air. All of a sudden the ground started to shake. The ground noise became louder and louder. Earth started to spit out four giant underground creatures. Partly looking like a huge mining machine, partly like some nightmare worm, they steeply stuck out of the ground like the front of a blue whale. The tip started to slowly open and the creatures started to growl. Steam came out of their mouths as they opened.

Aliens started to run out of the creatures mouths through the steam. They stopped in front of the humans. Their eyes were large and black colored and their skin was colored thick grey and covered in metal scraps and armor. They carried strange-looking guns.

" All right troops this was the moment all of you have been waiting for ! These bastards are so considerate, they're saving us a walk. When I give you the command, go into the forest on your own and start shooting the enemy." whispered Sergeant Bryan.

One alien walked in front of all the others . He wore a giant blue cloak that covered his left shoulder. He was larger and looked older than most of them. He put a translator badge on and adjusted it. The alien started to talk:"I am Ah-torrs and I am your contact between our races. I led the raid here last night. We are here to tell you to stop bombing the cities that my people live in. You have killed many innocent lives that didn't have to die today. This fight should be one of honor, between warriors, Not between soldier sand innocent civilians. If you stop now, we will help you return to your fleet and then we can resume fighting at some place where no civilians will be hurt."

"My name is Sergeant Bryan of the Martian Space Marines division and I am your worst nightmare. We have come to take over. Not to talk. Surrender your cities to us and none of your people will get hurt! Oh by the way, I think that you should step back now Ah-torr, you see we are anxious to kill all of you and I can't control all of these animals and I'm sure you'd prefer to die with your troops than out here by yourself."

The aliens looked puzzled at Sergeant Bryan. He grinned then shouted " NOW!".

The troops started to run forwards, taking cover in the forest and pointing their guns at the helpless aliens, The advance party of aliens started to run back to the ground beasts but the tanks turned their cannons towards them and started to fire away.

One by one, the aliens started to die, the advance party first, then the massed troops further back. The ground beasts sank lower into the ground with a handful of survivors.

Sergeant Bryan walked to the dead bodies of the aliens, He took off the cloak of the leader alien, then stuck it on the tip of his bashed up rifle. He took out a lighter from his pocket and started to burn the cloak.

"As I said before!, we move east to conquer the settlement!, So why don't we get going?"

The soldiers started to cheer for their leader. Bryan

had finally showed them that he was a powerful commander and was not going to show mercy for the aliens. The soldiers shouted out "Bryan!, Bryan."

Bryan stood up , waving the burning cloak and grinning. He pointed east then started to walk. His troops started to follow, and the tanks followed last.

Dark came fast, nothing was seen and nothing was heard.

" All troops start up your vision goggles, we're going to make a sneak attack!." whispered Sergeant Bryan.

Kim put on his night vision, he saw all the trees, and all the troops crawling in the dirt, he saw everything as if it was day.

" We're almost there troops, just over those hills and we will reach the city." whispered Sergeant Bryan.

They crawled for hours , then they stood and started to run and stop at every tree. Finally they reached the hills which were tall and covered in grass. There were a few jagged rocks sticking out of the hill, but otherwise it was smooth going. The troops bent down and pushed a button on their boots. Spikes came out of them, as if they were soccer shoes. They started to climb the hill, holding on to the grass and trying to avoid the sharp rocks.

Sergeant Bryan was panting and was tired, he weakly said; "Don't worry boys , we're almost there !"

With in a few more footsteps they would be on the top of the hill. A soldier ran up and reached the top. He looked around and knelt down. He held his automatic gun like a walking stick, waiting for the others to arrive.

Suddenly a gunshot was heard. Blood trickled down

onto the grass, the man was dead.

"We're busted boys. Get your guns ready. It's time to rock and roll, "

They raced up the hill then started to crawl over the top. Kim heard another gun shot, he ducked down and pointed his gun off to the side, he shot a few rounds then heard a faint scream.

Kim stood up and walked towards to where he shot. He came up to a tree, covered in ferns and flowers. Blood started dripping onto his boots. He looked up and saw a figure with a hand gun facing down. It was on top of a tree branch.Kim couldn't tell who it was but he was hoping to see who he shot. He climbed up the tree and saw the body. He turned it around and saw the three bullet holes in the forehead.

Kim saw finally saw the face - he had shot Linka.

Kim was shocked, he gently picked her up and carried her down, He sat down and held her in his arms, silently crying and hoping for her to be alive. He looked at her dark hair, her bright blue eyes , and her frail skin. Tear drops started to fall on her face. Kim took off her necklace and put it in his pocket.

Holding her in his arms, he whispered "I'm sorry Linka."

"Kim , you found one of our missing personnel. What happened to her? did the aliens get her ?" said Bryan.

"No, I killed her." responded Kim.

" Was this friendly fire ?"

"Yes. She thought that we were the enemy. She

killed one of our guys and I returned fire - killing her. I thought she was an alien. She was -"

Kim stopped talking and sighed. He Kissed her and laid her down onto the ground, then stood up. He said "Good bye". He took out a shovel and started to dig a grave for her.

" Kim we have no time for this. We are in moments of taking over a city."said Bryan.

Kim gave no answer.

Bryan grabbed Kim by the collar and started to talk to him.

"Kim ! Don't lose your head over one death. I am deeply sorry that you lost your friend but this is war ! You are expected to lose you loved ones and your hope, but that is what makes us stronger. That is what keeps us fighting , That is what gets us up in the morning - to kill even more than yesterday, do you understand me?, Now Private Kim are you with us or are we going to have to leave you here?!"

" I am going to kill the bastards and I am not going to show mercy ! They took my hope, my lover, and now they are going to pay ! They are all going to face my wrath." Kim shouted.

Bryan let him go and smiled.

Kim picked up his gun and started up his night vision goggles.

Sergeant Bryan ran in front of everyone.

He pointed at the city. He picked up the radio once more then said. " Tank squad 1 and 2 start the attack now."

He stood up on a rock and started to dictate. "Who

are we going to kill ?" he said.

"The aliens sir!" the troops shouted.

Bryan raised his voice and said "ARE WE GOING TO LET THEM LIVE UNTIL TOMORROW?"

The troops responded "NO SIR!"

"Then why don't we go and kill them now?" shouted Bryan once more. Bryan pointed at the city. He took out his automatic rifle and started to race to the city.

The troops followed him down.

They were firing all of their rounds at the buildings, Throwing grenades at houses and raiding them.

*   *   *

Morning came. The city was left in ruins. All of the aliens were dead, Every child, every baby and every adult. Slaughtered before the sunrise. There was no one left but the human invaders.

Chapter 7

The conclusion

In the room of the world senate, on Congress Moon, the lights were dim and the meetings were not yet adjourned

"Document 1, Translation completed. Message being played" said the Recorder.

September 12, 2437
Cadet's log:# 345

"The dawn of the new age for mankind. The discovery of the new planets though the wormhole has attracted colonists from the Moon and Mars. The date has been set for the first contact with the other life. This will solve the problem with our overpopulated earth, the mother home.

The first contact will, of course, be the last contact too and will end when we exterminate the other life to clear the way for the colonizing by earth forces."

The Leader of the Degos system said to the Joined Planets ambassadors on Congress Moon; "My scout soldiers found this document on some of the invaders debris. The humans have taken Degos and Arotasa and will reach Congress Moon here within three days. We must act quickly if we want to win this war with the humans. "

" Now Commander, don't jump to conclusions. There isn't going to be a war. Only a vaccine." said the Chairman, putting down her plasma gun..

" Most of our home planets are being invaded as we speak and you are not going to take any military action towards defense ?" came a voice. They spoke out loud to convey their strong emotions more clearly.

" They killed the ambassador of Degos right here infront of us. They own that planet now." said another.

"This is stirring up dangerous feelings in all of us. Be very careful. Once we agree to species-to-species violence, we will become as infected as the humans. And there may be no cure." said the Chairman.

"Diseased or dead. That is the choice. Forget all this medical stuff. Our very survival is at stake. Your plan is too cerebral. " said another ambassador. "All over the system, bands of fighters are forming, but alone they can accomplish nothing."

"I know. We are supplying many of them with plans and instructions for building living war machines . . ."said the Chairman

"We need a concerted effort. A huge commitment. Not just a few scattered pockets of resistance. Otherwise we are doomed." shouted another.

"We are doomed also if we infect ourselves with this disease." argued the Chairman.

"The Recorder said to follow your lead in this - and we've done that. But it isn't working. We're dying in droves. Yet the humans are not stopping. Let me talk directly through to the Recorder - Recorder - tell us. How did we defeat the humans in the past. Was it this way, or did we band together and embrace violence ?"

"You banded together. But it took thousands of years to get over it. This way there is a chance that you will not be infected. It will allow you to avoid truly ugly aftermath that nearly destroyed the United Planets before. We defeated the humans ten thousand years ago. Yet we've only had 4000 years of peace. Surely you can see the legacy violence leaves." came the unique thought-pattern of the Recorder.

Thoughts flashed around the room as all the ambassadors pondered this.

"This new way there is also a chance we will be exterminated. Let's go with what has worked before. I say we vote on total war ! All in favor of that say 'Aye' !." came an angry voice from one of the Ambassadors.

All of the ambassadors shouted out "Aye".

"Gods help us all"said Chairman Xentos to the excited group. " But I must accept your vote. Now what planets still have working armies or militias and where can we set up bases."

"There is the Terosian fleet, the one that was assembled to build the theme world and a few thousand survey ships, but I don't . . . "

Suddenly there was a giant rumble, the lights started to flicker on and off, there were gun shots heard all over.

"Warning ! Invader alert ! Invader alert. Support staff under attack. Support staff dying" said the building computer

" Oh Gods, It's the humans. I thought we had three days. They're going to destroy us!

They found out our plan!" whispered an ambassador.

"Don't be silly. They're animals. They can only speak out loud. They can't think nor can they hear thinking."

"But we held that session out loud !"

The screen came on. A person appeared, He was human. "I hope you are satisfied -we overheard your plan through these translation devices that you so thoughtfully provided us with, and we are not going to let you follow through with this embracing of violence and banding together. We told you to surrender peacefully and you did not , now you must face the consequences. Oh and thanks for the translator it really helps."

The message went off.

" Safety doors now locked , doors now locked!"said the building computers.

Gun shots were heard everywhere! There were faint screams and loud ones.

" Stay calm ambassadors. We have no weapons, but we have our dignity. And this plasma gun will hold them off for a while - it has really remarkable firepower. " thought the Chairman, picking up her strangely-wrought weapon.

" Chairman send the thought now!" said an ambassador.

"What thought ?" said the chairman.

" Send the thought to very corner of the universe, that we have declared total war on the human pestilence. That we will get together and crush these vermin once and for all. That , no matter how dismal things may look now, help is on the way. Overhear that - and die, human scum !"

The entire assembly cheered.

"That thought has been dispersed through the thought-throwers. We now have declared war!" said the Chairman.

All of a sudden, the lights went off. There was a giant hit towards the door. The ambassadors knew that the humans were trying to get in.

" Now all of you, stand fast. Stay behind me. If I fall, take this weapon and continue firing. If all else fails, spit in their eyes."said the Chairman.

The door became loose, The ambassadors stood tall and faced the entryway. A gust of mist started come out the corners of the door, then the doors came down.

The Chairman raised her terrible weapon.

"Ambassadors! Are you all right ? " the two Degosians, who had come in originally with the Chairmen, strode through the broken doors; smoking weapons in their hands.

"The humans came in the other side of the building from where we were. I'm sorry. We were too slow to react and many support people were killed. We hope that we got here in time - anyone hurt ?."

The ambassadors came out of their tight formation and sat down in relief. The Chairman pointed her weapon to the ground.

"You two alone defeated this force of humans " asked the Chairman.

"These weapons are frightening. Once the rage built in us and we accepted that we could kill other intelligent beings, they could not stand against us. The living guns sought them out and destroyed them. Their weapons are not alive.They are dead metal and laser beams. They depend entirely on the skill of the operator and on the luck of finding someone within sight of the operator. These plasma guns will seek out the desired lifeform, around corners, under ground, wherever - and destroy it. That is why two can defeat two hundred."

They walked outside and saw dead humans all around the sides of the building and laying piled in the alleys . When the ambassadors walked further they saw ships destroyed and more dead humans all around the front garden.

The chairman looked around and saw what was once a peaceful and beautiful garden now sprayed in blood and covered in dead corpses. He sighed and group-thought: "This was the dark day, the day where many lives were lost. Now the war has started, and there will be no stopping to it .There will be blood spilled on both sides. This will be a banquet for death itself."

An ambassador came up to the chairman, patted him on the shoulder.

" The humans started this fight, they tortured our

people , and they wanted us dead ! They wanted a fight and they will get it "

The chairman turned away from the ambassador then looked at the garden covered in blood and bodies. "But the victory will destroy us"

Chapter 8

Saving the prisoners from war

The morning sun shone dark, the clouds were stormy and it was going to rain soon.

The prison camp, which was once a pleasant home to many, now carried death through the air. All of the people who survived the napalm blitz and the invasion of the colonists were dying of hunger and disease.

In a cold, dark room filled with children lying on the ground, came a weak thought from a dying girl ; "Ah-ztes where are you ?"

" I'm here, I won't be going anywhere, you're sick, this is the time you need me most !" This thought came from Ah-ztes, now become a gaunt child, himself. He was sitting near Ah-Quasaferu; the girl who was sick .

He was looking at her softly and he was worried of her health.His eyes saw her gaunt body, and her pale skin. Her bones showed through her skin and her eyes, which were once dark blue, were now shaded pale grey.

" I can't see you any where ? It's all dark here. I 'm scared !" she thought, faintly.

" I am holding your hand, no matter the problem, I

will stay with you. Now go to sleep, I am watching over you , don't be scared." thought Ah- ztes.

There was a rumble in the ground and then there were gunshots over and over. The doors of the dark room start to open. Two humans with guns walked in.They roughly picked out some of the children and led them outside.

The doors closed.

Another round of gun shots were heard, this time the screams and cries were were those of children, quickly silenced by a few more shots.

The doors open once more and the humans came in again to try to take more children.

Ah-ztes was sitting on the floor and lying beside Ah-Quasaferu .

The humans reached for Ah-ztes, they picked him up and pulled him away. He was too weak to resist.

" Ah-ztes ? Ah-ztes ? Don't go away!" screamed Ah-Quasaferu in his mind as their hands were torn apart.

The humans took Ah-ztes outside, they tied his hands to a post then they walked backwards. They reloaded and their guns were pointed at him , Ah-ztes closed his eyes and sent a gentle thought; " Good bye Ah-Quasaferu."

A shot was fired but not to Ah-ztes, He opened his eyes and saw the guns facing the other way. Ah-ztes saw a Degosian like him in military colors. Ah-ztes was happy, slumped against his killing post. Finally, the war has been declared. The Degosians started to invade the area, They ran towards the humans , firing their plasma rifles at them.

The fire from the plasma guns twisted and turned and sought out humans, no matter where they hid, but never touched or harmed any other type of being.

Gunshots were heard followed by plasma shots .

"Don't move, son ! I am going to cut you loose."said a voice out loud, behind him.

"What is going on ? Are you human ? Who's side are you on?" asked Ah-ztes out loud.

The person behind him gave no answer. The roping broke and Ah-ztes stood shakily.

" Duck!," yelled the Degosian soldier. he grabbed Ah-ztes and pulled him to the ground. An explosion was heard, Pieces of hot shrapnel flew at Ah-ztes and the soldier.

"Sorry to speak out loud to you and scare you that way, but I wanted you to be scared, so your body would release fright chemicals. That would wake you up. You looked too weak to live. Are you all right ?" the soldier had begin thinking again, as they lay on the ground.

" What just happened ?" Ah-ztes thought at the soldier.

" We stopped the humans from calling any reinforcements. Are there any other survivors ?" thought the soldier.

" Yes." responded Ah- ztes, still dazed and still lying on the ground.

" Can you show me where they are?" asked the soldier once more .

Ah-ztes nodded his head and started to get up. He stumbled, then started to walk down the street. The soldier followed him. They walked to a domed shaped building

"They are right in here." Ah-ztes entered the building first. The room where they'd been held prisoner seemed much darker, there was no noise or thoughts of children anymore.

The soldier came through the door. He put up his right arm , a small monitor came out - a portable thought-thrower. " Home , home, this is scout patrol reporting in, we need a lot of medics and recruits, there are still human personnel in the area. Be careful. I repeat there are still human personnel around, all armed and dangerous. Land near the town square. We have that area secured. Baby scouts , Baby scouts come to the town square. I repeat come to town square ! " He put his hand down and walked to the door.

" Hey Kid," he turned back and sent a gentle thought; " I need you to help me set up a temporary hospital."

" No I have to check on a friend down there."Ah-ztes thought back, wearily, dreading what he was sure he was going to find.

" OK , but here take a plasma gun. There might be more humans." The soldier walked to him and handed him the squat, living gun. "Shoot what, Lord ?" the gun thought at him as soon as he touched it.

Ah-ztes took the gun and started for the stairs. The dark and misty stair case became cold fast. The stairs creaked every time he walked.He touched bottom and went for the door. Decompressed air hissed out, as Ah-ztes opened the basement door, Groanings were heard .

He walked into the room, " Ah-Quasaferu?, Ah-Quasaferu!" He looked on the floor, He stopped walking.

Ah-Quasaferu was lying on the floor where he had been pulled away from her. She was not breathing, her eyes were now white. She was dead.

Ah-ztes picked her up. She seemed to weigh nothing at all. A tear came down his cheek as he took her up stairs. He walked out the door, and, for the first time, the sunlight shone on him and Quasafaru together.

" Is she dead?" the soldier sent a gentle thought.

"Yes, I left her alone and I lost her. I broke my promise and she suffered for it. I should have died with her." responded Ah-ztes.

" I am sorry" the soldier sent his condolences.

A young thin girl with beautiful dark eyes walked up to the soldier. She stopped infront of him and started to think. "Sergeant Ah-Nik ! We have chased the humans to the hills, they won't be attacking soon, We got your message and the medical supplies are ready,"

" At ease , Commander Ah-Vessk, tell the medics to start setting up. There are a few survivors in the town square basement. Start taking people up !" Sergeant Ah-Nik thought.

Commander Ah-Vessk nodded her head and started for the town square. Within minutes the medics and other recruits came and started to treat the survivors.

Ah-ztes walked to the street, looking at the sunset.

"Hey kid I need your help !," said a thought-voice. He turned around and saw Commander Ah-Vessk calling him. Ah-ztes walked forwards to her.

" Here hold this little one's arm , we need to stop the bleeding ,"She handed Ah-ztes a medicine gun , grabbed his hand and put it on a childs bleeding arm. Ah-ztes, trained in medicine from early childhood, turned the child's arm, pointed the gun at the wound and pulled the trigger. The gun hummed and twitched, a living organism bred to cure minor trauma and infection. After analyzing the wound, the living gun shot some liquid into the wound and bathed the area with a bright light. The bleeding stopped immediately and a foam-like substance arose in the wound and rapidly hardened. The child stared in fascination at the process.

"You're very good with children" came the commander's thought from across the street, where she was tending to other wounded.

"When I'm not getting them killed" thought Ah-ztes back, still bitter about Ah Quasaferu.

There was a rumble deep in the ground. A Flying Saucer landed on the street near the Town Square, the hatch door opened up on the side of the ship and several people jumped out. They walked up to the town square.

A rather thin person with a frowning face came to the Sergeant and said." Sergeant Ah- Nik sir, we are the recruits you called for, I am their commanding officer Sergeant Ah-Vink, the medics are on their way with the supplies."

Commander Ah-Vink, I want your troops to track the humans down and destroy their communications to outside space, and I need all your medics to set up a hospital right here, right now !"

Commander Ah-Vink nodded and tapped some of his men on the shoulder, which told the soldiers to follow him. He walked to the street and moved his right hand in front of his mouth and started to talk out loud, " Medics we need you to come here right now, We have a problem."

He put his hand down and called his soldiers by mind, giving them more detailed instructions. Then his men swarmed into the area, and, in concert with the medics, began building an instant hospital, right in the middle of the square.

Three hours later, the huge hospital tents covered the streets like the air. The medics had cured and and helped most of the survivors that could have been helped,

The revived children and grown-ups scattered into the streets, looking for relatives and friends. The others, the ones who died or were expected to die were laying down on the grass of the Town Square with long cloaks over them.

The death count grew more and more, Fewer and fewer people were able to be saved.

"We need more replicators here," came a thought

" Pass me the biogenic viruses, we are going to lose her!"came another .

" My Gods who did this to you ? " asked a doctor.

"Humans" came the mumbled thought of the patient. "They use projectile weapons and fragments of stuff are always buzzing around."

"Body damage now reduced to 20%!" said the replicator, as the biogenic viruses quickly did their work.

" Ok , we can stop operating now she's going to be all right." thought another doctor.

Within minutes, the wounded officer. opened her eyes, she sat up, and looked around. Her eyes looked abnormal.

" Well I see you woke up Sergeant ! You almost died out there in the battle field. The Humans shook you up a little but we were able to repair their damages."

She stood up. Her biogenic breast shield was cracked and covered in blood. Her pants were cut, with sprays of dark red down to her all-terrain shoes. Her head was sore and aching. with a couple of bandages on her forehead and medical bit clips all around her face.

She looked around and saw the doctors, She put her hand on her head. She started to notice something on her eye but her eye didn't react or feel anything. She then felt around her eye and felt a cold bulky object on her eye socket.

" What the hell did you do to my eye? It's like I'm looking into a camera." she snapped.

A thin Doctor walked up to the confused soldier standing by the bed. He stopped in front of her and started to explain her question out loud, so she could concentrate on this slow means of communication. Thought would likely be too fast for her to grasp at this time.

" Sergeant Ah-Sarak , your eye was lost in your invasion to the colony. Don't worry your artificial eye is made of biogenic material, so your body won't reject it."said the doctor.

She nodded and limped over to the weapons shelf .

As she picked up a fully charged Plasma gun, a hand touched her on the shoulder.

" What are you doing?, You can't leave yet." said the doctor.

" And why can't I go human hunting ?"she asked.

" Because you are injured and you are to be transported to the Degos base setup #14. You are going to be assigned to another squadron." replied the Doctor.

Ah-Sarak looked at the gun and dropped it. She peacefully went to sit down on a stool. She realized that she was much weaker than she thought.

Outside, a faint motor sound was rumbling in the distance. The wind started to act up within the tents. The faint sound became louder and louder. A giant dome-shaped object came out of the sky. The glaring object started to shoot exhaust fumes all around the area and the ship finally came to a stop. The back cargo doors of the ship split with a hiss of pressurized air. The doors slowly came up and a draw bridge came out.

" Personnel numbers 14, 23 , 67, 32, 154, 35 , 33 , 27 233, any injured personnel and the surviving citizens, report to the landing port #1 now. You are ready to leave."said the speaker tower.

Sergeant Ah-Nik walked up to Ah-ztes, touched him on the shoulder and said. " I think you should go with the others, you are safer there, and you will get the proper treatment you need. Here I will bring you over to the landing bay."

Ah-ztes, still holding the medicine gun and still in shock, nodded and started to walk there with the Sergeant.

" Last call for any other evacuees, leaving to Air base #14."yelled the pilot.

" Wait , we have another one. I want you to take him there and give him proper medication, he has been through a lot."said Sergeant Ah-Nik.

Ah-ztes walked into the doors of the cargo ship, and went into the passenger room. He sat down and put a seat belt on. The cargo doors closed shut, the engines started up and a sudden jerk forwards followed immediately after. The Flying saucer took off and flew South.

Ah-ztes watched out the window as Sergeant Ah-Nik, still in the town square, looked up and waved good-bye.

Atmosphere flights were often longer than space flights. Hours went by. The night time came,and the saucer engines still vibrated through the floor and the air pressure continued to grow,

The cramped cargo hold was filled with injured officers and troops along with survivors from the colony. Medical supplies were stenching up the place, and there was rotting flesh on one side and moans on the other. Ah-ztes tried to go to sleep but was bothered by the painful groans, and the terrible smell of dead bodies.

"What the hell am I doing here " he asked aloud.

" Hey Kid, quit your whining!, I'm trying to get some sleep here." said a voice.

Ah-ztes looked around and saw a tall woman with an artificial eye looking at the ceiling .

" What happened to your eye?" asked Ah-ztes.

" Kid, it was a freak accident, and after this war is

over I am going to complain big time. Now let me get to sleep." she said.

"What resistance are you from? The Echo Artrosa Grookes, the Degosian Militia Army, the Daze Navy, the North West Border Defenses, or is it the Sivil Sand Warriors?" asked Ah-ztes, still a boy at heart, and excited to eb repeating the names he had heard whispered among the prisoners.

Ah-Sarak looked up at his stern face. She smiled then said." You won't me go to sleep until you get every answer you want from me. Why do you want to know?"

"I'm recording" He said. "I just want to know how the army came here so fast now and why didn't they put up a fight when the humans originally took over the colony?"He changed from talking to thinking in consideration for the wounded who were trying to sleep.

"To start things off, I am part of the North West Border Defense, I was once second in command in a squad, and the reason why we couldn't reach the colonies in time was because we didn't exist then. The congress on the third moon was invaded by humans twice - Ambassador Denos was killed in the first attack and . . "

"Gods -Ah Denos dead?"

"Yes - they say he died bravely. No-one knew what the humans were capable of - why did you know him?"

"He is my father"

"I'm sorry. I didn't know."

"Tell me the rest"

"Congress didn't declare war until a few days ago, after they beat off the second human attack. And, even then we had no weapons, no plan and no intelligence. We didn't even know what was going on over here until a few hours ago. Your thought throwers were all out of commission and no-one was getting any information out of here. Then, when we went into action, the human weapons held us off for a while, until we mastered the plasma rifles. Does this answer your questions at all ?"She said.

" How many people died in your squad?,"

"We've all lost people in this war" she thought back sharply.

"But how many ?"

Ah-ztes received no answer and, after a while, realized that that was the answer. Silence. She had lost everyone.

Ah-Sarak turned around and started to sleep. Ah-ztes continued to look at her. So much carnage and pain in just two people and in just a few days of war. He was concerned about the two great races, the humans and the people, and who would eventually kill off kill who. For he was sure now that this would be no short skirmish. It would be a battle to the death.

" We are now landing at base 14," said the speaker.

The engines started to slow down, there was a rumbling on the floor. The seats started to grip Ah-ztes , the Engines started to roar and growl. The windows closed up and the room became darker. Rumbling turned into giant chaos.

" Warning , back engine failed." called the speaker.

The neck snapping shakes started to slow and then stop altogether. The engines started to shut down . The cockpit doors opened up and the pilot came out. He looked around; " Welcome to Base #14, I am sorry for the engine failure but those things happen. This poor living ship was hit badly in the battle and was losing lifeforce all through the flight. Part of it is now dead, but we've learned much during this flight and can now cure our living ships in flight. So I assure you that it will never happen again."

He walked over to the back to the ship. He pulled a lever and the back cargo door opened. When the seats loosened up, Ah-ztes got up and went to the cargo door.

He walked outside, and the others followed.

He saw no trees and no sign of civilization around, nothing but the empty basezone. The base, itself, was a giant dome on the ground, colored green, and had no sounds coming out of it.

A door opened up in the dome and three Degosian soldiers walked out. One soldier was a woman, quite healthy and tall. She came out with no gun. "Welcome to Base #14, I am Admiral Rolik of the Arotosa Resistant. If you were part of the survivors group you will be treated, and you will be inducted into the new militia if you are well enough. Please enter single file and think your records at the identifications computer."

" Admiral, I am Sergeant Ah-Vessk . I have injured personnel, my squad needs new recruits. Sergeant Ah-Sarak is also here, she lost her entire squad. These humans are more dangerous than we expected."

"At ease Sergeant, this is now our stronghold. Unfortunately we can't give all of the Sergeants that will be coming in a new squad. The only new recruits we could spare are the militia. I need you and the other Sergeants to train the militia.

The healthy survivors you brought will become the militia, it may be cold - I know you expected a safe haven here - but we can't afford to have no defense forces at all."

The Sergeant looked up at the Admiral ." Yes Admiral."she said. Sergeant Ah-Vessk walked away into the base. She was not going to break her orders. She walked to the Medical room hoping to find people for the new recruit. She saw dead bodies and one doctor working on a badly injured patient.

" I need more bandages ! This one may have a chance to keep living. Come on damn it , live you bastard." The doctor stopped working on the patient.

" Patient lost, patient lost!" said the medical monitor.

The doctor looked around and saw the Sergeant. He stormed over to her and started to talk. "If you are looking for more recruits they are at the cafeteria, there are only dead corpses in this room. But save yourself the walk - and save me the trouble. Just take the dead ones. You'll make them all dead soon enough."

The Sergeant looked up at him." I see you got the new message as well" she said.

" Why do you have to take in civilians and try to turn them into warriors?, I am surprised that they are not left traumatized from the invasions they encountered already. Is it right to turn these peaceful people into brutal killing machines ?

Our people have believed in peace, We were so peaceful that we had to genetically replicate military high officials so they could train an army for us . Tell me Sergeant , Were you created in a lab ?"

She looked up to him, " I was not created, I was a natural born. I am doing this to avenge my people. The labs didn't create me - the humans did. The humans came and destroyed our colonies, They showed no mercy, they will not care if we are gone. I may be raised the Degosian way but I was taken into the military because I had studied the old rules of the Ancient tactics. And my study tells me this: now we are on a war footing. Martial law applies everywhere. And under martial law, orders are orders, so don't expect much democracy or much tolerance to come out of it. There are a group of us who believe that our peaceful ways will prevail and that the War Order was wrong, but until such time as we can gain control of the congress, we will do our duty. Just as you will do your duty and shut your mouth - or I'll kill you myself."

" Doctor we have another injured man." said the radio.

" We will continue this discussion later." said the Doctor. He stormed out of the room and disappeared.

"You should live so long." she sent the thought chasing him down the hall.

The Sergeant went on her way to start recruiting militia for the war. She came upon Ah-ztes who was limping up the hall to teh cafeteria and asked;" Where are you going - to get something to eat ?"

He responded . " I am looking for the militia, I want to join."

The Sergeant looked at him and saw that he was not playing a game , she saw his rage for revenge . She took out a data card and flashed it at Ah-ztes.

" Put your eye print on this and you are in." she said.

Ah-ztes put the card near his eye then pushed a thought into it. He took it off and gave it back to the Sergeant.

"Tomorrow at noon you report in for the pilot training outside the base dome."She said.

Chapter **9**

The start of the Air Militia

The room was filled with soldiers and people. People from destroyed cities and people from other places of horror. People with nowhere else to go.

On a table closest to the wall sat six people bunched together, they were all female infantry and were all trying to flirt with one man sitting on a chair at the table.

" Ah-Jord?, please tell us that story again, you know the one where you saved the wampek from getting shot by a human."said one girl.

" Wow you are a wildling!" giggled another. They spoke out loud because it was considered naughty and animalistic to do so.

The man bent closer to the table and started to grin. "All right, I will tell you the story again. This time, all out loud - so listen carefully. It all started when . . . "

The man wa rudely interrupted by the Sergeant.

" Ah-Jord , where have you have been ? Your Militia training started half an hour ago." she said.

" Oh my Gods I'm late. I will continue the story later girls ."Ah-Jord stood up from his chair and ran out the door followed by giggling thoughts from the girls and loud laughter from other tables.

He arrived at the docking bay outside the base. People were waiting for him. furious and tired. There were green sheets and barrels around so that it would not be detected easily from the air by the humans. The human weapons were non-living, so they had to see something before they could destroy it.

Ah-Jord slowly walked into the landing area where every one was waiting. " Attention, My name is Ah-Jord, I am your new squad leader,   I will be teaching you how to control a living flying saucer. It's not as hard as it may seem. They are all alive and pretty well fly themselves, but they depend on you for direction and strategy. I will put all of you through courses in those tactics and, if we're lucky, we all might see some real action in our training. Any questions?"

" Yes I have one?" said a voice.

Ah-Jord saw a beautiful girl coming up to him, She was thin and had one dark eye, her other eye was lumpy and mechanical-looking and obviously artificial. There was no attempt to disguise it.

" I am Sergeant Ah-Sarak . In the Identification key here says that I am now a private , Do you have any rea-son why this would happen?" she said.

Ah-Jord was not paying attention to what she said,

He was just amazed by her beauty.

" SIR!"

"Huh?, oh check with Sergeant Ah-Vessk or the Admiral, sweet heart" he said."I'm just a Saucer-jock. I don't know anything about the bureaucracy. Run along now and get your rank sorted out, then, when you're ready and you've worked up your courage, come on back and I'll teach you how fly to rings around the humans. "

She slowly walked closer to him, Her artificial eye hummed and focused into his face. She smiled."Do you know the design specs of the kind of fighters you will be flying ? Do you know what the humans are flying against you. Do you know that the humans have won 3 out of 4 engagements with the types of fighters we have. Do you know that the human fighters are non-living, so they are not susceptible to acid. Do you know anything or are you just assigned for this job because it's just a talking job and talking is all you know how to do ?

"Huh?, oh um yes I guess." He said.

" I've been fighting humans since Day One. I know how they fight. How they react. How they think. I, personally, with this gun, have killed over 300 of them - within the last few days. Yet you now have a higher rank than me. It's sad. But, look on the bright side. With your lack of experience, well, I guess I won't be seeing you around for too long. Nor any of your poor students."

She smiled again and walked away.

" Grit leader, are you going to show us our fighters today - or have you been shot down already ?" said a person.

" Huh?, oh yes I think I've been blasted. She's got the grit today and she's right. I should do some homework before I try to teach you guys what to do in a fight. So let's say, for today, it is canceled. No, wait before you all leave , I want you to take a look at the living fighters you will be flying." he said.

He walked over to the hatch doors of the base. He pushed a button on the side of the hatch doors and they started to open. 69 round oval shapes started to appear inside the room, they were brand new - straight from the huge replicator box - dark grey living skin that went right up to the transparent top which was the cockpit.

" These beautiful grashin pieces of bulk are Shecklak Raider Fighters, These fighters were around long before you people were born, the design is 10 thousand years old, so they should still last another life time." Ah-Jord said.

The people who were being trained walked up to the saucers. They were amazed at the size, the craftmenship and the strength of the ship. Each of them reached up and touched the skin of one ship, making mental contact with the rudimentary brain.

" Are you the squad leader ?," said a voice out loud.

Ah-Jord looked down and saw a short,young boy, 11 or 12 years old, with an artificial leg,

" Yes I am , what can I do for you ?"

" My name is Ah-ztes and I am one of your recruits."

" That can't be , you're much too young"

" No, I am an orphan - mother killed here, father killed on Congress Moon. So, by law, I am at the age of making my own decisions and I already signed a militia sheet"

"Do you know what type of fighters these are ? Are you qualified to fly one of these monsters ?"

" Yes I am , and if I am not mistaken" he paused a moment to consult the Recorder secretly - "I think those fighters over there are S. raiders, - the Shecklaks that were so important in destroying humanity before. And by the pattern on their wings they belonged to the Graunky Battleships, which are also being replicated."

Ah-Jord smiled, "Welcome to the team, rookie. Maybe you can teach me a thing or two."

" I have one question," Ah-ztes said.

" What?"

" Where did you get these fighters ? They were banned after the peace treaty among the civilized worlds 4000 years ago. When they voted for total war, did they also vote to lift the bans on all the living weapons ?"

Ah-Jord grinned, " They were stored in the Recorder and it has been ordered to send out the specs for all weapons, banned or not. We've got big replicators all over this area, so we have thousands of these fighters now, all over the Habitable planets, there are even more on Arotosa."

" Now when do we test these things out ?" Ah-ztes asked

Ah-Jord picked up a small thought-thrower, " All personnel report for the first test flight tomorrow at 0-800 hours, that is all."

*   *   *

The next day came , the dawning of the three sun's were very blinding and stunning. Ah-Jord was standing on a barrel and thinking into a portable thought-thrower.

" Good morning people. As I said before I had to do some homework. So I've been downloading information all night, right into my brain. I know the capabilities of this craft and I've talked to pilots who've flown them against the humans lately. It won't be easy as I thought to beat the humans, but it's possible.

We are ready to test these pieces of junk for the first time now, so if there are there any objections to why we shouldn't test these things fully, let's hear them now. " said Ah-Jord.

" Yes I object to testing. Let's not waste time. Let's fight right now. I swear, if there's no action within the next week than I am going to quit." said a female voice.

Ah-Jord looked down to his left, Ah-Sarak was smiling and looking up at him.Ah-Jord smiled back and got off the barrel.

" So what is the news ? Are you part of the group or are you a Sergeant again?"

"I am the second in command of your squad, so I have to stay here today - in case our glorious leader doesn't make it back. They want to be sure there's still a chain of command." she said.

" Do you know how to fly these ?" said Ah-Jord.

" Yes I know, so I can skip today's training."

" OK, see you later. All pilots to your saucers," said Ah-Jord.

The engines in the fighters shot out flakes from

the exhaust pipes, the hover engines gave out a loud, low growl, like powerful beasts awakening from a long slumber.

Ah-ztes and Ah-Ah-Jord walked up to a saucer colored red with a light silver covering.

" Are you ready to pilot this, skipper ?" said the mechanic/keepers .

" Yes I am." said Ah-Jord.

Ah-ztes nervously shook his head.

Ah-Jord climbed up to the cockpit and sat down. He put on his seat belt and strapped his left hand to the joy stick.

Ah-ztes climbed up and sat down behind him facing the opposite direction.

Ah-Jord was surprised. " So, you are my new co-pilot, gunner and bomb plotter."

Ah-ztes looked at Ah-Jord,

"Lucky you" he said. He smiled and took a pill from his utility pocket and swallowed it, Suddenly his eyes turned black . " Lets get it over with." he said.

Ah-Jord smiled and took a pill, his eyes turned dark black as well.

" Hover engines on, Waste materials now clearing, Plasma cannons are perfect, and our Master engines are still intact." came the thought from living the ship itself

"Close the hatch, we're taking off."

Ah-ztes pushed a small button. The top Hatch closed and locked.

" Hold on there is going to be a forward jerk."said Ah-Jord.

The Saucer growled, and the big ship bent upwards as if coming alive, shooting out clouds of air to the ground and snarling. It took off into the sky with a single burst .

There they met hundreds of other fighters ready for their training.

And their destiny.

Chapter 10

Interception attack by the Black Fighter

"**G**rit leader, this is Grit two." said the Wing Leader on the radio,

Ah-Jord smiled , "I hear you, Grit two."

" Should we try firing as well as flying ?" asked

" Sure, take half of the squad to practice targeting on the rocks on the mountain top."

" Roger that,"

Ah-Jord looked over to his left and saw thirty-five fighters pull away.

All of a sudden a small black Bird-like fighter appeared, all dented and spanged, with four rockets on the back of it. It was bulky and squarish, having big thick wings and the sign of a human skull and cross bones printed on its left wing.

" Attention all fighters. Attention all fighters. We have an unidentified flying object. Stand by for assault, I repeat , stand by for assault ! Don't worry. Your aircraft are intelligent, they know what to do. Just keep in thought-link and give it directions now and then and you'll be fine.

Trust your fighter. It's programmed to do this.".

Ah-Jord sent a private thought to Ah-ztes; "What is that - something Ah-Sarak sent up to spook us ? Is this a training simulation or something ?"

The Black Fighter started to go faster, turning from side to side, It started to fire on the saucers.

"I don't know. If it is, it sure seems real" Ah-ztes thought back at his pilot

" It has assaulted , It has assaulted, Red Alert. Destroy it now. Destroy it now !" Ah-Jord said. "Ah-ztes put a lock on it, We are going to fire the Charge Bombs on that sucker."

" Right away, sir" said Ah-ztes.

Ah-ztes reached to his left, searching for the Joystick. He strapped the joystick belt around his hand, and turned on the computer. Red lines appeared in the screen.

" Locked on target" said the ship.

The Black fighter started shooting bullets so Ah-ztes now knew that the Black fighter was a Human fighter. This was no drill. This was war.

" Ah-Jord sir, That is a Human plane sir. It's not a simulation. We are going to need something a little stronger to get that out of the sky."

" Load four Charge Bombs on that sucker,"

The Black fighter started to shoot again, it closed on to a saucer. The saucer, with its inexperienced pilot, didn't stand a chance against it . The saucer exploded in seconds.

" Grit leader, This is Grit Two, Ah-Sazer and Ah-Frox are gone,"said the radio.

" I want all fighters to try and shoot that thing down, It is not a practice simulation, it is a real Human Fighter."said Ah-Jord.

The Black fighter closed onto another victim, and shot bullets at it. The saucer was hit at the right wing, it pulled up, and started shooting plasma at the Black fighter.

" Grit leader, this is Grit four, I've been hit really bad, My gunner is dead, I am working on manual, the ship seems mostly dead. I need some help now. I don't know how long I can hold this fighter before he gets me." said the radio.

" Don't worry, Four, I am locked on him, Ah-ztes get ready to shoot the Charges at it when I give the command !"

Ah-ztes nodded and nervously put his thumb near the trigger.

Ah-Jord slowly increased the speed, the fighter came closer and closer,

" Wait"

Ahztes put his hands on the cannon triggers.

"Hold it."

Ah-ztes became jumpy, he began to sweat.

" Hold it."

" NOW"

Ah-ztes pushed the trigger but nothing happened, "MALFUNCTION, MALFUNCTION!," cried the computer.

The fighter fired on the student saucer, and sent it spinning to its death. Ah-Jord furiously pushed the triggers for the plasma cannons, and added the thought force that would target the weapon. This time it worked. Plasma flamed quickly out of the cannon barrels on the saucer, and chased the black fighter through twists and turns until it hit the fighter nine times on the wing . Fire came out as a quick gushes of flames.

The Black fighter spun around. It became stable and flew down towards the ground.

All of a sudden a skull and cross bones, laughing ,appeared on the screen of the Shecklak computer. A message came on, the translator on the computer translated: " Naughty, naughty - you amateurs."

A hovering sound was heard, Ah-ztes looked up and saw the Black Fighter, suddenly above them

" Ah-Jord , get us out of here," said Ah-ztes.

Ah-Jord quickly turned around and saw the fighter about to shoot.

"No Human is going to take me down," said Ah-Jord.

" Ah-ztes duck!,"

The guns on the black fighter started to shoot endlessly. Bullet holes were everywhere. Bullets were being flicked off and bounced all over on the living skin of the wings and in the cock pit . The shooting stopped, suddenly.

" Ah-ztes, are you all right?," whispered Ah-Jord.

" I am all right" Ah-ztes responded."But sometimes I don't mind being small."

" Hold on tight, We are going to kill that bastard. Slowly climb to the seat and strap on." said Ah-Jord.

Ah-ztes climbed up from the bottom of the seat, where he'd been hiding and sat down.

The fighter was gone.

" Ah-ztes push the reserve engines button on the side of the control panel."

" Reserve engines on!" said the computer.

Ah-Jord reached for the joystick , all covered in broken glass and scrap metal. Ah-Jord grabbed the joystick, hit the exhaust button and flew off.

" Ah-Jord, we should go back for repairs," said Ah-ztes.

"Not until I shoot that fighter down,"

"Ah-Jord this is crazy, we are lucky to be alive."

"Fine, you're right. I guess I've caught the disease now. I just want to kill that bastard."Ah-Jord sighed.

The saucer covered in bullet holes and broken shrapnel took a sharp turn and set a course back to the base.

" Grit Ground, this is Grit leader, I want permission to land" said Ah-Jord.

" Permission granted," said the radio.

The saucer stopped flying, the hover engines were on and it slowly landed into the cargo shaft.

" Ah-ztes , open the cockpit hatch."

Ah-ztes reached up and grabbed the handles of the smashed, cracked top hatch. He opened it .

Ah-ztes first climbed out of the saucer, tired and shakey from the attack. Ah-Jord came out second, now even more paranoid, shakey, and tired. The repair crew quickly ran to the wounded saucer, bringing gadgets and tools , like doctors ready to operate.

Ah-ztes and Ah-Jord walked to the door. As they

reached it, the door opened up. Ah-Jord looked up and saw Sergeant Ah-Vessk, She was startled from this surprising encounter and walked up to him.

" What the hell happened ? Where did that Black fighter come from?" she said.

" It was just one Human alone, on ambush patrol, he jammed our radar somehow. But that's not the scary part. The scary part is this: just that one shot down three of our saucers - even though we scored direct hits on him - I hit him nine times myself."

" Are your pilots trained. You're in charge of training ?" said Ah-Vessk.

" What?,"

" Are your pilots trained for combat - all I hear is that you sit in the cafeteria telling stories ?"

" No, they are still in the training stages of attack flight."

" Well get them ready , the humans have attacked the settlement again, Tomorrow you attack at dawn." said Ah-Vessk.

" Why can't you call any of the other squads to take them out. We are just not ready ?"

" Look, I don't like you and you don't like me, You should be ready. If you're not, then it's your responsibility. I wouldn't use you if I didn't have to. You guys are the last squad on this planet, all the rest are up in space with the fleet and every officer over me, planning their next freaking attack, This makes me in charge of you, the troops and this good-for-nothing base."

"Boy I bet that sure limits your career opportunities. Let me talk with my pilots tomorrow and we'll decide if I will attack the base tomorrow,"

"Don't worry about my career - I'll do just fine. You won't. You don't seem to realize you're under orders here and we are at war. I know where you come from - I have your entire history on file - And I know how flawed you are. I don't have time for your snivelling. You WILL attack the humans base tomorrow. Whether you want to or not. Is that clear ?

"OK"

WHAT ?"

"Yes Ma'am, that is perfectly clear"

Ah-Vessk , turned around sharply and walked away.

"You don't like her at all, Do you?" asked Ah-ztes.

" She is a pain, but she is just a messenger, no heart whatsoever, She was always out only for herself and this has just made it more obvious. She is Ah-Vessk. But who am I ? What's happening to us that we're squabbling among ourselves. This war business is more dangerous than we ever thought it would be." said Ah-Jord.

" So, since you are the Leader, shouldn't you be checking on your pilots ?" Said Ah-ztes,

"What - you want to insult me now, too. I don't know anything about this leadership stuff. Their business is their business. If they are in shock, the last thing they want is to see me and if they are scared, and who wouldn't be after today, they won't want me to see it." said Ah-Jord.

" Then what do we do now ?" said Ah-ztes.

" We wait until tomorrow, then we follow out the orders , and wait for other orders - is that clear ?"Ah- Jord joked.

Ah-ztes looked up at him then said, " Crystal. I think we should check the hospital deck, to see if we have any wounded."

" All right, I guess I should check the casualties. They could use a few words of consolation." Said Ah-Jord. He started walking down the hall and Ah-ztes followed.

They reached the hospital door and looked in.

" Doctor I need to see the casualties list," Said Ah-Jord.

" Shh !" said the doctor.

Ah-Jord saw Ah-Sarak there, lying on the operations table. Her artificial eye was taken off,

The doctor, wearing gloves and a mouth guard, was operating inside the empty eye socket. The doctor then put living machines over the operation cuts, stitches, scars and other damaged skin. The skin was repaired in a matter of minutes. The doctor took off the machines. He took out a needle from a shelf and injected her with a serum. Ah-Sarak woke up, immediately. She stood up and turned around. Her left eye now didn't carry the bulky monstrosity on her eye socket. She now carried a new beautiful working eye.

" Make sure that you keep this one working" said the Doctor.

She nodded and walked off.

Ah-Jord bumped into her , surprised and a little dizzy.

"What happened to you. I thought you were here on base, out of the action. Did you get wounded ?" asked Ah-Jord.

" That eye was temporary. It stopped working while

you were gone and I came here to get it fixed. I heard you ran into a human."

"Whew. Did we ever. He took out three saucers and just sailed away. I hit him nine times myself and a lot of the others scored too. Nothing fazed him. He could have shot us all down if he had the time and the bullets."

"You actually hit him ?"

"Yes. Confirmed."

"When you gave the thought-assist to your plasma, did you think human fighter, or human being ?"

"Human fighter, of course. That was the target"

"You know, I think that was the problem. Remember I told you the humans win 3 out of 4 encounter ?"

"Yes"

Usually the 1 out of 4 we win is where someone rams the human. We can't seem to hurt them by shooting them with plasma - yet the plasma rifles work well on ground troops. So I think I have the answer. Plasma was designed only to hurt living things. It leaves the environment alone. But the human fighters are non-living. The plasma can't hurt them. We might have better results if we think of the human pilots as the target. Then the plasma can chase the living part of the fighter."

"You'll get a chance to find out. We've been ordered to attack the human base tomorrow. We're having a meeting tomorrow at the Docking bay to talk about it. Be there. Tell everyone this new strategy then - and Ah-Sarak - I want you in the air for this mission. We'll need all the experienced pilots we can get."

" Good, I guess. But if it's a big mission then I am

going to need a gunner. I was never assigned one."

"Don't worry, a couple of pilots were hurt and their gunners are available. But I think you can handle your self without a gunner. Just be there - we'll get it all sorted out."

"Don't worry, I'll be there. I wouldn't miss it"

11

Chapter

The final attack on Degos

The next day came. The Sergeant, Ah-Vessk, was waiting outside near the docking bay. The entire squad gathered in front of her, worried and angry, Out of the crowd of the 100 pilots only one man, Ah-Jord, walked up to her.

" We are ready to do your dirty work now !" He said.

Ah-Vessk climbed up on a barrel and began talking into a microphone.

"You, and your damned squad are going to bomb the area on the ridge of the settlement, Sergeant Ah-Nik had to retreat from that area so it is our job to get it back. Ah-Nik will be piloting a squad just like yours. When you get there he will give your next orders.

The area that all of you will have to destroy is the canyon plains fourteen miles off the settlement. The area there is full of human infestation. Cure it." she stepped down.

Ah-Jord started stpeaking: "In order to do that, Sergeant Ah-Sarak has come up with a new strategy. You know what happened yesterday - one human and we couldn't touch him. We think we know why. Today, when you are think-assisting your plasma with targeting, think human, rather than ship or building. Let the plasma seek out living humans rather than their machines - and we should have better results - just like ground troops have such good luck with the plasma rifles. So think human. Dead human. That's it. Well you heard the woman, lets attack and kill. Divide and conquer. Erase and re-write." said Ah-Jord.

Ah-Vessk came up to Ah-Jord." You are not going to kill any of the humans on that territory. You should only scare them a little bit and make them leave." whispered Ah-Vessk.

"Official orders have changed. We're not to act intelligently anymore. Now we are supposed to kill, maim, and destroy. It's total war now - didn't they tell you. The orders just came in from Congress Moon."

"I don't agree with those orders. I think acting like that will doom us."

"As you so clearly pointed out yesterday, I only exist to take orders. So I'll kill all I can kill."

"It's wrong. Please, be civilized out there. There's more at stake than you know."

" OK - here's what I'll do - I won't shoot them first, but if they even throw a freaking rock at us, then we are going to have an extermination." said Ah-Jord

"No. That's not good enough. Do it my way. Only scare them. Don't shoot at them - even if you are under fire yourself. That's an order !"

"Sorry, orders from Congress Moon are bigger than orders from you. I only exist to carry out orders - and the bigger the better. So today, my inexperienced pilots, who I told you are not ready for this, will follow the Congress Moon order of total war."

Ah-Vessk , now furious, walked over to the side of the wall where the door was, She opened the door and walked through and. childishly, slammed it, then went up the stair case into a little observation room and watched the preparations.

The huge cargo doors opened. The crack of dawn shone through the bay and onto the saucers, The golden light created thin shadows of almost everything in the room. The preparations for destruction, for that one golden moment, looked like a work of art.

" Start loading up, we are now going to war. Remember - think dead human - and be careful. I want to see you all back here later."shouted Ah-Jord, breaking the spell.

The Mechanics started leaning ladders onto the sides of the saucers, they climbed up and opened each of the cockpit hatches.

Ah-ztes and Ah-Jord climbed into their repaired saucer. They sat down on the back to back seats, The cock pit was picked clean of every single piece of broken glass.

Ah-ztes strapped on the seat and the joystick, he turned the saucer monitors on and, with a flash of a button, all the ship awoke and came to life, feeding it's thoughts directly into the brains of the pilots.

"The gas is stable , the weight of the ship is equal, the computers are fully functional. This ship is perfect, it's like it was never in battle, the mechanic's did a perfect job in fixing the old bastard," said Ah-ztes.

"Are we clear to take it into the air ?" said Ah-Jord.

"Yes, as soon as the whole squad is ready , we can take this baby into the air."

"All right," said Ah-Jord. He turned the radio on, he spoke into it,

"All right, Grit squad, are you ready for take off ?"

" Grit Two ready for take off!, Grit Five, ready for take off, Grit Seven, ready for take off , Grit Ten , ready for take off !" The radio shouted out 67 'readys'.

" Ah-ztes, send a message to Ah-Vessk in the control tower, we are ready for take off," said Ah-Jord.

Ah-ztes nodded, he turned the plane's neon lights on, on each side of the ship the lights started to flash red and orange,

"The signal is on !" said Ah-ztes.

The engines turned on, the saucer slowly moved outside then stopped and the hover engines came on.

" All right Boy, I hope you have buckled up, we are now going into Human infestation!" yelled Ah-Jord.

Ah-ztes nodded, took out two dark pills, he took one then gave the other to Ah-Jord.

"Thanks for giving me my shades Ah-ztes, now hang on,"

The saucer shot straight upwards. It darted through the sky then stopped in the middle of the air.

" Ah-ztes , look in front of you,"

" I see nothing."

" Keep looking."

Ah-ztes looked harder. Suddenly other saucers , thirty-two of them, darted through the sky. They stopped in the air as well, in perfect formation - the living brains of each ship in perfect communication with the lead saucer.

" Where are the other thirty-five?" asked Ah-ztes.

" They are heading for the first bombing, with Ah-Sarak. I like her. She really knows her stuff. I think this new strategy will work."

"So what are we waiting for ?"

"Ah-Sarak and I came up with a plan. She'll bomb them flat - then when the fighters come out in response, like bees from a broken nest, we'll sneak up behind them. We are going to attack when we get her signal."

A blinking red light on the joystick went on,

"The signal has reached us. Send the message in thought that we are dropping on them from behind."said Ah-Jord.

Ah-ztes reached for the control pad, he pushed the red flashing light , The message was sent. The other saucers started to move closer together,

" Why are the fighters moving closer together ?" asked Ah-ztes.

" Remember what happened yesterday. That one guy cut out saucers from the group and got them alone so he could attack them - like a predator does. We learn from our mistakes - so today we bunch together in a different formation to prevent separation and ambush by the enemy. This way we should have a better chance from surprise attack . We should be at the target area now"

" The mist is clearing, the target is right under us ."

" I don't see any fighters - let's use our time constructively - Ah-ztes, aim two charge bombs on to the target, we are going to give a little aftershock shot for the humans who survived the first strike. They're going to wish they had never messed with the Degosian defense"

Ah-ztes put his hands on to the joystick, he looked into the targeting computer on his left.

" 90%, 97%, 100%! , charge bombs have dropped." said Ah-ztes.

Ah-ztes opened the bottom screen on the floor of the saucer, he looked through the bottom screen at the base, a bright light from the explosion caused the saucer to rumble, Ah-ztes closed the hatch and looked at the sonar computer.

" Ah-Jord, we've attracted some trouble, the black fighter and a hell lot more fighters are coming our way."

" That can't be, they should be after Ah-Sarak. It's too early for them to notice unless -"

" What - Unless we were followed ?"

"Or unless some-one, who disagreed with the new total war order, informed the humans of our plan. "

Ah-Jord quickly reached for the radio, " Attention all units. Attention all units. Prepare for combat. This is the action you all have been waiting for. Remember - think human. Think dead human."

Ah-Jord looked at Ah-ztes, " Ah-ztes, get ready, we are going against the Human Henchmen !"

Ah-ztes grinned, " Bring forth the Henchmen!"

Ah-Jord grinned and turned around.

Ah-ztes looked at his sonar screen, then at his view out the cockpit wind screen, "Ah-Jord!, They -, um, they are looking down on us, literally!"

Ah-Jord looked up and saw the black fighter and hundreds of other fighters swarming the sky.

" All saucers, all saucers load plasma cannons, the enemy is on top of us. Start thinking dead human now !"

" Ah-ztes, hold on!, it is time to kill."

Ah-ztes looked worried, he closed his eyes and thought human. Thought humans laughing as they killed his mother. Thought humans uncaring as Ah-Quasferatu died.

The saucer pulled up suddenly and the plasma cannons erupted in a hatred of fire.

The thirty saucers soared upwards out of the clouds like streams of light. Human fighters, racing down towards them, began dropping, out of control, as the newly directed plasma found it's human victim, time and time again.

As more and more of their forces began spinning away with dead men at the helm, the human fighters began to realize that they were outgunned, but, rather than retreat, they pressed on, faster and faster, toward the saucers, hoping to get within bullet range so they could inflict some damage.

" Grit Leader, they are everywhere. Too many for my plasma. I can't lose them. Help me!" cried the radio

" Don't worry Grit Five, I 've locked on to that

sucker, Think - dead human."

Ah-Jord turned the radio off, he cracked his knuckles watching the target computer cry silently as it flashed information on his face, seeking another target.

"Thanks Grit Leader. I owe you one."

"You owe me 3 - Grit four"Said Ah-Jord, then grabbed his joy stick and began to fire plasma. Shot by shot the human fighters fell out of play as their pilots were hunted down by hate-directed plasma.

" Ah-ztes, wake up!"

Ah-ztes opened his eyes. "Leave me alone. I'm smoking humans."

"How many so far ?"

"I count 23"

It's too easy. Open your eyes. We are going after that Black fighter that outgunned us last time. Get ready and think-assist those charge bombs, We don't want the same thing to happen."

Ah-ztes nodded, and turned the info-read to maximum,

"Ah-Jord , I found him, he is a trouble making bastard, that one. We don't have to even look for him, he is coming this way !"

All of a sudden bullets came flying to the wind shield. Bullet holes once more haunted them, letting in whistling air and cold high altitude weather,

" It's time for the reckoning" said Ah-Jord.

Ah-Jord grabbed the Joystick, he started to fly after the Black fighter. The Black fighter swayed side to side but Ah-Jord always managed to catch up.

Suddenly on Ah-ztes' screen, strange writing started scrolling by.

" Ah-Jord, a message is coming in, it is not Degosian I could tell you that !"

The ship's brain, updated at manufacture with the new human language, translated the writing out loud.

" For those who try to offend me, death shall come in the most painful suffering way..."

The computer printed out a small sheet of plastic, which contained the writing. Ah-ztes handed it to Ah-Jord and Ah-Jord quickly browsed through it and frowned. "Is it the translation, or is this guy really that melodramatic ?"

Ah-ztes shrugged and shook his head. He sent a lash of plasma chasing the fighter.

" Ah-ztes are those charge bombs still locked and loaded ?"

" Yes they are,"

" You've redirected them at the human ?"

"Sort of - they're a lot stupider than plasma."

"OK - when I give the command, We are going to shoot the black fighter."

" Just say when"

" Now!"

Two bombs dropped out of the saucer, and followed the Black fighter, like shadows as it swerved to avoid them. The two bombs hit the black fighter right on the cock pit, seeking the human within.

The fighter exploded into a thousand pieces of shrapnel.

" Finally we have killed him !." cried Ah-Jord. "No - look. He's ejected "

"Where, I don't see"

Suddenly another strange message came into the communicator again.

" Ah-Jord, another message is coming in," said Ah-ztes

The computer read, "Lucky shot ! But you missed me !"

Ah-Jord furiously hit the computer

"DAMN!" he shouted," That monster is still out there ! If we can't trust our eyes then how can we fight him ?"

" Ah-Jord, We killed the Black fighter, it's over. That message was made before he was hit !"

" But how could he know he was going to be hit?, I am not convinced that he is dead!"

"I sent a plasma jet at him - that's the one that missed."

Suddenly the radio was calling out a "Must-hear" signal, Ah-Jord picked it up and switched to "listen".

" Grit leader, Grit Leader , This is Sergeant Ah-Sarak - I'm on the ground, we have taken back the base - the humans seem to have left. You have to land your vessels on the settlement streets now!."

" Roger that Ah-Sarak , but there are still human fighters up here"

" I just intercepted a signal. Sergeant Ah-Vessk just sent a vapor bomb coming your way ! You will be safe on the ground but not in the sky. This explosion will not effect anyone under a height of 20 feet."

" Oh My Gods !," Ah-Jord said; "Is she nuts ? The whole squad is up here dogfighting. If we turn tail, the humans will blast us."

"If you don't, the vapor bomb will blast you worse"

"Roger that. Let me inform my squad." He turned the radio on to the squadron frequency.

" All units damaged and perfect we are to land immediately ! This is an emergency ! Do not hesitate for questions this is a life or death situation ! There's a vapor bomb incoming. I repeat, vapor bomb. Disengage. Land. Now. Over and out." Ah-Jord turned the radio off, He shut off the main engines and put on the hover engines and quickly fell to the ground.

One by one the other saucers landed. The pilots and gunners quickly got out of the saucers and took off into the settlement buildings.

Ah-Jord opened the cockpit hatch. He slid down the side of the saucer, flipped over and sprawled in the street. He got up, turned and saw that Ah-ztes didn't make it out.

" Ah-ztes, get out of the cock pit, that bomb is going cause a gigantic explosion and there'll be a huge suction hurricane right after when air rushes into the vacuum that it creates. If you don't get into a shelter, you might get sucked into it."

Ah-ztes looked at Ah-Jord strangely. He stood up and said quietly; " I can't go into the settlement. It brings back too many memories of killing and torture. My mother and everyone I knew died here."

"If you don't get out you will die here too !"

" I guess that I will have to take that chance!"

All of a sudden a human fighter came diving down from the sky. It started to fire on the landed fighters. Ah-Jord was startled by the gun fire. He fell to the street and quickly crawled under a broken piece of scrap metal lying beside the saucer. Ah-ztes closed the hatch, sat down, and turned on the plasma cannons. The human fighter came back to finish off the saucers firing many rounds of bullets.

Ah-ztes aimed the plasma cannons at the fighter and closed his eyes, think-assisting every stream of plasma. The plasma shots arced out over the field, torching the cockpit and trying to get at the human pilot inside. The human realized he was in trouble and began trying to avoid the flaming streamers, but they followed every twist and turn he made and eventually one got in some minor crack and smoked him.

They watched the human fighter go from a tightly controlled machine to a brainless meteorite in a split second. It went straight down and crumped into the ground raising a cloud of dust. There was no fire -and no-one got out of the wreckage.

Ah-ztes quickly opened the hatch, he slid down the side of the saucer and ran to Ah-Jord,

" Ah-Jord , are you all right ?"

" Yes , his shots didn't even come close. Now that you're out, where can we find shelter ?"

" We should be safe in the Gate Tower."

" All right, we don't have much time, where is it ?"

"Just over there."

Ah-ztes helped Ah-Jord up and they ran over to the Gate Tower.

All of a sudden a siren went off. Giant rusty, gritty walls came up from the ground sealing off all of the doors and windows on every standing building.

" Ah-ztes do you know why the buildings-"

" The automatic defense was placed in every house seven years ago. It was designed for meteor showers." Ah-ztes sighed.

" Damn!"

" Now what are we going to do ?"

"The program doesn't work on damaged houses, Quick we have a chance in one of the ruins. I know some. They aren't very far away !"

Ah-ztes grabbed Ah-Jords sleeve, he ran to a torn down building. Ah-Jord saw a door, partly destroyed but intact. He tried to open the door, but it wouldn't move. Ah-Jord furiously kicked it several times until it opened.

" Quickly , the explosion won't kill us because it is in the sky but it could suck us into the explosion. Ah-ztes, tie yourself to anything sealed to the ground !"

Ah-ztes took a piece of cable off a broken outlet and tied himself to a sealed-off water tap dispenser. Ah-Jord took off his belt, tied himself to some broken pipes sticking out of the ground and held on to the pipes very tightly.

Ah-Jord looked up, seeing the human fighters flying in their formation waiting for the aliens to attack them. Thn he looked to the left side of the sky . The bomb was coming , it was small, flaming and coming in like a bolt of lightning.

" Ah-ztes , cover your eyes, It's going to be so bright that people in Sivil will see this explosion !"shouted Ah-Jord. Ah-ztes saw the bomb coming closer and closer. Ah-ztes started to close his eyes.

The bomb finally detonated.

The explosion was extreme, all the fighters turned into flaming scraps of wasted metal. The sky turned from dark blue to a bright yellow and actually started burning.

The explosion started to die down, the winds of death pushed and pulled on Ah-Jord and Ah-ztes . The winds pushed extremely hard on them, like giant weights.

The winds then started to suck in air because of the pressure of the explosion, the winds became weaker for a while then became almost a vacuum as air rushed into the space where it had been blasted away.

Ah-ztes started to hold tightly to the cable tied to the rusty water displacer. He opened his eyes and saw millions of small flaming pieces of metal hitting the ground like hot rain. The remains of the human fleet.

Ah-Jord opened his eyes and saw the pale sky with nothing flying in it. No life, no machines and no humans.

The winds started to suck up dust and falling debris. Ah-ztes felt that he was being lifted from the ground, so was Ah-Jord. The pull on Ah-ztes became stronger . He began to fly around dangling on the cable tied to the dispenser.

" Ah-Jord!, how long will the suction last for ?"

"Just a few minutes. Just hold on to the cable !"

The winds sucked up everything that was not tied

down.

Ah-ztes , having his life on the line , pulled his way to the dispenser. He climbed down the cable, hoping to get a better grip on the pipes. He finally grabbed the pipe and held on tightly. only to feel it suddenly come loose.

Ah-ztes became scared. He started to fly upwards to the vacuum explosion, sucked right out of the window of the ruined house. Then, a giant net attached to the side of the house to catch falling building material, caught him.

Ah-ztes was relieved.

The explosion started to die down and the suction stopped gradually.

Ah-ztes, tangled in the net, fell to the ground. Debris once more started to fall to the ground. Ah-ztes tried to get loose from the net but he was trapped.

Ah-Jord quickly untied his belt from his hands and ran over to Ah-ztes . He took out a pair of rusty blade pliers. He bent down and cut Ah-ztes loose from the net, helped him up and tried to make him stand.

Ah-ztes stood for a while but then fell.

" Ah-ztes your leg might not work for awhile, the explosion caused an electric storm , there is going to be a magnetic impulse all over this settlement that wil prevent anything electronic from working."

" Damn!, now how are we going to get out of here?"said Ah-ztes.

" Most of the squad and troops are in the sealed off towers, They are going to be trapped for a while unless there is another way out."

" All the doors here are electronic, there is no way

out for them."

" Ah-Jord, how long exactly do we have to wait until everything is working?"

" Possibly four hours, these magnetic ikmpulse storms rarely last for days."

" So do we wait ?"

" Yes , we have to wait for a search and rescue team to fetch us."

" Wouldn't they be effected by the storm ?"

"Not really, the storm only effected the electronics that were in the area of the explosion - they should be all right."

Ah-ztes sat down on a rock and looked at the sky. Ah-Jord lay down on the floor and looked at Ah-ztes.

" Why are you so scared of this place?"Ah-Jord said.

" This is where I used to live. I grew up here. I knew everyone and every corner and alley. It was my whole world. The funny thing is that learning about the legend of the humans was part of my education. It was such a fantastic story that I just didn't believe it. It couldn't be true - intelligent beings that killed and warred ? Couldn't be. I lived a normal life here, right in these streets, until the Humans came and invaded.

Here I was shot in the leg, they came and took me somewhere where they cut my leg off. My family, friends, people I liked , all died here either being executed or dying of something else.

Here I am scared and I can never be the same as I was when this war started, Now I am no longer that carefree happy boy I was. And I never will be that again. Now

I am a killing machine driven by hate, revenge and the hope of their extinction."

" I am sorry."

" Sorry about what ? This event has opened my eyes, I now realize my true meaning in this war. I am the rememberer. I'm recording it all. I remember what we were like and what has been lost. I remember so well so that I can hate so well. Kill so well."

" I am sorry that there is no hope of you thinking of peace. They traumatized you, I know that will never be fixed, but that's what's required for the humans to get what they want - and what they want is this land.

You, the ordinary people, are brought into this war because the humans would rather die fighting than die of extermination in their home worlds. They fight for their very lives. You on the other hand fight for revenge. That is not the way that you should fight."

"How should you fight ?" asked Ah-ztes." With a song in your heart ?"

"No, you should fight like scratching an itch. Do what is necessary to make the itch go away, then don't scratch anymore. After a certain point, you only hurt your-self."

"You have never killed anyone before, have you Ah-Jord ? Even today, you only piloted the saucer, it was me who sent the plasma and bombs on their way. Let me tell you this, once you have killed, with your own hands , your personality changes, you are not the same person any more. You become more respectful, more anxious and much more skilled. Gods - if my family were alive, I wonder if they would recognize me now. Do you know that I had my birthday when I was lying int hat filthy cellar and that girl was dying. Now I'm 12. I was hoping to get some action figures for a present - but my parents said it might be a bad influece and make me violent. I'm glad they can't see me now.

"I envy you your family. They sound very warm and friendly"

"Envy - they are all dead except my brother - and he was on a survey ship - so he was likely the first one the humans ran into. I don't hold out much hope of him being alive either. What's to envy ?"

" I have no family at all nor any memories of any. I was created in the vats a month ago. I am one of the military weapons that was replicated. But I am flawed somehow. Killing and violence are supposed to be in my DNA, but I can't seem to find them. No matter how big I talk or what stories I tell, I believe in peace. If I had to vote, I would side with Ah-Vessk. I just can't kill. So I envy you on two counts - you had a family - and because you don't have them anymore, you can kill.

Killing shouldn't bother me as it would bother other people. I was created for it. But it does and I just can't force myself to do it."

"Then I envy you, my friend. It seems to be the only thing I can do now."

Ah-Jord stood up , something caught his eye . He walked over to see what it was

"Ah-Jord !" came a voice, out loud. "Ah-Jord is that you?"

Ah-ztes stood up and limped over to Ah-Jord. The figure came closer , then turned into two figures - one squirming and the other dragging the squirmer.

The dragging object became clearer, it was Ah-Sarak pulling a human in a strange uniform. The human had a very dark skin color from the other ones that the Degosians had encountered, the clothes that it wore were all black with pattern and other signs on the jacket. It was trapped in a net and squirming like a snake trying to break loose.

" Ah-Sarak ! How did you escape the vacuum?"

" I landed in a cave not too far from here, before the vapor bomb went off. I called it in, remember.

I landed right inside the cave to avoid the magnetic pulse. I wasn't alone either, I found this little monkey hiding in the shadows and armed to his ass. He almost shot me but I still caught him. I didn't realize we were so much stronger than them."

" So did you get effected from the pulse ?"

" Nope. I stayed inside so I wouldn't get exposed, see, my eye still works and my saucer still is functional."

" The thought thrower still works ?"

" Yes."

Ah-Jord quickly ran towards Ah-Sarak, he put his arms out then grabbed Ah-Sarak and hugged her.

" Ah-Sarak you are a life saver" said Ah-Jord.

Ah-Sarak smiled."I wondered how long it would take you to notice."

" Ah-Jord ? Just what are we going to do with the Heum ?" asked Ah-ztes.

Ah-Jord looked down at him, he then recognized a small black patch on his left shoulder, it was the same skull and crossbones picture he remembered from the Black fighter.

" It's him!, he is the Black fighter."

" Well, he is black skinned, but that can't be. That was the one we shot down. Disintegrated it." said Ah-ztes.

" Then they're all part of the Black fighter group ?"

Ah-Jord looked at the human tied uncomfortably in the net. Ah-Jord became angry , blood ran to his head and fists and his eyes became watery. He then ran to the human and started kicking it in the stomach.

Ah-Sarak ran to Ah-Jord trying to stop him from killing the human,

" Ah-Jord!, what are you doing?"Ah-Sarak quickly kicked Ah-Jords right leg, tripping him onto his ass.

" What has gotten to you? Five minutes ago you were happy to see me , the next you're trying to kill this poor heum ?"

Ah-Jord looked up at Ah-Sarak , he closed his eyes.

" I have a problem with that skull symbol. I am going crazy, I have an urge to kill every human I see. You are going to have to put the human out of my sight. If you don't, I will have the urge to kill it."

" Ah-Jord, snap out of it, This is not the pilot of the Black fighter you want to destroy ! Besides, the pilot of the black fighter should of died from the charges we sent him."

"I saw with my own eyes that the pilot ejected out before the fighter exploded. I know that he is alive."

Ah-Jord yelled, then closed his eyes and calmed down.

" Anyway I am all beaten out, it is safe for you to let me stand up,"

Ah-Sarak moved out of the way, Ah-ztes limped over to Ah-Jord and stuck his right hand out at him, Ah-Jord grabbed his and stood up.

" So now what ?" he said.

" Do we wait ?"asked Ah-Sarak.

Ah-Jord smiled," We'll use Ah-Sarak's thought-thrower to get help, then we wait."

Ah-Sarak sat down on a rock, looking at the Human Ah-Jord sat down close to her .

" What do you think we do with the Heum now?" asked Ah-ztes.

"Let's see if he knows anything that we should know." said Ah-Sarak. "Is there a translator around ?

"I have one" said Ah-Jord, pulling a button from his pocket.

"Give it to me. "Ah-Sarak reached out for it. "Ah-ztes, go and use the thought thrower in my saucer to send for help. It's in a cave by . . ."

"I know where the cave is."

"Meanwhile, we'll see if we can find out anything from this dog."

Ah-ztes went off toward the cave. Ah-Jord went to the window and stared out at the devastated town. The human began moving around inside the net.

"Tell us what your kind want" Ah-Sarak spoke aloud into the translator

The human spoke curtly. Ah-Sarak laughed out loud.

"What's that ?" asked Ah-Jord

"Maybe it's the translator, but it claims that the human said "Have sex with yourself and I will tell you nothing.""

"Perhaps it's a deal - you know, if you have sex with yourself, he will tell you nothing. If you don't, he will tell you everything."

They laughed aloud at the possible interpretations. The human got angrier and angrier, thrashing around in the net.

"Let's think about this" said Ah-Sarak and the two immediately went into think mode. "They say humans cannot detect thought communication", she thought at Ah-Jord, "and don't even suspect that we speak this way."

"I've heard that" Ah-Jord thought back.

"Let's double-think him. I'll ask the questions aloud, you read answers from his mind - then feed them to me."

"Sounds like fun, I'm ready" came Ah-Jord's thought.

"How many fighters do you have"said Ah Sarak to the human out loud.

"You'll get nothing from me" spat the human

"900" came the thought from Ah-Jord

"900 - eh ? That's not many " said Ah-Sarak out loud.

The human jumped. "Where did you get that figure from ? Is there a traitor ?"

"We have our sources. Now how many starships, human ?"

"None, alien bastard"

"4000" came the thought

"Just 4000 you say - I thought you were a much more

formidable enemy than that. We have more survey ships than you have starships."

"I said nothing. Where are you getting this information, you bastard ?"

"We know everything, we just want to see if you will tell us the truth. Like, how many troops do you have "

"I'll tell you nothing"

"500,000 - isn't that right ?"

"You think you're the only ones with spies" the human began shouting. "We've got traitors in your high command. They not only give us data, they will act against their own kind."

"Who ?"

"I'll never tell"

"He doesn't know"

"High Command sent the Vapor bomb that blew you guys out of the sky - is that treason ? " Ah-Jord asked out loud, switching around with Ah-Sarak

"Ha !" the human said

"Gods - he thinks that they were told about the Vapor Bomb. But they didn't believe any one of us would kill our own fighters - so they ignored the warning !"

"And Vessk never told us about the bomb - but told them ?"

"Vessk is the traitor ?"

"Couldn't be "

"She isn't happy with the total war thing "

"Who do we tell ?"

"No-one, until we're sure"

The human was getting nervous as the two friends

thought together.

"Your people fell for the traitor ruse - when we called up and told you about the Vapor Bomb, human - you believed that ?" Ah-Sarak pestered the human again. "We warned you and you still were destroyed - your race is not fit for civilization"

"Who are you getting this data from ? Tell me !" the human screamed

"Who do you think it is ?" prodded Ah-Sarak

"Shut-up !"

"The Supreme General is the name that popped into his mind." thought Ah-Jord

"Why disappoint him the" Ah-Sarak thought back. "The Supreme General Nevel Thomas tells us everything - we've promised him his own planet after you humans are defeated. We have no fear telling you this, because we are going to kill you in a couple of minutes anyway."

The human was now so angry he could barely move. Just stared hate looks at them

" He has been through a lot, I think we should just let him go." thought Ah-Sarak. "Besides, now he will spread rumours of our vast knowledge and of our revealing who the spy is - it could cause quite a bit of trouble for the humans" she continued her comments in thought-speak,

Ah-ztes walked up and rejoined them. "What are you guys up to - torturing poor dumb humans are you ?"

Ah-Jord sent him a thought summary.

"You guys are so devious" Ah-ztes thought at them

"You're right. We are. He's become a time bomb.

We are going to let him go and then watch him tell tales that will help destroy the human hordes." thought Ah-Jord

"OK - Let's kill him now" Ah-Sarak said out loud for the translators sake. "Let him go now Ah-ztes" she thought; "but be careful. It's like freeing a wild animal"

Ah-ztes looked at Ah-Jord, for his approval.

" Go ahead" Ah-Jord thought, "but listen to Ah-Sarak. The is one dangerous human"

"Don't be silly. He thinks we're going to kill him. He'll be totally passive" Ah-ztes thought confidently.

"They're not like us " warned Ah-Sarak in his mind

Ah-ztes laughed and took out the same pliers that had cut him loose earlier. He limped over to the scared human, bent down, took a sigh, then clipped the net. The human stood up really quickly, started cursing loudly in its human language, then turned to Ah-ztes and punched him.

Ah-ztes was knocked off his feet. He was knocked unconscious.

The human then went after Ah-Jord, quick as a reptile. Within a couple of steps, the human took something out of his pocket. He took out a handle, then he pushed a button and a blade flicked out. He came closer and closer to Ah-Jord , The human started waving the blade about trying to cut Ah-Jord. Ah-Jord dropped to the floor and quickly reached for the gun holder on his back. The human started to holler and then fell on top of Ah-Jord. Ah-Sarak was suddenly there, holding the human away from Ah-Jord. The human held by Ah-Sarak, swung his arms comically, trying to stab Ah-Jord, missing every time. Ah-Jord smoothly pulled out a medium sized Plasma gun, He aimed it at the humans head.

" You are going to wish you never ever stepped foot on Degos, Asshole!" he said out loud. "What the hell do we do now ? " he thought at the same time.

The Human felt the gun on the side of his temple. The human dropped the blade nervously, then quickly stood up and walked back wards.

Ah-Jord stood up holding his gun near the Human and following him backwards, step for step.

" Ah-Jord don't do it!, he is just a human, he is not worth the pride of being killed with a Plasma gun." yelled Ah-Sarak out loud. "Oh quit fooling around. Let the poor creature go before he hurts you " she thought-spoke.

Ah-Jord held the gun too close to the Human, His fingers were twitching, as if he were eager to shoot him. He pushed the human to the floor, then backed up as if to get a better shot.

The Human got up and ran away, twisting and weaving to avoid the shot he was sure was coming after him.

"Great acting" thought Ah-Sarak

Ah-Jord sat down, put the gun back in the holder and faced Ah-ztes.

"Is he dead " Ah-Jord asked in thought.

" No, his eyes have not turned grey, he is knocked unconscious. he'll be all right - and he'll never believe humans react like people again . Did you see him. He had such a shock on his face till he fell over"

Ah-Sarak walked over to Ah-Jord. She sat down

close to him and looked at him." Was that really acting. I really thought you were going to shoot that heum."

"I was working myself up to it."

"Our game didn't matter that much. You could have shot him. I don't care. And you know that. So why didn't you shoot the Heum when you had the chance ? "

" There were two reasons, One, I was only trying to scare him, as part of the game and Two , my plasma gun was custom made, It's electronic. It doesn't work in this atmosphere after the Vapor Bomb."

Ah-Sarak started to laugh,

" What's so funny ?" asked Ah-Jord in thought.

" You never intended to kill him,did you ?"

" No, not really."

Ah-Sarak smiled ,

" How do you think this war is going to turn out ?"

"One little starving human system against 50,000 civilized worlds - I think we'll win eventually. We have to. They can conquer a world a day for 100 years and we'll still have lots left. We're sure to win. As to the cost of that victory - well, I don't think about things like that."

" Then what do you think about ?"

Ah-Jord sighed, but was saved from answering by a groan. Ah-Sarak heard it too.

Something groaned again.

" I think Ah-ztes is coming to" Ah-Sarak said in mindspeak.

Ah-Jord ran to Ah-ztes and tried to help him up.

" Ah-ztes ? Can you hear me ?"Ah-Jord said.

Ah-ztes opened his eyes, he saw Ah-Jord and Ah-

Sarak.

" What happened ? " he thought at them.

" You took a bad fall when the Heum hit you, are you all right ?" said Ah-Sarak in mind-talk.

"How could he do that ? I was just trying to help. "

"He didn't know that. He thought you were going to kill him." thought Ah-Jord.

"Even so, he should trust me - I'm his elder brother" Ah-ztes sat up and shook his head.

"He was under orders to resist" Ah-Sarak explained.

"Can you see right down the street there. I used to live there. One day, right there, at the corner, my mother once told me something. She said that the mother doesn't take orders from the children, the children take orders from the mother. I thought that all of the animals and these humans were the children of us higher races. We observed them , we trained them and we, once in a while, punish them, so why then have they now gotten the guts to revolt ?"

"I could answer that question," said Ah-Sarak.

" What is your answer ? "

" My answer is that they grew up."

Ah-Jord smiled.

" But they grew up bad. I take your point, though. I won't make a mistake like that again.Has the rescue team come yet - they said they'd be here soon?"

" No not yet, but -"

Suddenly there was a great hovering sound over them. Ah-Jord looked up and saw a giant P.W. transport Saucer over them trying to land somewhere in among all the rubble of chewed up Shecklaks.

" Quick, Ah-ztes, Ah-Sarak , get over here out of the blast zone ! The damned thing wants to land !" shouted Ah-Jord out loud.

Ah-ztes quickly stood up and limped over to where Ah-Jord was standing. Ah-Sarak followed. The hovering sound got louder, the wind was stirring up again as the giant P.W. saucer landed. The cargo shaft opened up and twelve armed troops ran down,

The leader of the troops was Ah-Vink, he was tall dark and thin. He walked over to Ah-Jord, Ah-Sarak , and Ah-ztes.

" Sergeant Ah-Jord Sir, I am Sergeant Ah-Vink - say, aren't you Ah-ztes. I remember freeing you from an execution post."

"Yep, that was me. Thanks again."

"We got your message. We would have been here earlier, but High Sergeant Ah-Vessk sent us a message that a Vapor Bomb exploded here. She said everyone was in the air and there were no survivors. Are you three the only survivors - or are there others ?"

Ah-Jord looked at Ah-ztes and nodded. "Yes, " he said out loud. "Ah-Vessk was mistaken. There are dozens - they are all locked in the Gate Towers , the doors were electronic, so they were stuck in there when the Vapor Bomb went off and zapped all the electronics."

Ah-Vink walked back to the saucer."Bring me the blood suckers!" he shouted. The soldiers walked back into the ship, they came out with strange weapons. They went to the closed off doors of the towers and started to shoot the door, the plasma ate a hole through the door, revealing the lock mechanisms, which were living creatures. Once they could touch them and use their minds , they convinced the mechanisms that it was OK to open the doors.

Once the doors were open, the soldiers ran in. One came back out immediately; " Sir, the survivors are alive and well !"

"You'll probably have to do that with every house in the city." Ah-Vink said, then walked over to the towers. He walked in then ran out.

" Where are your saucer fighters?" asked Ah-Vink.

" Most were blasted on the gound by humans. See all the rubbish. If any survived, they must of been sucked into the vacuum storm, why ?"responded Ah-Jord.

" High Sergeant Ah-Vessk has ordered an evacuation as soon as she heard there were survivors ."

" Evacuation , why?"

" There is more bad news, only the troops can be evacuated, the fighters have to fend off the enemy."

" How do we do that?"

" First we are going back to the base, to get you more fighters and supplies. Sergeant Ah-Vessk and Ah-Nik will answer your questions."

" I thought Ah-Nik was here?"

" That was a lie to get your pilots jump started for the attack. Now could you please get into the cargo hold, like now ?"

"Too many lies, it seems" Ah-Jord nodded. and walked into the cargo hold. Ah-ztes and Ah-Sarak followed.

They sat down and waited for lift off. As more and more people started to board the cargo hold, the stench of unbathed skin and unminted breath filled the air.

Ah-ztes looked at the other surviving pilots, some who lost their limbs from the doors closing on them too fast, some who lost their sight from over exposure to the explosion light. Some seats were empty, identifying to Ah-ztes that those pilots who left the seats empty were counted either dead or missing in action.

Ah-Jord stood up as the people boarded the ship, The cargo doors closed.

" All right, I am the Squadron leader and it is my duty to fill out who is here and who is not." He said.

" Ah-Sarak!"

"Here"

" Ah-Drewa"

"Here"

"Ah-Qwelax"

" He didn't make it sir!"

" Ah-Dellik" " here"

"Ah-Transha"

" The door closed on her, cut her in half!"

" My Gods !,

"Ah-ztes"

"Here"

"Ah-Fronk"

 " Here"

"Ah-Wal"

"Dead - in the Vapor Bomb Suction"

"Ohhhhh. It's so sad. I don't want to hear any more."

said Ah-Jord, with tears forming in his eyes.

Ah-ztes walked over to Ah-Jord, he looked up at him and said." These people have been through a lot, I think that we should let them rest through the whole trip."

" All right, I'll just pass the roster around. Before we get back get to the base, tick your name if you are on it. That will be all."

Ah-ztes smiled and walked back to his seat. Ah-Jord went to look for his seat, The seat was taken by another person but Ah-Jord saw his raw cuts all over his body, his terrible stench of sweat and Ah-Jord thought that asking for his seat back would make himself feel even more guilty than he felt in the first place.

He looked for another seat , but there were no more vacant seats around. Ah-Jord looked around once more and saw Ah-Sarak lying on two seats; she was trying to sleep.

Ah-Jord smiled and walked up to her,

" Is this seat taken?" he asked.

Ah-Sarak looked up and saw Ah-Jord." Are you coming here with an excuse or are you having a big crush on me?"

Ah-Jord smiled and waited for Ah-Sarak to move over.

" Sit down!" she said.

Ah-Jord sat down in the vacant seat, he looked over to Ah-Sarak and smiled again.

" So , have you ever been in one of these before?" said Ah-Jord.

" Yes I have, I met Ah-ztes in one of these when I

came to the base."

Ah-Jord was going to say something until the radio interrupted him;

" Attention all passengers, we are now going into hover stage and will be in the air within a couple of minutes, The seats will be working soon!"

Ah-Jord looked at Ah-Sarak; " What does the radio mean by the seats will be working soon?"

" These seats are part of the new biogenics equipment that the old factories used to produce, Don't you know that ?"

"No, I haven't been around for long. So I've never trusted any new style equipment. Only what I've been programmed to use - that is why I stick to S.R. Fighters and the D.k.I. fighters"

" You are a strange Degosian, I've got to tell you that"

" Oh yeah , what s wrong with -"

The floor began to shake, giant growls came out of the engines like an animal going to attack its prey.

Ah-Jord suddenly saw his chair begin to change form, two giant straps came out near his shoulders and came down to his chest. The fabric became harder then another band came out near his leg and wrapped around his hips.

" My Gods, what is this material?" said Ah-Jord.

Ah-Sarak smiled and closed her eyes. " Just enjoy the ride!"

Ah-Jord was still amazed at the sorcery he had experienced, he laughed and closed his eyes.

Chapter **12**

The war brought among themselves

The Sun rose to the top of the sky on Arotosa. "The Young Earth" was the new name that the humans called it because of it's similarity to the pristine Earth of legend. Seven thousand years ago.

The Sun shone on to the Army beach headquarters, set up in the ruins of the city that they had taken over a few months before.

The planet Arotosa had changed drastically since the first human set foot on it, Now there were human settlements on every corner of the planet. The Japanese colony, The American Fort, the Martian BeachHead, The Moon Colony, and the United Asian Colony - naturally - in the Far East side of the Planet.

Most of the troops were training on the old streets of the alien city, Tents and cement mixed into the ruins gave the perfect hide shelter for human habitation.

Kim was still asleep dreaming about the attack a few months back, dreaming of the victory and dreaming of his lost love Linka. Suddenly he woke up, covered in sweat and tears.

Kim looked around. It was a warm morning shining through his tent in the ruins of an old room. There was nothing but rubble and barrels of supplies. Kim quickly got out of bed and went to the barrel filled with water.

He washed his face in it , then he walked over to put his uniform on. He grabbed his shirt and buttoned it up, he then went for his pants, and last he put his boots on and laced them up. He wiped his face and went out.

He looked down and saw the drill Sergeant giving his orders in the plains where the city dome once stood. It was now fallen to the ground. He smiled and walked down steps that were once part of a three story building.

He went and took a walk down a broken up street, looking at all the tanks parked on smashed buildings, jeeps blocking the broken roads , barrels of water, food and ammunition leaning against walls.

He kept walking down the street covered in rubble and stones passing the drill sargeant's students . He continued down the road to a small round Bungilo - an instant dwelling area that came in a pack and could be set up in seconds. It had a red Martian flag on a pole outside.

Inside, he saw broken glass all over the floor, a few tables set up and a radio system still intact. There were dirty floors covered in glass, dust, pieces of wood and cement crumbs.

" Kim I'm glad you're here,"

Kim turned around and saw the tall commanding

Sergeant Bryan.

" Sergeant Bryan sir, is it true that General Nevel Thomas is coming to this base?"

" Yes, he is going to land here at 16:00 hours, He is landing near the border of the city."

" Why is he landing here ? He is supposed to be controlling the U.S.S. Mayflower up in orbit, and he was not part of the Martian alliance."

" The word is that the American soldiers are joining forces with us, The reinforcements they are going to give us number around one thousand, and they are arriving with the General."

" So how many shuttle crafts are going to land exactly?"

" Roughly twenty shuttles , Ten carrying tanks , hummers , you know, all those things, why?"

Kim looked at Bryan then went to the radio.

" Kim , what are you doing?"

" That area is not big enough for that many of those types of craft, we are going to have to clear off the trees in that area."

Kim turned on the radio and he brought the microphone close to his mouth. " Attention all units, Attention all units ! We are going to need assistance, we have an problem in the outer ring of the entrance of the base, all flame thrower units and attached soldiers needed for this activity - all such troops needed immediately !" Kim turned off the radio, he went over to Bryan. " How long do we have ?"

" Roughly three hours until they land."

"Strap on a flame suit sir, we are going to need all the help we can get."

Kim ran out of the Bungilo and all the way back up the road, panting into the storage unit in his tent. He quickly went to the barrels, then found a box labelled: " Fire use only"

Kim quickly opened it, he found the flame thrower and the flame suit. He put on the white strap suit, grabbed the flame thrower and ran out of his tent.

Kim fan down the stairs, he quickly jumped into a Jeep, he looked for the keys, but they were not there, He crawled under the seat and ripped off the ignition junction box and hot wired the jeep, then drove off down the road, stopping to pick up 5 or 6 other people in fire suits.

He arrived at the border of the base, got out of the jeep, grabbed up his flame thrower and ran to the forest. He saw hundreds of soldiers dressed in fire suits ready for action.

He ran up to them , took off his mouth piece and shouted out;

"Attention , all of you, We only have three hours to clear off thirty feet in width and one mile in length of trees, be careful in what you burn and try not to fry your-selves - OK - start now."

Kim put his mouth piece back on, he put on the dark eye protectors that were strapped to his helmet. He turned on the flame thrower and started to torch trees.

Kim ran from tree to tree, torching them and torching them down for hours , until there was no more trees in his sight. Smoke and dust filled the bright sky until it was dark.

Kim ran to a soldier, "Is that area all finished?" he yelled.

" Yes, the trees are all now dust over in the north and south side!" the soldier yelled back.

" Tell all of them to stop flaming , We have to stop now !"

" Right sir !" The soldier ran to tell the others to stop.

Kim ran to the Jeep and took off his helmet, He picked up the radio in the Jeep;

" Some of the tree-trunks are still standing , the trees are still standing, we are going to need something to plow the trees down, over."

Kim got a response;" The trees shouldn't be a problem , the shuttles have just entered the atmosphere, tell your troops to move out of the way quickly, the shuttles range around 100 tons apiece, so a few tree trunks won't present any problems. Twenty five ships coming in. They would be flaming when they land, so stand clear."

Kim threw down the radio speaker and ran out, He started shouting , " All soldiers out of the way ! Out of the way !"

The soldiers did not hear his calls to stop, they continued to torch trees. Suddenly great lights came through the smoke. The shuttles were coming in to land, One soldier saw the flaming shuttles. He took off his dark protective glasses and looked up to clarify what he saw.

He ran to Kim: " Kim sir, there are meteorites coming through the atmosphere! What are we going to do ?"

Kim looked down at him;

" The meteorites are shuttles, they are coming in to land, Quick tell the others to go back into the city. The Supreme General is coming in. "

The soldier quickly ran back into the flaming plains to tell the others.

Kim went back to the jeep to take off the Flame suit. Once he reached it, he quickly jumped into the back and unzipped the suit. He took off the boots, the vest, glasses,helmet, mouth piece and gloves. Kim immediately felt cooler, he was sweating all over. He quickly cleaned himself up with a cloth and a bottle of water, put on his old uniform and took his shotgun.

He got out of the Jeep, seeing the soldiers running by him out of the flaming plains and going back to the city. Kim waited, Sergeant Bryan came up to him and said nothing,

Kim looked up at the sky, The flaming objects came falling through the sky, He continued to look up and saw the flaming balls turn into the first ten shuttles shooting through the air. They started to land on the far north side of the plains, Ten more of the shuttles came crashing down from the sky and they shot over to the south side of the plain, There were only five left still unseen, somewhere up in the sky,

Kim looked up at the smoking sky, thinking "Wow - what an entrance !" Two ships were coming in fast, intending to land right in the middle of the plain, Bryan got nervous .The ground started to rumble, the air was getting stirred up. The air became incredibally hot. Kim saw one shuttle right above them, it was flaming like it just came back from hell. Kim stepped back to let the Shuttle land.

Bryan was amazed.

The flaming ship slowly hovered to its chosen landing spot, only inches from the jeep. Kim watched the ship land. It was still burning.

Kim turned to Bryan " Why are the shuttles still flaming?"

" The air in this planet is much thicker than many other planets, the flames wouldn't hurt anyone though, the shuttle is now going to cool off."

The shuttle doors suddenly opened up.

Kim turned around to watch. The cargo doors opened now, and were flaming at the tips and corners of the cargo ramp. Thirty men came out carrying their guns and supplies. They walked slowly out of the flaming ship, looking around cautiously.

A six-foot man with dark hair and sun-glasses came out last. He had no guns and carried no supplies but dressed like the troops. He slowly walked down the cargo ramp. He stopped right in the flames for a few seconds, then walked through them, as if he were used to walking through fire.

He walked over to where Kim and Bryan was standing. He stopped and stood there.

Bryan came up to him,

" Private , may I ask why you are not unloading the supplies like the others ?"

The person smiled and gave no answer .

" Private , I am going to ask you again, Why are you not unloading like the others ?"

The man gave no answer and stared at the shuttle. Bryan became furious and stormed up to him and grabbed his arm," Are you damned mute boy ? I asked you a question and I hope for an answer !"

A soldier saw the man getting grabbed by the arm and ran up to Bryan.He pointed a small automatic hand gun at Bryan's head.

" Sir, I want you to take your hands off the Supreme General right now, Sir !"

Bryan was stunned; he quickly removed his hand from the Generals' arm.

" Oh, I'm shocked. I thought that you would be in one of the main shuttles where . . . "

" I like to be an equal when I travel, not a leader. This protects me even more if any enemies get strange ideas." The General interrupted. Then he walked to the dying flames of the torched trees.

"Now Sergeant are you doing a strategic plan or are we going to destroy the atmosphere just like our mother home ?"

Kim came up to him and tapped his back." This was to clear a path for your landing here." he said.

The General looked surprisingly at Kim" Oh my God ! You've got a damned Jap with you!,"

Kim was confused, he looked at the General to get an explanation.

" Why didn't you hear Sergeant ?" The General said.

" Hear about what?" said Sergeant Bryan.

" We , the Americans and you Martians are allies. We are competing with Asia, Europe and the Moon colony. They are now the enemy,"

Kim was silent, Bryan just looked at him. The General walked to the jeep, passing them. He sat down in the passenger seat in the back.

Kim and Bryan turned around and slowly walked to the jeep. Kim sat down in the drivers seat and turned the jeep on. The General leaned over to Kim and Bryan;

" Now , where is the command tower ?" he said.

" Don't we have to wait for your other soldiers ?" asked Bryan.

" No, they have their own supplies , they will be staying outside the perimeter of this city, or base whichever you would refer to it as."

Kim and Bryan gave no answer.

" You are all shocked about the news of the war , why is that ?"

Bryan turned around and faced him," I am shocked that the mission of settling citizens has now turned into chaos. We're fighting a huge technologically superior race, who has us outgunned and outnumbered - and now you say we're fighting among ourselves - how can we go to war with our allies ?"

The General laughed and leaned back to his chair.

" I am surprised Sergeant, I didn't know that you felt that way about people. I thought that you killed everything in this area - Alien , civilian or veteran on sight ?"

"That's different"

If you could kill aliens then why can't you kill a

human?"

Bryan was furious, he became very silent.

The General looked at him,

" Ah, I see, you are Xenophobic, you kill Aliens because you are frightened of them, not because you like to kill. That's the difference between us. That's why I'm a General and you're a Sergeant - I like to kill. I'll kill anything I can get my hands on - and I want my officers to feel the same way.

I'll work on you until you want to kill everything - including me Sergeant. Then you'll discover that you can't can't kill me. I am the eternal human spirit. I am the violence and madness and bloodlust that makes us great. I am like energy, I can only be transferred but not destroyed - if you kill me, Sergeant, it will only because you have become me."

Kim stopped the jeep, he walked to the back of the jeep and opened the trunk:" Sir I am sorry , I am going to have to ask you to step out of the transport unit."

The General grinned he walked out. Kim walked up to him and took off the General's hand gun from the side holster and took his knife from the opposite side,

" What is the point of this, Jap ?"

" I am confiscating your weapons, Sir, for a precaution. We are going into the command station , there are some Martians of Japanese and European descent that I don't want dead because the temper of the General is too great."

The General grinned and nodded, he walked back into the jeep and sat in his seat. Bryan grinned as Kim jumped back into the Jeep.

" Very smart Kim," said the General.

Kim turned the jeep on and kept driving. The General looked out the window of the jeep assessing the base. He saw housing destroyed with barrels leaning on the wreckage, jeeps parked in unorderly fashion, tanks parked in damaged houses, soldiers marching on the road, and five jets parked on the side walks.

" Is this where you all set up base?" asked the General.

" Yes , this is the area where all our training and supplies are put, all parts of the city are occupied, but it's all pretty much ruins. Unfortunately their technology died with the Aliens, we don't know what to do with it, so we use the area for simple things like storage." said Kim.

Kim stopped the jeep.

" What are you going to do, confiscate my clothes now ?" said the General.

Kim laughed, " No Sir, we are now at the base."

The General got out of the jeep. He saw a giant tower with three fallen pillars, the building was beautiful, covered in rust with the gentle glow of silver, marred by dents and fractures all over the building.

" What did this use to be?" asked the general.

" I think this was some sort of a shield generator, but now it is just a building." said Kim,

Bryan came out of the jeep," Kim , I just got a contact from the outside patrol - they found Sergeant Will Fecod !" said Bryan.

"My God, that maniac is still alive ?" mumbled Kim.

The General grinned, " So you are not the real Sergeant, you are just a temporary second in command ?"

Bryan was quiet.

Kim ran to the jeep. "Bryan we need to meet him, where is he located?"

" He is at the outer ring on the fifth pillar,"

" Fifth pillar, fifth pillar, ah, then that means he is at the south side of the ring, can we drive there ?"

"Yes ," said Bryan.

Kim ran to a seat in the jeep, Bryan sat in the drivers seat. The General grabbed onto the door before Bryan could close it. " I hope you were not going to leave me behind."

"No sir." Bryan looked away from the General.

The General opened the back trunk and sat down in the passenger seat. Bryan closed his door and turned the jeep on. By the time they reached the south side it was dark and raining heavily. Bryan and Kim ran got out of the jeep and ran to the medical tent. They came in through the tent opening , where they saw a medic, and Sergeant Will was on the bed with his left arm amputated.

"What happened to him?" Asked Bryan.

" The ambush we had a few months back where his body was never found, he was wandering around in the bush. He got shot in the arm with the Alien's acid guns, so he has ben carrying the dead limb for three months. I had to cut it off before it caused any more damage to him." said the doctor.

The General came through the tent opening, he looked around the medical tent and stood there.

"This is your commanding officer ?"

Kim walked up to Will not knowing what to expect. Kim saw William knocked out, drugged from the operation. Bryan came up and joined him at the bedside. As if sensing their presence, Will woke up. He had blood shot eyes.

" Sir, should I take command till you recover?" asked Bryan.

Will looked to the left side of his shoulder where his arm used to be. He started to grin."Do you think that this small injury is going to stop me from commanding the Martian Marines from hell ? I love pain ! This is only a scratch." Suddenly his good arm reached for the left shoulder. He ripped off the life support wires going through his shoulder. He crunched his teeth together and closed his eyes.

All three of them, Kim, Bryan and the General Nevel knew that he was in pain. William stood up from the bed, His left shoulder was bleeding, blood drizzling from the amputated wound to the floor. William walked over to Bryan dripping blood all over his boots, and said. " No, I will be resuming my position in command, you are dismissed."

" Sir, you should rest, you are losing blood ," said the Doctor.

William grinned at Bryan " Don't think that I can die, I am too tough to be hit seriously."

Suddenly William became pale , he closed his blood shot eyes then fell to the floor.

" Damn ! Kim , Bryan help me put him on the bed."

said the doctor.

Kim grabbed Williams feet, Bryan ran to his hands and they picked him up. They slowly moved William to the bed and swung him to it.

" How long will he be out for Doctor?" asked Kim.

" A few hours, but he will be fine if he listens to reason. He will have to have an artificial emplacement on his body by tomorrow."

The General went to the doctor . "So he will be fit to command by tomorrow morning?"

" Yes, that I can guarantee" said the doctor.

Bryan walked out of the medical tent. Kim looked at the doctor then left the tent. The General followed.

" Damn!" yelled Bryan.

Kim went to the jeep then hit the hood.

" Is that madman going to lead us again ?" said Kim.

" What's wrong with you two ? You should be grateful that you are going to be led by a real leader rather than a pitty excuse for a commander." yelled the General. "That's one hell of a man in there - even without an arm."

Bryan looked up to the dark raining sky , he furiously looked at General ." What is it that you want from me ?" shouted Bryan.

"I'll give you an example of what I want from you, Sergeant." The General walked over to Kim, reached into his commando Jacket and pulled out a gun which was plugged into his hand and hard-wired right into his brain.

" What are you doing ?" said Kim.

The General grinned; " I can't abide a damned Jappo . . ."

He pulled the trigger on the gun,

Kim fell to the ground holding his stomach, His eyes filled with tears and blood.

"That's what I want from you, Sergeant" The General took out a tissue from his pocket and ripped out Kims gun from the gun holder. Suddenly the General heard a loading noise and felt a blunt gun barrel pointing at his back.

" All right you damned ass plucker disconnect your cyclone gun from your hand, Now!" said Bryan. "Or I'll give you what you want from me"

The General quickly took off his gun and threw it to the ground.

" So what other tricks are you going to pull out your freaking bag of magic Nevel?"

" Oh I just have this one final trick left." said the General. He quickly pulled Kim's gun from his left side and shot through his jacket, hitting Bryan in the chest. Bryan fell face down into the muddy ground .

"But it's a goodie" said the General.

He quickly walked to Kim and dropped the gun near him.

He picked up Bryans' gun with a cloth and ran into the medical tent , shot the doctor in the head and shot William three times in the chest.

"Pity" he said, patting William's dead hair, "I thought you were a bloody good egg - but, after all, I am making an omelette"

He grabbed a pair of small tweezers and walked back out saving one bullet to put the final touch on his little drama.

He went over to the now-dead Kim and turned him over. He stuck the tweezers into the gun shot wound and grabbed the bullet, pulling it out and putting it in his pocket.

The General quickly stood up and pulled out the gun wrapped in cloth and shot Kim again, directly into the open wound.

He walked over to Bryan and threw the gun near to Bryan's outstretched arm.

He walked over to the Jeep and sat in the drivers seat, then picked up the radio

"Anyone who can pick up the message, I need some assistance, there has been an assault. I need help. Please come as soon as possible!"

He turned the radio off and sat in the jeep laughing.

It was the end of the of the reasonable reign of the Sergeant from Mars. The new era of Nevel would begin tomorrow with more power and skill.

And nothing would ever be the same.

Chapter 13

The day of the invasion

The next morning shone softly through solid grief.

The newly conquered base of the humans from Mars was in mourning. All of the restored alien gates of the base were now wide open. The American soldiers, who had arrived with General Nevel Thomas, filled the broken up streets of the base with activity. The Martian Marines, for the most part, stayed out of sight and kept to themselves.

The Martians were becoming uneasy in the presence of the Americans. The reason for it was that the American troops had infested the entire north side of the base and were scattered thinly everywhere else. They outnumbered the Martians 2 to 1 and their fire-power was much more sophisticated than the Martians old-fashioned power weapons and transport units from the 22nd century.

The Martians, though, were listless. They were sad about the strange and unexplained deaths of their

beloved commanders who had led them to such stunning victories against the alien forces. And they were
weary after months of solid fighting - they had been
part of the original invasion force and had never had a
moment's rest.

A large group of Martian Marines stood silently
on one side of a street near a huge red flag with a picture of a burning cloth on it. The flag was the symbol of
their commanders , Sergeant William and Bryan. It echoed their mood - it hung limp and unmoving in the
windless city.

The Martian Marines stood quite silently, grieving
and building up a slow, powerful resentment against
the Americans, who were not giving any respect to the
dead leaders.

Grief, anger and confusion, fueled by disrespect,
has always been a sure recipe for a nuclear explosion in
human civilization, and this time was no exception.

In fact, the Americans were making things worse.
Although they stayed on the other side of the broken
up road, they were laughing, drinking all of the hard-
won water supply, eating up valuable food rations, telling jokes and playing loud Jolt musi .(Ancient Jazz,
Rock, Heavy Metal, Rap, newscasts, TV show sound-
tracks and normal conversation all mixed together to
make one unending song and played loudly enough to
hurt.)

Although they seemed happy and unorganized
the Americans all had hand guns and rifles lying nearby.
Ready for anything.

And anything happened - sooner than expected.

One grief-stricken Martian took matters into his own hands; he calmly walked over to the American side of the street, pulled out a hand gun and shot the music box.

" What the hell did you do that for ?" said a furious American soldier.

"It needed more bang" The Martian replied, turning to return to his fellows.

The American grabbed the Martian soldier and pushed him around. Another Martian walked up to the soldier and sandwiched him."Let him go you damned ass ! We all just want a moment of silence for our dead leaders."

" You can just shut it ! Do we give a damn if your freaking losers are dead?, Besides it was Bryan that went crazy and started to kill. It's his bullets in Kim and Will and the Doctor. Lucky that Kim got him with a dying shot or the traitorous son-of-a-ho would still be in command, instead of our glorious General Nevel " said the soldier.

" YOU SON OF A BITCH!" yelled one of the Martians .

"SHUT UP YOU GREEN MAN WANNABE!" said an American soldier.

The Martians all ran to the Americans. Fist fighting broke out between them. Noises of hitting and the smell of blood started to cover the street.

Suddenly a gun fired, everyone stopped fighting. They all looked and saw the General on a Jeep.They all backed away and made a way in the road.The General jumped out of the Jeep, He walked down the street seeing blood and broken pieces of wood all over.He stopped in the middle of the road between the Americans and the Martians.

He held his right hand up.

" Do you see this ?"He pointed to a Red Circle over the American flag on his sleeve.

" Do all of you know what this circle symbolizes ? It symbolizes unity between all human armies ! Where is the Unity we need ? "

One angry Martian soldier - the boom box shooter - walked up to The General . " How are we going to co-operate with these piss heads ?"

An American - the boom box defender - walked up;" How are we going to co-operate with these crybaby Martians ?

"This is how !" said the General. He crooked a finger and summoned them both closer. "Stand side by side right here in front of me" he said. Both soldiers, bloody and angry, were nevertheless conditioned to follow orders, and marched smartly to stand in front of the General, side by side, like brothers.

The General pointed a finger at both of them. "These two soldiers represent the future of this fighting force under my command" he said. "Those who cannot work together . . . "

He clenched his upraised fist and his cyclone gun, hard-wired to his wrist, shot out of his sleeve and into his hand, fired twice and zipped back up his sleeve in two blinks.

" . . . will die together " he finished, as the two soldiers dropped together and lay like clumsy lovers. His upraised arm still pointed at them. "I am ashamed of all of you. Be soldiers, not children. From this moment onwards, the punishment is death for all parties involved in human to human fights."

The General put his hand down.

All of a sudden a building exploded.

" THE DAMNED JAPS ARE ATTACKING ON THE EAST SIDE, THE BRITS ARE ATTACKING THE SOUTH, IT'S A FREAKING INVASION OF THE FOUR CORNERS OF THE EARTH. BATTLE STATIONS NOW!"shouted a towers man.

All of the Americans ran to grab their rifles on the street. The Martians quickly put their helmets on and grabbed their automatic shot guns and jumped into the jeeps parked all over the Streets. The Americans ran to the tanks parked on the side walks of the road.

The General ran to the Jeep and opened a box in the trunk. He took out a gatling gun half the size of his body and connected it to a set up pole in the open back. He loaded it with explosive bullets then jumped off and ran to the troops loading up a nearby jeep.

" I want three tanks and two armed jeeps to cover the north."

The troops said yes.

The General put on a helmet and checked the connection of his cyclone gun to his wrist. He then ran to the Martians loading up,

" All of you cover most of the south and east, where your troops are stationed. The Japs are not going to be soft, so I advise you to convert your fire power to explosives wherever possible. Explosive personal guns, cannons, gatling bullets, every freaking thing that can be fired should be explosive. Tell that to all Martian personnel ."

He ran back to his Jeep, and strapped a bullet-proof vest onto his back and chest. He quickly jumped into the drivers seat and turned the engine on then drove north to the Japs location, seeing, with approval, that every other jeep was armed to its wheels.

The driver of a nearby racing jeep shouted to him " The Moon colony just dropped in and sided with the invasion force, they are already on the ground heading this way towards the Alien Gate !"

" Thank you for the information, soldier" shouted The General. He stepped on the gas and his super-charged jeep sped away from the others and headed for the border of the base. He dusted to a stop in front of the newly created firewall over the old alien gate way.

He jumped out of the Jeep and ran to one of the sides of the Gate. He looked out of a small newly-created window to see how many Moon people he would be dealing with.

" Where the hell are they?" said the General

"Sir, we have made it. We got the firewall up just in time. We are set up and ready to waste those green cheese, moon-man bastards."

" I like your confidence soldier, they are probably dressed in fog suits, We aren't going to pick them up on sensors. We likely won't even see them until they're right on top of us. Set up the Gatling guns and just start blasting. They would likely try to come in right though there."He pointed out at a nearby section of still-burning forest.

" Right sir."

The General kept looking out the window, hoping to see something.

" Target spotted ! 10 O'clock. Waste the suckers!"shouted the tower men.

The General kept looking, but saw nothing. Suddenly, exactly where he had pointed previously, giant white tanks lumped out of the mist of the burned forest.

" Start the Gatling guns!"shouted the General. He climbed up to his jeep to use one of the Gatling guns himself. He set up quickly, put in three chains of bullets then started to fire. The explosive shells hammered the white tanks, blowing one to pieces and stopping another in its tracks.

The remaining tanks stopped in a line and began to fire back.

" Duck!" shouted the General.He jumped off the Gatling gun. A whistling noise became louder .The defense tower fell to the ground flaming all over .

" We must call for recruits, We can't compete against that kind of fire power." said a soldier.

Another whistling sound became louder and hit a

building .

" Quit whining. Fight, damn it!" shouted the General. He climbed back up on the jeep and began answering fire, his explosive shells tracing curved lines through the fog. All of a sudden he saw a ghostly tank coming towards the fire wall.

" They are going to ram us! Stand clear !" he shouted, still firing. The soldiers ran and scattered all over the rubble of the supplies and destroyed monuments.

The General bent down in the back of the Jeep and took out a Tank Piercing Bazooka from the trunk.

He leapt down to the ground, lay down and aimed it at the wall. "All of you , run back a ways and get ready for our defense in case this doesn't work !"shouted the General.

The wall suddenly explodedas the tank oxed its way through. Hot debris shot everywhere. The General calmly shot one shell to the tank, which exploded, blowing a larger hole in the firewall.

White-clad MoonTroops ran in and were invading the entire Gateway area. The General carried the Bazooka on his back, picked up a rifle and zipped the Cyclone Gun out of his sleeve and into his hand. He jumped behind barrels and began to shoot, not wasting any ammunition. Every shot resulted in one or two MoonTroops falling down.

Three soldiers joined in, they started shooting with the General. The other soldiers stopped their retreat and started to run forward to stop the invasion and reinforce the General.

Once they arrived beside him, he ran to the jeep and turned on the Gatling gun again, laying down his rifle and retracting his Cyclone gun. He started to shoot the huge explosive shells at point blank range. The MoonTroops didn't fall - they vaporized as the explosive shells did their wet work.

The invaders fell back and retreated into the smoking forest of blackened stumps. The street outside the alien Gateway was covered once again with bodies. Human bodies lay mutilated with limbs separated from the connecting joints. A red rain of vaporized blood and guts fell lightly over the street and over the defenders of the Gateway.

The soldiers stopped firing and sat down.

The General turned from his Gatling gun and lifted his face to the gentle downpour.

"Feel that ? Taste that ?" he shouted. "The Mist of War ! GOD I LOVE IT !"

The General stepped into the front seat of his Jeep and picked up the radio.

"This is General Nevel, How is everything holding up on the East and West side ? We've got MoonTroops here in the South. We've got them stopped here - but not for long."

" The East side has been invaded, We have lost. The Japs are in !" said the radio.

" Contact the Mayflower for help , we might get some assistance there !"

" It is too late we have lost !"

"Bull. It's never too late. Fall back quickly and call on Mayflower to send Death from Above. Lure them in, then smoke 'em. Do the unexpected, you sucky bastard.Have some fun out there. And that's an order!"

The General heard gun shots, he turned around and saw Japanese and European soldiers coming up their road behind their position.

"The games afoot!" he cried and climbed to the Gatling gun,turning it around and spraying the incoming soldiers with his explosive shells. The Americans quickly grabbed their automatic rifles and joined in.

The European and Japanese soldiers fell like dominos. But suddenly incoming fire began to arrive from the burnt out forest again.

"Bloody MoonTroop bastards are back!" the General cried and swung his terrible gun around again, whirling like a toy and spraying death in all directions.

They were fully surrounded by now. The incoming fire was so solid you could almost see it, yet, strangely, nothing touched the mad General, who continued his bizarre dance of death.

The American soldiers one by one were picked off as the bullets hit them. The General saw that he was losing and he stopped firing the gatling gun.He leaned down to the radio and called out: Mayflower. Mayflower. Get your fingers out. I need some help down here. "

"General we have your position, but we have our own troubles up here. It looks like the Brits are setting up an attack up here. We cannot help at this time."

"You pussy bastards, you'll pay for this !"

"I'm sure we will, but that's still the answer. No help. Fight your own battles."

He put his hands up into the air and screamed like a madman. He got the jeep going and tinkered with something on the back, then climbed behind the Gatling gun again. The jeep began moving. The General used one foot to steer and another to prop himself up as he took the jeep in a huge circle, firing all the while at the soldiers on all sides. Although the fire continued to pour in and pick off his American soldiers, he seemed charmed and nothing even came close to him.

Finally, after completing a full circle, the General pulled back into the centre of his huge circle and climbed down from the Gatling gun.

He put his hands up and waved a white handkerchief. "Give it up lads, he yelled. "There's no point in dying for nothing." He looked around and grinned.

The firing stopped. His few remaining men stood up cautiously, laying their weapons down.

The incoming troops approached warily. A rough circle of MoonTroops, European and Japanese soldiers stood in the rubble at about the same distance that the General had driven around in his last mad defence.

One tall man dressed in a green British uniform left the circle and came up to him," If you try to play any bloody games with us we will kill you , you know that, laddie?" The soldier grabbed his arm and looked at the shoulder. " Well, well. We have a high ranking General with us."said the Brit.

" I take it that you are a sergeant and your General should be here with you, am I wrong ? I'll surrender only to another General."

The British sergeant grinned . " You are smart General , and you put up one hell of a fight, but your mouth is bigger than your brain ."

The sergeant continued grinning as he tipped over slightly and karate kicked the General in the stomach.

The General fell to the ground and was choking up vomit.

"While his highness here is puking, take his men out of the area and secure them as prisoners of war."

The Americans were quickly pushed into a rough column and marched away, back into the city by the Japanese and European soldiers, leaving only the whitesuited MoonTroops to fill out the circle.

The General turned over and tried to stand up. He struggled up and tried to show no pain to his enemies. He finally made it to his feet, grinned and just faced the sergeant with an evil look.

" Now I hope you two are not going to bust each others handsome faces to pieces, this is our first victory against the Americans since the Revolutionary war."

The General looked to his left and saw a woman wearing dark round glasses and a grey officers hat and a black trench coat. She had on tall black boots with grey army patternless pants and a grey army shirt with four yellow stripes and the Union Jack with a small white circle in the center .

The General smiled and looked at her.

" Nevel, my love."I heard that you died when you took the MayFlower into the Wormhole ?" she took off her glasses and walked over to General Nevel. She hugged him tightly not wanting to let go.

" Grace, rumours of my death are greatly exaggerated not to mention greatly anticipated. Once I saw those Neatsi-Nazi uniforms, I knew that you would be around here somewhere." Nevel then kissed her on the lips softly.

" Excuse me , mum but isn't this sad bastard the enemy ?" asked the sergeant.

General Nevel stopped kissing and looked up at him. " Speak to your superiors with respect son, or suffer the consequences. I am on your side, and, technically, your superior officer."he said. General Nevel turned to Grace to back up his outrageous statement.

"That's right Sergeant-Major. We had an agreement with General Nevel long before we left Earth. He works for us."

"Well mum, he does it in a bloody funny way. He must have killed a hundred of our boys single-handedly within the last ten minutes, while 300 top shots couldn't put a bullet near him."

"My God, I thought you had orders not to hit me - you mean you were trying to kill me." The General was pleased. "Maybe I am invincible after all."

"Mum, this is all too complicated for me. With all due respect, I'm going to have to take this trickster into custody and report back to High Command and see what they say ?"

"Sergeant-Major ! You will do nothing of the kind. You will treat General Nevel Thomas with the utmost respect and obey his every whim"

"Begging your pardon Mum, but I will not. I think he's cast some sort of spell on you, and I am relieving you of command until this is sorted out."

" Gracie, may I ?" The American General asked the British General calmly. Nevel caressed her waist.

The sergeant was puzzled, but pulled out his hand-gun, nevertheless.

"Sergeant-Major" The woman General barked. "Will you reconsider your position"

"With all due respect, I cannot mum"

She grinned." Yes, you certainly may Nevel, dar-ling"

Suddenly Nevel pulled out her hand gun and pointed at the sergeant. He pulled the trigger and put a bullet through his head. The sergeant fell to his knees, His head was gushing with blood all over the boots of Nevel and Grace. He finally flopped down and lay still. Nevel kicked the sergeants head and walked over the body.

"You must quit doing this, Nevel. It's bad for mo-rale" Grace laughed.

The circle of MoonTroopers were uneasy. They were pointing their guns at the couple.

"Oh come on Gracie, just one more ?" The General asked with a smile.

A sergeant of the MoonTroopers spoke up; "I think we'll have to follow the Sergeant-Major, Mam, and relieve you of command"

"Oh go ahead, Nevel, you impetuous boy."

The General snapped his fingers on a small remote control button. The entire ring of Moontroopers were instantly vaporized in a wall of explosive force.

"I never liked those bloody Moontroopers - dressed all in white - that's reason enough to die right there." said Grace, shaking her head. "How did you do that ?"

My last gallant defence with the jeep, I laid a trail of Blast as I drove around. Thought it might come in handy"

Hearing the explosion, backup European and Japanese troops ran out and surrounded the two Generals, who were laughing and dancing.

"This is General Nevel Thomas. He has been been working with the Americans, but he is one of us. He holds the rank of General and will be obeyed without question."

"What happened to the Moontroopers ?" asked one.

"They questioned." said Grace.

"That goes for the rest of you,too. Learn from this. Don't ask questions about my authority. If I want you to do something I want it to be done. If I say jump what do you say soldier" the General pointed out one of the Europeans.

"I say 'How high ?' Sir ?"

"Wrong. You don't have time to say anything. Why ? - Cause you're already in the air."

The group laughed.

"Now, here is my first order. Listen carefully . . . JUMP !"

There was the sound of 200 pairs of combat boots, landing. And more laughter. He had them now.

"Good. Here is my next order. Execute all of the survivors here. Every one of the Americans and every one of the Martians. We now own the base ! Dismissed."

" Sir, yes sir !" yelled the soldiers, in a good mood and full of their victory.

The soldiers ran to the Jeeps and started them.

The General went back to Grace. She was grinning with an evil look in her eyes."You're so good Nevel, it's a pity you're so bad."

" What will the New British Embassy think of this?" asked General Nevel.

Grace smiled and slowly walked closer to him.

"The British embassy will gladly give you a badge of honor for disobeying the Americans. And make you a Knight Commander for taking care of 1000 American and Martian troops, single handedly."

They heard the pops of small arms fire. The executions had begun. By tomorrow the Japs will attack the Mayflower. and the entire sector will be ours. We will also be expecting some new reinforcements and they will include a couple of new Generals to command in our place while we . . . "

" While we do what ?" interrupted General Nevel.

" While we take a much deserved rest on the flag-ship St. Victoria."

" St. Victoria? the Flagship of the Royal British

Navy ? That's no fun. Can't kill anyone on the flagship. Why would-"

" Shh, this is all top secret info wink wink," said Grace. "It's enough that your commanding General orders it "

General Nevel smiled . "Yes ma'am"

"Besides, after the Americans and Martians and the Moonies hear what you've done, there is nowhere in heaven or earth that you will be safe"

"Maybe a sport of R&R on the St. Vic is just what we need. When are the new Generals coming ?"

Grace touched her ear, activating the implanted radio receiver; " They have landed and should be ready for us on the North side."

Nevel smiled and walked to his Jeep, He turned it on." Let's go over there and turn over command right now. The sooner the better. I'm in urgent need of some deep debriefing right now ?"

Grace smiled and walked over to the other side of the Jeep.

Chapter 14

The Freebooters of the Frotnerk

The P.W. shuttlecraft powered through the the
dark and misty atmosphere upper atmosphere of Degos.
It was so high it was almost in space and the gravity
was much less than it would be on the surface.

Inside the P.W., the atmosphere was also dark -
filled with cold air and the stench of vomit. Some people were dying. Some were injured. Many were dead.
Most of them were so badly wounded that they would
never pilot again.

Death filled the interior more than the cold air
which surrounded them. Defeat kept the temperature
down. Depression kept it dark and silent.

Whether history recorded that they lost this war
or won this battle wouldn't matter. They would still
have suffered these feelings. Seventy fighters had gone

into Degos, proud and invincible. Only thirteen made it out.

The Humans had suffered more casualties but no one was cheering. The whole Human force of fighting troops all together out numbered the troops from the planet of Degos ten to one.So the humans could afford to lose many. Each Degossian was worth ten humans. Although there were 50,000 planets in the Confederation of Worlds, so far only the small planet of Degos had managed to find troops that would fight - that were infected with the war virus. It seemed the only sure way to create fighters, was to let the humans destroy a planet - the few survivors would catch the disease. Otherwise, civilized people could not be persuaded to fight by any means.

In fact, the biggest problem of Congress Moon and the ambassadors was to find a way to get re-enforcements and better fighters, without allowing entire planets to be destroyed.

In a few days the depleted squad would be going to battle again, First in space and then on another planet. There was no end in sight.

*   *   *

" Ah-Jord?, Ah-Jord." said Ah-Sarak,

Ah-Jord got up from his long slumber, He looked around, the air was humid and strong scented .

" How long have I been out?" asked Ah-Jord.

Ah-Sarak smiled, " Almost three hours, We had

some turbulence trouble, so we'll be a little late coming back to the base."

Ah-Jord looked at Ah-Sarak " Aren't you at least concerned with what Sergeant Ah-Vessk did ? What is she going to order next, a suicide ?"

" Calm down. There's no proof she's a traitor. She had good military reasons not to tell us about that Vapor Bomb - Humans have translators now and understand anything we say out loud. If she didn't send the Vapor Bomb, we might have been slaughtered out in the battlefield. And most important, her action didn't kill any of us. And did kill a lot of heums."

"I guess you are right," Ah-Jord sighed and shifted a little in his seat.

Ah-ztes got up from his seat and walked over to where Ah-Jord and Ah-Sarak was sitting. " Hey, I think that we're going to have to stop the fighting soon. Otherwise it'll just be us three. We started out with seventy pilots, now we only have around twenty alive and of those, there are three dying and four that are going to need artificial limbs. And that's just our squad. Look at this plane. It's full of the remnants of other squads who fared worse than us. This war is more destructive than even I imagined - and I'm a bloodthirsty kid."

" I know Ah-ztes, but we are going to get a new squad of recruits, I heard. These guys need a rest. Tomorrow, I hope, we'll get a whole new squad ,"

" Ah-Jord, we are not going to be here tomorrow, Tomorrow we evacuate to Arotosa for the take over."said Ah-Sarak.

" Yes that is what I am talking about, I have the idea that the wounded should stay and logically we should probably get the new squad to fill out the ranks."

" I hope you are right." said Ah-ztes, "but where would they get new recruits from. So far, only Degosians are angry enough to fight."

"I heard they found a resistance group on Sivil."

"The desert world ? Did the humans attack there, too ?"

"Yes - and left it worse off than Degos."

"Good - those guys will be really angry."

Suddenly the cockpit doors opened up and a person walked out.

"Attention all passengers, we are going to land at Base 14 soon. We'll be re-entering the atmosphere and full gravity will resume. Please make sure you are strapped into your seats and help strap in any of the wounded that can't do it for themselves. Then be ready for departure from this shuttlecraft immediately - we have to turn right around and go back for more." he said. He walked back into the cockpit and the doors shut behind him.

" Well Ah-ztes you heard the man, go back to your seat before you get hurt. It would be a pity, after surviving all these battles, that you get killed in this landing. "

OK lovebirds - I hear you. " said Ah-ztes and walked back to his seat.

Ah-Jord turned to Ah-Sarak ," I guess it's obvious how we feel about each other. I wish times were different. All we can do, now that we're finally alone, is get ready for the landing."

" If times were different, we never would have met. In fact, the labs would never have created you - so don't complain. And don't worry - there will be lots of time. Now strap in."

Ah-Jord faced up to the ceiling and pushed a button. The seats began to grab his legs and arms. The pressure of the seats became harder and the outer windows of the craft became darker. The floor began to vibrate and the engines became louder.

Suddenly Ah-Jord felt a giant jerk forewords. That was the sign that the hover engines had become functional. The craft slowly came down through the atmosphere. Ah-Jord could feel himself slowly falling deeper into the seat as the gravity increased and then became normal for the planet.

The craft came to a stop.

The engines went off-line and the seats lost pressure and released their occupants.

" You have arrived at Base #14," said the ship's computer.

Ah-Jord stood up and looked down at Ah-Sarak. She stood up, too and together they walked over to the cargo doors. The cargo doors began to open allowing a gust of planet-scented wind inwards into the interior of the ship.

"I remember this smell" said Ah-Sarak, breathing deeply; "my parents and I came here once on a vacation. It was supposed to be one of the most beautiful parts of the planet - on one of the most beautiful planets in all the universe. They used to say "Come to Degos Prime - and die - they meant you would never see anything as beautiful so you might as well die happy."

"Come to Degos Prime and die - it has a whole new meaning now" said Ah-Jord as he walked out the door. The base was dark and cold all over. It was night time and windy cold - refreshinating after the close smells of the P.W..

He looked at the rubble and destruction which stretched away in the moonlight, as far as he could see. There was no life in it. The former beauty of the area was erased, like the beauty of a living creature is gone after its life has been snuffed out.

The only standing structure was the temporary domed green base - and all activity would be inside it. Nothing was outside but broken memories.

The others, injured, sick and well came out and stared at a planetscape which used to bring joy and happiness to millions, but now was smashed and gone forever. They were silent, each dealing with their own thoughts.

Ah-Jord went to the entrance of the base. He entered an airlock and the outer door, behind him, shut tightly.

" Please establish your identification by code word," said the door lock.

Ah-Jord gave a code " A72 4469."

"Voice-print/retinal print verified. Enter Sergeant Ah-Jord."

The inside door opened and he walked in. The

others followed, each having to go through the same process. It took a long time.

The lights in the base were, if anything, too functional. It was very bright inside.

Two guards came up to Ah-Jord. "Captain Ah-Jord, you are to meet at the commanders room right now. See that blue flag - go inside the cafeteria. It's in there" one of them said, pointing. "Don't worry, we will take care of the wounded ."

Ah-Jord was puzzled as to why they had called him captain, but thought that it was a bit of an efficiency-slip in the midst of this confusing war. As he thought, he walked through the base among the crowds, hearing the many conversations taking place out loud, and he was amazed at the change in his people.

Before the war, everything was done mind to mind, in thought-speak. Talking out loud had been slightly barbaric. Something only violent mental defectives or animals did. In polite conversation, speaking aloud had only been done to convey the most powerful passion, emotion and tension which could not be sent with thought. Now almost everyone spoke aloud and did it almost all the time.

The door to the cafeteria opened up and Ah-Jord walked in. The shelter here was even more filled with life, than the outside had been. The cafeteria was wall to wall with tables of people eating and talking. Many of the ground soldiers were asleep against the walls and the homeless civilians were helping with the work of feeding and caring for them and for each other.

Ah-Jord walked up to a door that said Commanders office. He took a sigh and opened the door.

" Ah-Jord I have been expecting you ," Ah-Jord looked at where the voice came from. He saw Ah-Vessk sitting down on a chair near her desk.

" The Admiral has sent a message to you, Because you were created in the labs and all the experience of war was grown into you, you will be the commander of a starship starting tomorrow and you will be receiving a crew of three hundred. I am now the new squad leader of your squad."

" Why have I been promoted?"

" The Admiral saw your record. It's quite a good record - the best, in fact, of all the lab specimens. There seems to be something wrong with all of them. They don't want to fight. They don't want to kill. You are one of the few who hasn't committed suicide."

" Still that should not matter, you should of been the starship commander. You have even a better record and no threat of suicidal tendencies. In fact you're so bloodthirsty, you send Vapor Bombs after your own pilots."

" The Admiral doesn't see it that way. She is not going to promote me for a while. I disobeyed the orders that she gave me. I was the one who almost killed all of your squad with the Vapor Bomb - but she doesn't think it was bloodthirsty. She thinks it was treason.

But, since we last spoke about my beliefs of peace and love, my entire family has been killed by humans. So I've been re-educated in the worst way.

Unfortunately, now that I've finally become a raving hater of all things human and a stone killer, I have to suffer the consequences of my earlier life."

" I cannot accept the offer." said Ah-Jord.

"What are you talking about?, isn't this the big thing that you have been waiting for. That you were born for."

" I cannot trust you with my squad no matter what you say now. I hold your earlier actions against you too. You cannot escape your past actions by just saying you've changed. You have to earn trust again slowly, once it is broken, That is the truth.

I do know how to command and I would be better at it than most others - but part of command is the caring for your troops - and I would not trust my squad to you under any circumstances. So tell the Admiral to forget about this promotion unless I can keep my squad."

Vessk was puzzled." I am not going to kill them, you know ?"

" I don't know. You already tried once, just because you disagreed with an order from the Admiral. Who knows what you'll disagree with now - you're a disagreeable person. And also, there are very few people in my squad left. I started out with 70 healthy pilots, now I have 13 who are not injured, 6 are almost dead. After all we've been through, I could never leave them behind."

" I thought that you would be used to this kind of thing"

" What are you talking about ? Is it because of my back ground ? Yes -I am born to kill, but - and maybe it's because of that - but I seem to feel more deeply than anyone else too. So my loyalty is as strong as my killer instinct. I thought otherwise before - but this war has proven me wrong."

" I am not referring to science fiction come to life, I am referring to your experience so far. Even the most innocent child among us, like young Ah-ztes - he's what 12 or 13, even he has become a hardened killer and a resourceful survivor and it's not just something he does because it's his duty. He loves it. As do all of us. Let us just take off this thin clothing of civilization and beneath it we find some naked growling, blood-thirsty beast.

I was right before - that surviving this war would destroy us - but I don't care any more. So long as I get to do some destruction too. You probably feel the same way too."

"I was born feeling like that" Ah-Jord lied, not willing to reveal his secret to this woman who he had always disliked and now hotly hated.

"I envy you." she went on, not seeing his feelings; " It's a feeling I've come to love and you had it all your life. But I'm getting off-track here. Here's what I meant: this is war, good things happen and bad things happen. The only certain thing is that things will change. Live with it !"

"No. I'll stay with my squad. Thanks anyway."

"OK then - I'll tell you what. The new squad that I will be training are going to be all new recruits.

I'll have to start them right from the beginning and your people have been through that already. I'll transfer all your people to your command - so don't worry."

" Fine then, I accept the offer, but I don't take orders from you anymore.."

Ah-Vessk smiled." You are still the same even when good things come to you."

Ah-Jord looked at Ah-Vessk," If you are not telling the truth, then I pity you, because if you betray those recruits, their young lives will be on your conscience for the rest of your days.

If you are telling the truth, I pity you more, because when you train those recruits, for all your talk about the hardness of war, you'll come to love them and when you send them off, without being able to go with them and lead them, it will break your heart. It will be like sending small children out into a dark and dangerous forest without you. So, for your sake, I hope that the war up there is not too dangerous."

"I accept your pity - and I hope you accept my apology for the Vapor Bomb. I was wrong and I put a lot of people in danger. It won't happen again." Ah-Vessk smiled. " You can leave now."

Ah-Jord turned around and headed to the door.

The door opened, and he went out. He never saw her again for years.

He walked over to the medical room. He looked around and saw his squad members asleep in the medical beds. Ah-Jord smiled and realized that Ah-Vessk was right. You could only see it when they were sleeping, but they were really children. Not one adult among them. Maybe adults just could not break the conditioning that had kept the Great Races peaceful for 4000 years. Only children could learn war.

He sighed as he stood there. He was going to miss being squad leader , flying the Shecklak fighters, seeing the air battles, and seeing young Ah-ztes by his side. He would be responsible for hundreds now, but he would never get to know any of them as well as he knew these 13 ragamuffin children. For all the wisdom and authority of the ambassadors and the Generals and Admirals, it would be dirty-faced children like these who would save civilization, if indeed it could be saved.

Ah-Jord walked out of the room and went toward his room. He walked down the halls, seeing all of the soldiers posted everywhere, the civilians that filled the rooms with their sad belongings and few little treasures that survived the bombings by the Humans. He looked at the outside cargo bay from a window, remembering the first time that he taught students how to fight , fly and do the tricks of war. He smiles as he remembered how tough little Ah-Sarak, a child herself, had challenged him to train these children better. The only reason any of them were alive today was because he had listened to her. He sighed again and kept walking down to his room.

When he reached his destination , he was stopped by Ah-Sarak,

" Did you hear the news ? We are leaving the base and going into space. Aren't you excited to be going into space again ?"

" I guess, there are good things and bad things about it." said Ah-Jord, opening his door and letting them both in.

" What's wrong?"

" I am not squad leader anymore." he said, closing the door behind him and going over to sit on a bench.

"What do you mean ?" She followed and sat beside him.

"I have been promoted to Captain of the starship that we will be going in."

" That's great. Why are you upset about that ?"

" I got Ah-Vessk to agree to put the squad on board, but I won't be close to any of you anymore. I may never fly with you or with the squad again."

" What are you talking about ? We will be in the same ship."

" The Captain's cabin is a long way from the squad room, believe me. I was born for this. I know the distance that has to be maintained. I feel that we are going be separated, like I or you are going to-"

" Die ?" said Ah-Sarak.

" Yes"

" Don't worry, We will always be together."

Ah-Sarak then looked into his eyes. She quickly gave him a hug and she didn't let go for a while.

" Ah-Sarak , I never knew that you thought about me this way -"

" Shh ! Just listen to the silence and remember it."

Ah-Jord saw that she wanted this moment to last.

He slowly put his arms around her, he laid his head down on her shoulder then closed his eyes.

Ah-Sarak slowly stopped hugging. They were both children in a way, and didn't know how to go any further from this point.

" I guess that this is good-bye till tomorrow."

" Yes, I guess, I will see you tomorrow. Take care of Ah-ztes for me from now on."

" I will."

Ah-Sarak walked out of the room and closed the door. Ah-Jord sighed and thought the lights on full. He took off his breast shield and left it on a chair. He took off the bottom part of his boots and left his Plasma gun leaning against the wall.

He took off his clothes and climbed into the slumber unit. He closed his eyes while the clear glass top came down. It sealed shut. The air became hotter and the glass became dark. Ah-Jord fell asleep.

The next morning came fast. The Glass opened up, and the air was cold. Ah-Jord shook his head at his forgetfulness the night before. He hadn't cleaned his clothes. He went over, naked, to the anti-bacterial sterilization box and put his clothes in a small compartment which read: 'decontamination laundry".

He stepped into a larger stall that said : "decontamination personnel". Steam came out of pipes all around, he closed his eyes and waited for the pipes to stop. The pipes slowly stopped vibrating. Ah-Jord got out, dry-cleaned, and walked over to get his clothes from the laundry cleaner. He quickly put them on , then strapped on his breast-plate and gun and heard a tap at his door.

Outside his room, there was no-one there, but he saw a small package propped against the wall. He opened it up to find it was the captain's traditional red cloak. He looked at it and then put it on, then walked down the hall, clean scented and depressed.

He walked over to the main cargo bay for starships, which in this station was underground. He went into an elevator, silent and not able to show emotions of joy or happiness, although he felt them.

When the elevator stopped, he took a shade pill, assuming some part of the bay would be open to the sun. His eyes turned black as the elevator doors opened up and Ah-Jord walked out into the thirty mile long under-ground launch site.

Ah-Jord saw three giant survey ships, all slightly different from each other. One ship was not operational. Rusty and old, but beautiful in it's unique design, it was Shent and it was being totally refitted.

The second, Skellio, was getting a few minor problems fixed.

The third ship was brand new. It shone its newness out from every gleaming surface. It was the first new battleship made in over 4000 years. The ship's name was Frotnerk, Ah-Jord remembered that this name meant 'savior of the people'. And that was the ship which would be his to command.

Two new creations, living man and living ship, both made especially for war and put together in an unholy alliance. A marriage made in hell.

Ah-Jord went forward and put his hand on the living side of the huge ship and made mental contact with the ship's brain. It was eager to fight, unlike the survey ships that were being converted. They wanted to avoid battle and protect their crews. Frotnerk didn't care. Battle was it's goal, never mind the outcome for ship or crew.

The two survey ships were around three miles long, made up of one mile of cargo space , half a mile of escape pods all over the ship, and a mile and a half of eating areas, and sleeping and battle stations.

" Captain, that is a beat isn't it?" said a voice.

Ah-Jord turned around and saw Sergeant Ah-nik standing proudly in front of him. Ah-Nik was also wearing the red cape.

" I am going to be commanding Skellio," Ah-Nik announced.

Ah-Jord looked at him. " You, are going to be the commander of the Skellio ? Who has Shent ?" asked Ah-Jord,

" Yeah - I got Skells - Ah-Vink has Shent - that bucket of trouble. It's one of the oldest survey ships, so they almost had to build it again from scratch, for battle. I don't know if it'll hold up. Mine's much newer. Say - Congratulations on your Captains cape. What have they assigned you to do ?"

"They've given me a ship."

Which ship - wait - have you seen Ah Vink yet ? Is that him ? He should be coming down soon. What are you doing here - is your whole squad on 14 ?

"Yes, what's left of the squad is all here."

"So are you spacing with me or Ah-Vink - What's your assignment ?"

"We're on Frotnerk here" Ah-Jord patted the side of the ship. " I'm in command."

"Gods - you lucky dog. Yes. You said you had a ship and I wasn't listening. Boy. The newest ship in the fleet. Are you worried ?"

" Worried about commanding?"

" No, I mean about surviving, we are going up against the most dangerous disease in the Galaxy. We fight the Human Race !

The evillest creatures to have ever walked through our system. They kill without mercy and hunt things for sports. And when thy can't find anything else to kill, they kill one another. I heard they were killing each other in Aorotosa. Ah-Jord did you forget all you know about the human race ?"

Ah-Jord grinned;" Well if you put it that way I'm not scared at all. After all, we've got hundreds of dirty-faced little kids, who cry in their sleep and call for their mothers. We've got these old untried, cobbled-together pieces of junk to save us. And 49,000 out of 50,000 worlds who won't fight or even think bad thoughts about humans. What do we have to be scared of."

Ah-Nik laughed." Ya, I guess that you're right. Those heums must be shivering in fright.""

Ah-Jord grinned at Ah-nik.

The doors opened once more, and suddenly there

were thousands of troops, some in the standard uniform and some wearing rags and religious head bands.

Ah- Jord looked at the troops marching towards the ships.

"Are these the new recruit ?" asked Ah- Jord.

Ah- nik walked to see the troops." This recruit is from the desert world Sivil, I think,"

Suddenly a thin man with hard eyes walked up to the two. " The south side of Sivil to be exact." he said.

Ah-nik laughed ." General Ah- Drake! So the heums didn't cut your throat after all.."

The General smiled." They didn't get a chance. You see, these troops have been through the test for the disease. And they all have it - real bad."

Ah- ztes spotted Ah-Jord from his position loading up the cargo bay. He walked over to him." Hey, lazyboy, why aren't you helping us load up. We're on this new ship now. " said Ah-ztes.

" Well I was checking a couple of things and I guess I lost track of time." said Ah-Jord.

"Not only that, he's commanding this ship" said Ah-Nick, " So if you don't want to be flogged, better fall to you knees and kiss his ring."

"Really ?" Ah-ztes asked his co-pilot, finally noticing the Captain's cape.

"Really" Ah-Jord nodded.

Suddenly a man walked   up to Ah- Jord. He was the same size as Ah-ztes and was wearing a standard pilot uniform." Captain, I'm part of the new flying group from Sivil and I hope to be fighting the humans with you." he said.

Ah- Jord smiled ."Glad to have you aboard, pilot."

Ah-ztes suddenly began to recognize this man. He
was skinnier, paler, but sounded so familiar. Ah-ztes
then took a closer look ." Ah- Nawo ?" he asked .

The man looked at him sternly, but he then began
to recognize Ah-ztes The man looked at Ah-ztes from
head to leg.

" Ah-ztes?" he asked.

Ah-ztes smiled. It was his brother which he
thought to be dead. "I heard Shama was totally destroyed. I thought you were dead."

" Only I survived. Then I joined up with Ah-Drake
and did some fighting on Sivil.. ."

"He's a tiger" interrupted Ah-Drake. "He's put
down over 250 human fighters"

Ah-Nawo wasn't paying attention to the compli-
ments his General was giving out. He was staring at his
brother in horror.

" What happened to you ? "he said, putting his
hands on Ah-Ztes' shoulders. Your leg is artificial, your
scars . . . My Gods you have changed!." he said in as-
tonishment. "When I left you were playing with toys
and now, you look like a warbird."

"Things changed." said Ah-ztes softly.

"Mom and Dad ?"

"Dead. Both dead. Mom killed in the house, Dad
killed on Congress Moon."

"Uncles and and aunts ? Cousins ?"

"All killed"

"Gods. Only us left. Maybe we should go and hide somewhere till this is over."

"Not me" said Ah-ztes. "I'm too angry to hide. Look at it another way - there's no one to miss us or to be hurt by us getting killed. "

"So we may as well - dun dun - have some fun" they said together, repeating the old song they used to yell out loud together in happier times.

The brothers walked off, arms around each other and headed into the huge ship.

Ah-Jord turned around and walked along the length of Frotnerk, trailing his hand against the warm skin. He looked at the 500-foot tall monster that stood above him. It almost seemed that this huge ship could never be controlled by such a small and insignificant being like him. But it would be. Already the ship was welcoming him and passing him information that he would need to command. He felt the missing part of his programming clicking into place as the ship fed him data, and the eagerness to fight.

This is what had happened to the other lab specimens. There had been no partner for them. No soulmate. And they had killed themselves from loneliness. He knew what he was created to be now that he had the ship as a partner.

Thousand of troops passed, but did not notice him staring. He was almost part of the ship now, and even his friends could barely see where he ended and the ship began.

Ah-Jord walked up to the loading platform and was whisked up. Even at speed, it seemed to be endless.

He opened the air pressured door and walked in. Seeing all of the troops standing guard, Ah-Jord was surprised when they saluted him. He saluted back and walked to the control tower of the ship. All of the crew was there, the weapons targeters, the navigators, the gravity engineers, and the engine experts.

A man came up to Ah-Jord. "Captain sir, we are ready for take off, all of the passengers are on, there are no fighters that are unaccounted for and the air supply is fit to last ten years. We are ready for take off."he said.

" All right, where do I sit?"asked Ah-Jord,

The man smiled. He walked and led Ah-Jord to the center seat of the room. It was black and file data were showing on each side of it. Ah-Jord walked over to the seat and sat down slowly.

" Is this biogenetic material?" asked Ah-Jord.

" No , we could have it replaced though."

Ah-Jord smiled and laughed." No that will be all right. We'll talk through it, this ship and I."

Ah-Jord sat down fully on the seat. Arm and leg restraints slipped into place. A slight shimmer of electricity slid over Ah-Jord as the ship checked him out to make sure he was the one who was authorized to command. Then the data flow began between them that would never end until one or the other was dead.

"Let's cure this disease once and for all" he said. And with those words, Frotnerk sailed off into history.

*   *   *

For four long years Frotnerk fought the humans to a standstill all over the galaxy. The combination of lab man and lab ship was invincible.

Daring tactics, outrageous tricks and utter ruthlessness pushed the Frotnerk and Ah-Jord from being a merely a great ship into being a legend.

Part of the legend were the two Shecklak pilots from Frotnerk who called themselves the Nothing-to-lose Brothers. They sat, back to back in a pure gold Shecklak that had more than 5000 human fighters confirmed on its kill record. The brothers had out fought and out risked any other fighter on either side. There were rumours that they had flown right through the inside of a human battleship, through the living areas and supply holds, killing everyone aboard. But they seldom spoke of such things. They didn't care for kill records or confirmations. They weren't after status - only humans. And they were so good at it, even humanity had learned to fear their names.

After an initial success with 30, 000 of the 50,000 planets, the tide began to turn. The humans were pushed off more and more planets and pushed back towards their home world.

They left stubborn human colonies on thousands of worlds, but the main force was on the run, slowly but surely, unable to withstand the irrational hatred and cruelty of the small alien force that hounded them throughout the entire universe.

The humans were now losing more battles than they won and their forces were fighting among themselves and splitting up to settle on fertile planets. The fighting force which was left could never return to Earth and, as the aliens chased them further and further away, could never realize the dream of having planets of their own. So the human force was beginning to feel backed into a corner. And that is one of the most dangerous places for humans to be.

*   *   *

"Are the other captains ready ?" Ah-Jord asked. His Captain's cape, once blood red, was faded now, after years of radiation and exposure to hard vacuum in accidents and near-misses.

Ah-Jord's skin was white. His face was wrinkled with the years of responsibility. But there was still a twinkle in his eye.

They had landed on a planet, far from the fighting, for much needed repairs and rest. Shent and Skellic had joined them on the surface and Ah-Vink, Ah-Nik and Ah-Jord had enjoyed their time together.

" Yes they are , they are ready now, we could contact them   if it would make you feel more comfortable."said the communications officer, joking He knew Ah-Jord's hatred of radio calls or the old thought-thrower calls, when he was in mesh with the ship and in the process of taking off.

" No that's all right, I trust you and my crew. So start the engines, lets take off."

" Right sir."

The man walked over to one of the ten control panels in the room.

" Attention all personnel, we are going to launch, please evacuate the cargo bay and enter a secure area."

The man came up to the Ah-Jord." Captain, we are in the process of lift-off now."

The crew quickly sat down on their specific seats, the whole ship began to rumble, the ships thirty hover engines were on and fully functional. The ship slowly lifted off the ground, the landing legs of the ship began to lift up, the main engines came on, the ship began to slowly move out of the area. It flew over the temporary base slowly and turned upward.

Suddenly the main engines came on and wind rushed through the trees a mile below. The ship quickly built up speed, going faster and faster as it kept reaching for the sky. The ship was now at a speed, so fast it couldn't be seen. For those aboard, the sky seemed to disappear, the atmospheric mist of the planet became dark, and they were in space now.

Small animals on the planet's surface came cautiously out of the underbrush and looked up, with wonder in their eyes.

The comm officer got up from his seat and walked over to Ah-Jord. " Sir, we have broken through the atmosphere. We are now in orbit.

Where are we hunting this time ?" asked the man.

Ah-Jord stood up and let the shipskin fall away from his arms and legs. He walked over to the view screen in front of him, he looked for the two other huge ships, commanded by his friends.

" Are the other two ships in orbit?" asked Ah-Jord.

" Not yet, they should be coming through the atmosphere in any minute."

Ah-Jord kept looking at the view screen. He saw the other ships shooting through the atmosphere like fast birds coming out of a forest. They began to slow down when they reached orbit, also discussing their next jump.

The radio was bleeping on the captains chair and Ah-Jord walked over to the chair and pushed the button.

" Captain Ah-Jord, Ah-nik here. where are you headed. We were thinking of going back towards the wormhole ."

Ah-Jord sat down on the chair, he pushed the respond button on the handle of the chair.

" Ah-Nik, this is Ah-Jord."Ah-Jord opened a file on the data computer,"What a co-incidence. According to our plan, we are to join the Admiral at the system where the worm hole is"

" Isn't that where the Sivil fleet is located too ?" said the radio.

" Yes I think so, I think that the fleet is planning an attack on the Humans Mother home. Set a course for the Wormhole, and we'll see you there." Ah-Jord said.

The radio turned off.

Ah-Jord looked up at the gravity valve. " Well all of you, don't just sit there, start the jump engines and let's head to the Wormhole."

The crew scuffled all around to restart the engines.

Ah-Jord stood up from the chair and walked around the room. He walked to the radar monitor, the radar showed three fighters coming fast at them.

" Hey, does the other monitor show Fighters?" asked Ah-Jord.

A member of the crew came up to the radar monitor, " Oh my god!, we have enemy fighters coming in from the North.,"

The crew became silent , Ah-Jord ran to the weapons status monitors.

"Call the other ships" Ah-Jord said to the Comm Officer. Ah-Jord turned on the speakers all around the ship." Attention all gunners, we have incoming, Get ready for attack raids,"

Suddenly the room turned dark grey, the alert system was on. The room became silent again.

Ah-Jord walked over to the chair. he sat down and let the ship cover him again, so they were in total mesh.

They waited for impact.

The Plasma cannons all over the ships were becoming alive, the cannons began to move around as Ah-Jord flexed his fingers and stretched. He was one with the ship now.

Ah-Jord looked into the outside monitors. He began to hear a faint plasma fire, as the gunners opened up.

The radio came on.

" Captain, the fighters have stuck onto the ship."

Ah-Jord looked around in shock. " Tell all of the people on the outside decks to move inside, now !

" But sir, the . . ."

" Just do it !" yelled Ah-Jord.

The man ran to a microphone: " Attention all units on decks 1 to 5 - get further inside. Repeat. Get away from the outer skin of the ship."

"If they're stuck to the ship, they must be planting charges, but I can't feel them anywhere. I should be able to feel the ship's skin being cut. I should be able to feel where they are stuck on - but I can't feel anything. I can't see anything."

"Maybe the report was mistaken. Maybe they are not stuck on. Maybe they went right by. "

"No. I smell them. They're here somewhere. Send out a fastprobe. Shoot it out a few miles and have it survey the ship"

"Aye, Aye sir" came the reply from one of the workstations.

Almost immediately one of the monitors started showing a probe's eye view of the inside of Frotnerk, then the outside as a piece of skin opened and the probe was launched. The view was of deep space, then suddenly swung around and showed Frotnerk, still gleaming and beautiful after all of it's action. It began to look as if the ship was revolving, but it was the survey probe, flying around and around.

"Hold it there" said Ah-Jord. "There they are"

The view showed three human fighters, landed together on the ships skin.

"Zoom"

The view expanded to show three space-suited humans working at something on the skin of the ship.

"Gunners, they're on Sector 51, close to the retros. Program your plasma for humans."

As he spoke, the three figures jumped up and ran back to their fighters - as if they could hear the conversation within the ship.

"Can they hear us ?" asked one crewman.

In the monitor, one of the humans waved to the camera on the probe

"There's your answer " said Ah-Jord. "We don't think anymore. We only speak. So they can pick up everything."

The fighters took off from the ship, leaving a human figure stuck onto the skin. Plasma arced around the ship from the nearest gun and hit the place where the fighters had been.

Suddenly, in the monitors, they saw a huge explosion. Everyone was in shock. A few seconds later, like a big wave arriving, the control centre shook and vibrated.

"It's the human figure. They know how plasma works now." said Ah-Jord. "They made a human-shaped bomb and our plasma sought it out." his fingers twitched as he tracked the escaping fighters with the guns under his control. Plasma shot out from Frotnerk and all three suddenly went out of control as their pilots were killed.

"Damage control" shouted Ah-Jord. "I can't feel anything down there."

" Sir, Decks 1 through 34 on the right quarter of the ship have been destroyed, We are losing air fast."

" Gods. 30 decks ? Seal off the remaining decks that lead to those areas," Ah-Jord felt a little lighter.

" What the hell is going on with the gravity?"

" Sir, that is a minor problem, I took some gravitational energy and switched it to give power to the damaged decks so we're losing a bit of gravity. Not much, just enough to notice."

"Good thinking"

Ah-Jord then became silent, communicating with the ship on a mental level. He pushed the sending message button near the receiving button.

" Commanders Ah-nik and Ah-Vink!, Be careful. Three human fighters have just blown 30 decks. I don't know what they're up to. I've never seen this before. Don't let anything near you." Ah-Jord took off his hand from the button.

A man's head rose up to from his work station:

" Sir, Other fighters are coming our way,"

Ah-Jord looked at him." Are they Heums or Degosians?"

" They are Human."

" I want all plasma cannons to hit any fighters in a range of 5000 yards, if any get too close tell the crew to evacuate that area. Remember with the plasma - think human - but don't let them get too close."

" Yes sir"

" I want to find out where those fighters are coming from. Set a course for the north, and we'll come around the planet behind them."

The man ran to a control panel. He was sending messages all over and working hard. Ah-Jord stood up and went to the viewscreen.

" Sir where are you going?"

" I need to see. The ship feels something strange is happening, but doesn't know what. I have to see."

" Sir, use the probe mon. You have to stay in mesh, if you get hurt, the ship might not recognize anyone else !" shouted a man.

Ah-Jord looked at the man. "There's something not right"

Suddenly the probe's view screen showed a small pointed fighter, it was heading at full speed to the control tower.

" That's it ! Everyone off the deck!" shouted Ah-Jord. He ran to the center of the room and began pushing people out the door. Ah-Jord turned to the view screen, the fighter was almost at it's destination.

Ah-Jord ran to the door last. He closed the door and locked it shut. He looked through the thick door glass and saw the fighter crash right into the view screen, and come out in the Command Centre bridge.

The ship began to rumble, clouds of dust came out inside the room. The hard vacuum of space sucked all the air out of the room, creating gale-force winds for a few seconds.

Ah-Jord stood back, the door was pressure-boomed into the room like a giant fist had given it a good punch..

He feared the door would not hold.

"Into the hall" he shouted, pushing crewmates in front of him. Ah-Jord was not willing to stay and witness what else would happen. It was too late. The inner door was buckling. He could hear the air begin to hiss out into space.

Suddenly Ah-Jord floated off his feet. Ah-Jord tried to swim to the next door, but he couldn't get near enough to anything to bounce off of it. A man opened the door and floated to Ah-Jord, trailing a rope behind him. .

" The gravity is off line, Sir !" said the man; "The others are all right, we just need to get you out."

" Better hurry. the control tower door is going to explode, we have to get out of this deck before . . ."

The man saw the pressure boomed door, quivering. " We haven't much time, get to the door, Sir !"

Ah-Jord pulled on the rope and floated to the other door, and the crewman followed, watching the inner door carefully. Ah-Jord opened the door and floated into the other room.The crewman was following Ah-Jord's every move.

Suddenly the pressure -boomed door broke a hole through the glass and the air started rushing out to the vacuum. The man was getting sucked in toward the small hole in the glass. He would be cut into pieces if he was sucked through.

Ah-Jord quickly grabbed the trailing rope and pulled up until he had the man's hand.

" I have you, don't worry !"Ah-Jord held onto the handle of the door leading to the other deck tightly, and pulled the man towards him.

" It's not smart to save me captain."

" Shut up and hold onto the handle."

Ah-Jord pushed the close button and the door slowly closed. The man and Ah-Jord stepped on the door, and it finally closed shut.

Ah-Jord floated to the crewman; "Are you OK ?"

" Yes, thank you Captain."

Ah-Jord floated around, trying to see what the damage was.

" The crew would probably be at the back-up control room,"he said."Deck 89 "

The crewman, in shock, was now confused. " What shape is the ship in - can we move 85 decks anymore ?"

Ah-Jord put his hand against the living wall of the ship and was in instant communication.

" Are the engines still online, is anything on line?" the crewman asked

" Everything is still functional except for the Gravity. Get in the lift " He pulled the man over to the wall with him. He pushed a decorative rock sticking out of the wall and the wall opened in two. The man floated in, Ah-Jord followed and they were both instantly encased in a big bubble.The walls closed up behind them.

"Deck 89!"shouted Ah-Jord.

They both floated in liquid, yet could still breathe

since they were inside a blood cell of the living ship. They zipped through the vein like children on a water slide.

Suddenly they stopped and stuck to the wall of the vein. The wall opened spilling liquid into the hall causing Ah-Jord and the man to slip and hit the opposite wall.

"Sloppy, but here we are." said Ah-Jord bouncing off the wall and kicking of out the door. He saw injured crewpeople milling about and soldiers quickly floating over to man outside space plasma guns.

The remaining crew, all stood, in precise military formation, all right and all ready for the next command that Ah-Jord was going to give them.

Ah-Jord was angry. He floated upwards. He yelled at them from above: " I am a bastard. I have no father. I have no mother. I was created in the labs to wage war and I have failed.

I am the bastard that led you into this defeat. It is the first time we have ever been so badly hit in over 4 years and 200 battles.

I am responsible. I should have foreseen this ambush. I should have foreseen this tactic. We are safe for the moment and I want to do something we've never done before. I want to take a vote.

This defeat proves to me that we must change our tactics. I say we must fight them like we are them. It is time for us to become the pirates. For us to become the bad guys. I think we must become even more barbaric and more like animals.

It will be more risky. We will sustain more damage like we did today. We will do more damage to our souls too. So it is not a decision I can make for you. It is your decision to make. I will abide by your vote.

I will turn around now. If you want to follow my new plan, take one step forward. If you do not want to put your lives and souls in this kind of danger, stand fast.

He turned around, in mid-air and faced the wall. There was a long shuffling sound, then silence. Ah-Jord turned around again to see the entire company still standing in straight lines. Not one person was out of place.

"I see." he said. "I will honor your decision. Especially since it is unanimous. I am surprised that not even one of you stepped forward, but I can understand, I will do as you say . . ."

"Sir" a voice interrupted

"Yes"

"We all stepped forward, Sir"

The people began to cheer. They started to call out his name over and over. Injured men began to feel stronger and even the ship seemed to have a new purpose and resolve. Ah-Jord saw their cheers and raised his hands in the air. His eyes were suspiciously moist.

" Now, man the battle stations, go and run out the plasma cannons, we are about to give those heum ships, the last surprise of their lives."

The people quickly floated to their stations. Ah-Jord floated down and saw his crew, waiting, and forever loyal to him.

" Captain, we are all ready for your command ."

Ah-Jord looked at all of the twenty members of the brifge crew.

" Lets open up the new bridge !" he said.

One man floated to a giant door. He pushed a code into the box and the doors opened up and there was the second replica of the original bridge.

A man came up to Ah-Jord. "Sir, I am here to tell you that the Gravity will be coming back on. So have your feet pointing downwards"

"Thanks Engineer Sinter." said Ah-Jord. He felt a pull on his legs and, suddenly, he was no longer floating. He walked into the replacement bridge which was in the centre of the ship and halfway back along it's length, unlike the original bridge which was on the top of the ship at the front.

The lights became bright in the room as they walked in, set off by brain-wave detectors. Ah-Jord saw the command seat brilliantly placed in the center of the room, having most of the monitors for the functions of the ship. Ah-Jord walked to the seat, he sat down and turned to the bridge crew.

" Are the Jump Engines functional ?" Asked Ah-Jord.

Sinter came up to him, "All of the ship is 83% functional sir."

Ah-Jord smiled," Set a course for the north, Keep this ship on red alert, we are going head first into the Human fleet !"

Sinter smiled," Yes captain sir" Sinter quickly ran to a main frame station on the left side of Ah-Jord. The crew sat down quickly and started turning on machines on their control panels. Ah-Jord sat facing the view screen, linked to the ship

" Sir we are going into thrust mode, hold on ,"said a crew man.

Ah-Jord felt a jerk to the side. The ship stopped and went forwards to the North, around the planet.

"Send this probe out a hundred miles, and let's see if we can see what the humans have on the other side of the planet."

"Aye, aye"

" Sir, we have some more fighters coming towards us !"

Ah-Jord looked at the man." Shoot them down and try not to let them come too close to the ship!"

" Sir they are not that type of fighters"

" What do you mean ?"

" These fighters are Shecklak!"

Ah-Jord was silent. He looked down. The message button was bleeping,

" Captain Ah-Jord this is Sergeant Ah-nik, "I've sent over a few top people,to help you clean up that mess. Ah-Goldis is one of my best - a little too ready to do things by the book, but it looks like you need that right now. That looks like a serious wound."

Ah-Jord pushed the respond button: "Thanks, Ah-Nik. I'll take them in, but we're trying new tactics here. Things we've never tried before. So stay out of it and

just observe. If they don't work, it's up to you to tell the
Admiral that we died gloriously !"

Well, if you do die gloriously, the Heums will pay
for their crime - I swear it."

Ah-Jord was quiet and faced the viewscreen. The
probe showed 5 big Human ships lurking on the dark
side of the planet.

"Are the fighters aboard ?"

"They're in"

"Make sure everybody is at least 10 decks in."

"Done"

"Ready the Jump Engines"

"Jump to where, Sir ?"

"I want 5 jumps in 5 seconds."

"We can do that sir - to what coordinates ?"

"I want to jump right into the inside of each of the
human ships. One at a time. Then, assuming we survive that, jump to Sivel. Plot the jumps"

"Gods" came the reply, then; "Plotting"

"We fight them as if we are them "said Ah-Jord.
"Surprise is another name for victory."

"Plotted and ready, Sir."

"I believe this will work."said Ah-Jord. "We are
materializing inside a hollow solid object. So the object
should give way. We have more mass, so we should
shove aside the mass that exists in that space. But I may
be totally wrong. Physics was never my strong point."

No-one objected.

"Jump"

Chapter **15**

The squad of Katheren Jewel

(Earth. Philadelphia space port - in the last days)

A young woman in her twenties was looking up at the sky. Her soft eyes gazed at the sun as it was dawning over the buildings of Philadelphia. Her short dark blond hair reflected its beauty over the grey uniform that she wore.Her thoughts were filled with excitement since this was the day that she would be joining the fleet in the new galaxy.

This was a day that she wondered , wondered if she would ever see the earth under her feet again, wondered if all that she would find out there would be destruction or death. She was scared, but she was excited too.

She knew that there was a war going on for the very survival of the human race. Every time she thought of the war, she thought of the war dramas she had seen. Of course she knew that the war was nothing like the movies, but she still used her imagination for the most of it.

" Kathie?" said a voice.

Katheren turned around. She saw a tall slender man, dark skinned and quite stern looking. It was her favorite instructor from the Academy.

" Kathie, You should be getting ready for the take off," he said.

" I just wanted a last look at Philadelphia before I go to the new galaxy. I fear that I may never return."

The man smiled. " Don't worry, you have the safest ship that this world is ever going to launch. Don't worry about coming back, either. Come back to what ? You are going to start a new life somewhere else that hasn't been gutted and used up."

Katheren looked at him; " I don't know. Did you hear about Deborah whatsername - you know the one who discovered the wormhole ?"

"Sollent. Debra Sollent. I thought she was dead ?"

"No, she was shot down on Sivil and captured by aliens. She got away and walked right across that desert to a human base and she's back on earth now. She claims the aliens told her that humans are alike a lab experiment for them - and that they'll never let us live among them out there."

Then we'll just have to win their hearts and mnds - then kill them all. "The man smiled again; " Now go to your ship, you should be taking off soon."

"Thanks for everything." Katheren picked up her helmet with the three stars on it and her duffle. She turned on the cement and walked over to the docking tower door. Inside, there was a line of people standing in order and waiting to board the giant triangle-shaped craft .

" All personnel, the U.S.S. ARIZONA is ready for take off. All sergeants and officers, please check in at the fifth deck of the tower."

Once inside the docking tower, Katheren turned to the top-seats elevator. It was stuffed with officers, other sergeants and captains. She quickly folded into the open cage.

"Is this elevator heading to deck five?" asked Katheren.

"Yes" said an officer.

Katheren smiled and walked in just as the elevator doors closed. The floor began to rumble.

" Deck five!" said the elevator finally, after a few other stops.

Katheren walked out of the cage into a connecting bridge leading to the front of the ship. She started to walk to the entrance of the ship but stopped to look out the window briefly, surprised to find she was almost ten stories up from the ground. She kept walking and went into the entrance of the ship where a stewart guided her to her seat.

Fortunately, it was a seat near a window, but unfortunately, to her point of view, the wall was the floor and the ceiling was the wall, and the seat was five feet off the ground and facing straight up. But there was a ladder -bracket and she was quite nimble, so, even carrying her helmet and duffle, she was seated in seconds.

She noticed some of the older officers, the men especially, had to be helped into their seats by one and sometimes even two helpers. She smiled at her own vanity sat down comfortably in the seat.

Exploring her environment, she found a helmet connected to the seat by a long plug. It was a protective unit for her head and was sitting in its own little shelf in the seat-back in front of her. She unplugged it and pushed the plug into her own helmet. It connected her to the ships intercom.

She was just strapping up the 5-point safety belt, when she felt a bounce beside her and heard a voice: "So, you are the new sergeant who's got everybody talking. Are you being recruited as well, or is this just a training flight ?"

Katheren was shocked she quickly turned around to her left. There was a young man in the seat beside her; six foot tall, dark blond curly hair, green eyes and all dressed in Battle Grey.

"Who are you?" asked Katheren.

" I am Sergeant Lorance O'Conner . Squad leader of the Giants."

" I am Katheren Jewel, Sergeant of the Desert Strike Unit, Cactus Spike."

" I know. You're famous. Best scores in the Academy. Best record in training. Most kills in the War Games - you're a legend already. It's a pleasure to meet finally you, Katheren. What's your secret. How did you do so well ?"

Lorance stuck out his hand at her. It took her a

moment to realize that he wanted to shake her hand. It was a gesture that had gone out of fashion.

"It's no secret. It was just fun for me. And when it's fun, you never want it to stop. " Katheren stuck out her hand , grabbed Lorance's hand and shook it vigorously. She let go and faced him."Have we met before ? I have the strangest feeling that I've seen you somewhere," asked Katheren

"That's supposed to be my line. But I don't think so. Not that you'd remember anyway" said Lorance.

" Your face seems so familiar, Yes. Yes. I have seen you before. You were one of the pacifists in the hall of congress debating about the Agreement of the Extermination Policy. Yes, I was there trying to hold you all back from high-jacking the congress hall in D.C."

Lorance smiled and looked at her as if she was his hero." Yes, I know. I didn't think you'd remember. Even though I was screaming and yelling, I never forgot your face. I thought of you all the time I was in jail."

"You went to jail for that ? I thought you were just expressing an opinion." She said.

"It wasn't a popular opinion. But I kept seeing your face. All those publicity photos in the papers from your success at the Academy. You were doing so well, while I was in jail. "

"But it worked though. It changed your mind. Now you're a stone cold killer like the rest of us."

"No. I still think it's wrong to go out there and kill everything we meet. I think we could have done things so much better if we had not come out shooting. But you did inspire me to be a sergeant."

"So why ? Why are you a sergeant for the new re-cruit ? Especially if you're still a pacifist ? " she asked.

" No choice. Didn't you hear ?" asked Lorance.

" Hear what?"

" All of the people in the Americas are being re-cruited against their will for the war, even nerdy paci-fists like me.

You can't go into space unless you are in the mili-tary. Now that we are against Asia , the Moon, and Eu-rope, as well as all those aliens, the War has become another World War . They need every body they can get."

"That's right. Mars is our only friend - and we never much liked them anyway." Katheren was silent and closed her eyes.

Lorance looked at her, he smiled and lay back in his seat. He began to laugh.

"What?" asked the smiling Katheren,

He continued to laugh." You are truly amazing" said Lorance."You know as well as I do that we're los-ing out there. We're being pushed back every day. We're even fighting among ourselves. What we're heading for is likely to be the Final Battle - and we're probably go-ing to lose that too. But you still think it's all fun, don't you ?"

Katheren was silent a moment and sat in her seat, looking out of the window. "Yes. And that's what will save me " she said.

" Attention all passengers, we will be taking off ,

please be seated and strapped in - or you'll regret it !" said the speakers of the ship.

The floor began to rumble and vibrate. Lorance looked at Katheren," Our old selves are now dead."

Katheren looked at Lorance and shook her head. "Don't worry about our old selves being dead. Worry about our new selves being dead. That's the one to worry about."

Lorance smiled at her. "Why worry. It's all in fun."

The ship took off into the sky like a giant submarine coming to the surface of the ocean. It kept going up into the sky until there was no more sky left.

It went up to the clutches of space not stopping for a minute's notice of the gravity which wanted to hold the ship dearly like a mother holds her child.

Within minutes, the ship was finally out of the gravitational pull of the Earth and was in orbit. Katheren looked out of the window seeing the Earth covered in its polluted atmosphere of gases. She looked at Lorance," Don't you want to see this ? It's beautiful."

Lorance smiled at her ,

" I have seen it too many times in documentaries and video diaries. I have a running picture in my mind of what it looks like. But go ahead. Have fun."

Katheren looked at him, then looked back at the window.

" Attention, all personnel, we are now in space, There will be no one getting out of their seats. There is no gravity at all in space so I rorder that you all stay in your seats through out the trip."said the radio on the ship.

" If you think that's fun, how about this : where do you think the Wormhole really is ? In the asteroid field, in the planet Mars or in the far depths of space ?" Katheren asked. "And is there really a worm in it ?"

Lorance smiled," Don't you know ? The best student in the Academy doesn't know what every schoolkid knows ?"

" Know what?" asked Katheren, looking dumb and confused; "I'm only a poor little country girl. And I just want to have fun."

" The Wormhole is in the Sun, little girl - and yes, there is a worm in it."

Katheren looked at Lorance, pretending she was shocked.

" My God ! A big worm. In the sun ! We're all going to die!" whispered Katheren.

Lorance laughed "Roger that. " he said.

Katheren looked at him thinking about what she just had said. She became very quiet and kept looking out the window. The windows became dark. Suddenly a giant metal sheet covered the window.

" Attention all personnel, Please sit tightly, we have just entered the last boundaries of the habitable areas. We have now entered the orbit space formerly held by the late great planet Mercury. Expect some turbulence soon ."said the radio.

" Well, we are going to be in the Wormhole in no time" said Lorance.

Katheren looked at him. she was going to make

another joke, but the turbulence had begun. The lights
flickered on and off,

" Why is there turbulence here anyway ?" asked
Katheren, when the lights stabilized.

" Parts of the planet are still flying around and the
wormhole caused big solar flares that won't stop, so it
gets shakier and shakier the closer we get. Besides, we're
going so fast by this point, that any little piece of dust
will shake us up."

The rumbling stopped and the metal sheets on the
windows opened back up.

"Boy, you really studied up on this stuff, didn't
you ?" Katheren looked out the window andsaw the
brightness of the sun . She then noticed a Hole, very
dark, very large , off centre in the sun. Like a huge drain,
it was pulling everything into it.

" Oh my God ! That's really the wormhole isn't
it ? I knew it but I didn't know it, you know." She wasn't
joking now.

Lorance bent over to the window." Yup, that's it
all right."

The ship turned slowly. The window's picture of
the full sun slowly disappeared as the ship began pointing directly at the fiery star. The metal sheets closed once
more. There was no explanation from the radio this time.

"Are we going into the wormhole now?" asked
Katheren, suddenly not so sure of herself.

Lorance grinned, " Head first !" he said.

The ship began to get strangely hot. Steam came
out of the floor. The seats also became incredibly hot.

Katheren became worried, she held the seat arm rest very tightly. The ship started to rumble about and pressure steam began to shoot out everywhere.

Suddenly the ship became incredibly bright, even inside. Katheren closed her eyes in fright, although she knew what to expect.

The ship became calm, the rumblings had stopped and there was no sound to be heard. She opened her eyes cautiously and looked around. The ship was normal.

"Katheren !" She jumped in fright, not so cool as she pretended to be.

" Katheren, we have reached the new system. Now the fun really begins." said Lorance.

" How did we reach it so quickly ?" asked Katheren; "I thought it just put us out in space. Not right into another solar system."

Lorance gave no answer. He was as much in the dark as she was and for once, all of his prison studies did him no good.

Katheren looked out the window, It was beautiful, the unfamiliar blue stars glowing in the darkness of space, the cluster of other new constellations never seen from Earth and the promise of the millions of new planets that could become new outposts of the human empire.

As the ship turned, she found they were very close to a beautiful light brown planet. It was incredibly large and grand.

Lorance bent over to see the planet.

" That planet is New Earth. The aliens call it Sivil - which means Endless Beautiful Sand. It is a desert world, but habitable. See that big spot of greenery. That's the Primary Oasis. That is where we are probably going to land and set up base."

Katheren looked at him." You love this stuff even more than I do, don't you ? What a waste. Instead of giving in to your bad attitude and being thrown in jail, you could have been in the Academy or in some other school. Then I would have been reading about you "

" I guess ," said Lorance.

Katheren didn't bother to ask what he meant. She lay back on her seat. Suddenly the windows closed up, the lights turned red and the air became cold.

" What is going on?" asked Lorance.

" This is one thing I know more about than you " said Katheren; "We are under attack,"

Suddenly they heard gun shots from the top of the ship, Katheren looked up and heard some more shots.

" The tower gunner" whispered Katheren."That's serious. Activate your pod."

There was a sudden jerk to the floor and Katheren heard clamping noises.

" Katheren , what do I activate ?"

Lorance was interrupted by a someone yelling :

" Shecklak fighters! God. It's the golden Shecklak. It's the Nothing-to-lose Brothers and their whole squad. We're done for. They never show any mercy."

The Sergeants and passengers that had any

knowledge of the Alien War began to scream and panic. The ship began to point down. Gravity suddenly started to pick up on the ship. Katheren felt a pull forwards.

" Oh my God, we are falling into the planet !" said Lorance, his studies not preparing him for this kind of examination.

" Stay calm" said Katheren. "Press the big red button by your elbow. It will activate your escape pod if we get in trouble ."

"No. That'll eject me. I'll wait til . . . "

The screamings of the passengers began to get louder as the ship's interior increased in temperature. Suddenly there was a rumbling noise. The top of the ship exploded. Katheren covered her eyes, Lorance fell off his chair and crashed onto the air chamber door. Pieces of shrapnel shot everywhere.

Katheren was in pain, her arm was covered in cuts and pieces of shrapnel stuck deeply into her arm like pieces of hot glass.

"Lorance" she cried. "Get into a seat. Any seat. Activate the pod !"

The ship was still falling all covered in flames. A giant hole through the top floor right on the top of Katheren and the other passengers sucked out everything which wasn't tied down. Katheren was in agony, she bit her tongue to try and forget about the pain but the cuts were too deep.

Suddenly transparent domes slid over almost all of the seats. Katheren felt herself being ejected out of the plane. She saw the many seats shoot out into the air like seeds from a poppy flower. As the giant 1000 foot ship fell over in slow motion, spouting great sockets of fire, the ship stopped releasing seats.

Katheren looked at the ship turning slowly, burning rapidly, as it tumbled away from her, hoping for a chance for Lorance.

She saw nothing.

As the parachutes began to pop out the top of the dome, she looked to her left, she saw thousands of other passengers and supplies all parachuting down with her. Her arm was still sore; she could barely move it.

With al her training, she realized that there was nothing she could do - so she did nothing. She just lay there in pain looking up at the top of the dome.

Finally Katheren felt a jerk , she had hit bottom. The dome shot open and Katheren saw the parachute blown off with it. She stood up slowly from her seat. She saw a small city of tents set up near the crash site of the ship. She looked up and saw the sky covered in thousands of domes and parachutes as supplies and passengers floated down.

Two men ran up to her.

" Sergeant, we have to get you to the surgeon ! You're not looking too good."The man said.

Katheren, in shock, said " What happened to Sergeant Lorance?"

One of the men was quiet. The other said: " We don't know any Lorance, but I'm sure he's safe. Don't worry. There are lots of survivors. But right now, we need to get you to the first aid tent."

The two men grabbed her arms and started to help her walk to the medical tent. The men put her down on a bed and quickly ran out of the tent to help with more of the wounded.

A man walked up to her. It was the Doctor .

" Oh my God, looks like you have seen some action. Welcome to Sivil." he said.He quickly grabbed a needle and a bottle of serum." This won't hurt you a bit" he said as he grabbed her arm and injected her. Katheren fell a sleep in a matter of seconds.

Katheren came to. Her body wasn't throbbing with the pain anymore. Her injured arm was wrapped around in a cast. She got out of the bed and walked around. The tent lights were on and the Doctor was nowhere to be seen.

Katheren opened the tentdoor. It was dark outside. She looked aroundand saw other tents set up , supplies set down, and the lights in the far distance where the crash site was. but noone to be seen anywhere.

Suddenly she heard thousands of gun shots and commands screamed out where the crash site was. She ran back into the Medic tent and opened a weapons chest. She was trained for this too. This was the fun part.

She grabbed an automatic rifle and checked it while she put on a bullet proof vest. She strapped on the night vision glasses and slowly walked to the outside area.

She loaded her rifle on the run and followed the lights leading to the crash site.The closer she got the louder the gun shots got. Suddenly the ground seemed to vibrate when she got closer and the screams got louder.

Fun, in the extreme.

Katheren saw the others shooting at something but she could not tell what. She ran to them.

" Sergeant, we need your man power!" shouted a soldier. She didn't bother to correct him. She became scared but only in a way that gave her strength and power, not in a way that paralysed her. She still held her gun in her hand tightly. and she still grinned, ear to ear as she ran closer to where all of the soldiers were, not firing until she had a definite target. The fear kept her cool, while others, who were fearless, panicked.

The ground began to shake and she fell and rolled into a sharpshooter position, ready for anything. She saw all of the soldiers backing up, leaving only her in front. Fine with her. No need to worry about shooting them anymore.

Suddenly a giant thirty foot-tall whale-like creature exploded out of the ground sticking it's pointed snout up to the air. Dozens of tentacles spun out of control under the giant snout. Probably the boring tools that let it go through the sand, she thought, as she brought her weapon to bear.

Katheren felt a thump beside her and looked left to see a Captain of Infantry lying beside her."Sergeant ! We are having a sneak attack from the Aliens !"

"This is an alien ? I thought it was the worm from the wormhole ?"

"Ha ! That's a good one." said the Captain.

"No that's not a worm. It's a troop carrier. Just you watch. It'll spit out a whole squad of aliens any minute now."

"Why wait"

"Nothing we have will touch it."

"Smell that - that's fossil fuel. It must be coated in some kind of petrochemical as a lubricant. I'll bet a big spark or an open flame would smoke it"

"No time to experiment. Sergeant. Get ready, lads" he waved his squad up around them. "We've already fought off the Jappos today. We're not going to lose to these baldie bastards." Said the Captain to his squad .

" The Mole is opening up!" shouted a man.

The Captain took out a grenade and stuck it in the grenade launcher of his rifle." Get ready for a Close Encounter of the worst kind, Sergeant !" he said.

Katheren then heard an unhuman growl. She turned around and saw the whale-like creature opening its snout. Katheren looked at it, scared as ever. She held out her rifle as more soldiers began to run towards them and take cover.

Suddenly fifty Aliens ran out of the creature shooting their plasma slime at the soldiers.

Katheren calmly picked off three of them, then saw the giant worm-creature had moved and was now on top of a crushed Hummer. "Steel Hummer. Steel-coated bullets." she thought and smiling grimly, took careful aim at a piece of Hummer closest to the Worm. Her bullet hit at an angle and Katheren saw a spark fly to the creature. She quickly stopped shooting and shouted out." Back away !"

The creature exploded slowly, like old footage of the Hindenberg, and spewed hundreds of burning pieces onto the battlefield.The burning debris slowly started to sink to the ground and further explosions hurled burning alien bodies out to the sky.

Katheren saw the aliens looking back at their burning comrades and took the opportunity to pot 3 more, before they came to their senses and started the attack again, shooting blobs of plasma with deadly accuracy. She was amazed that virtually every shot claimed a victim, even when the aliens were wounded and not aiming very well.

She saw the Captain beside her, looking at a small handheld computer.

" Any record of a Sergeant Lorance O'Conner?" Katheren asked .

The Captain pushed a few keys. " He never made it. Sorry. Friend of yours was he ?"

"I just met him, but yes, I guess he was. "

The ground started to shake once more.

" What happened to the two squads from the Academy. We're supposed to meet up ? The docs put me out for a while when they fixed my arm." yelled Katheren.

" They were hit by the Japs when they first landed. Wiped out to a man. They gave a good account of themselves, but they were doomed. The Japs hit them before most of them were even on the ground. Me and these two squads came along and wiped out the Jappos. Now the bloody aliens are popping out of the ground.

It's like a video game."

" Jeez. Everybody I know, the whole graduating class, all dead ? How many people are left in your two squads here ?"

"We had 120 this morning. I'd be surprised if we had 30 left. And we're about all that's left on the planet."

" Get ready another attack, Cap." shouted one of the squad.

Katheren suddenly felt a great shaking under her and immediately rolled to the right as the ground began to break up. The Captain rolled in the other direction. The wrong direction. Another whale-like creature came out of the ground , right beneath him, slicing his back up and killing him instantly.

Katheren stood and backed up, holding her gun on the monster. There was no steel around this time to try her sparking trick. The mouth of the creature opened up and another batch of aliens ran out. Katheren pulled the trigger of her gun smoothly, hitting three aliens in three seconds. Ten soldiers ran to where Katheren was and they all started to shoot at the aliens. The worm began to sink back into the ground.

Katheren stopped shooting and took out a grenade . She pulled the pin out of the grenade then threw it into the mouth of the monster. Katheren fell to the ground and threw away her night vision goggles.The blast was strangely muffled. She faced up to see why and saw n worm at all - only an Alien pointing a plasma gun at her.

A soldier ran up to the alien firing off his gun

The Alien fell down on Katheren dripping black blood all over her. She pushed off the dead body and picked up her gun. It was light which meant that it was out of ammo. She then saw the plasma gun and took it. She stood up not knowing how to work the plasma gun, but the moment she put her hands on it, it spoke to her, in her mind. "What should we shoot, Lord" it said.

She almost dropped it in shock. It felt warm. It felt good. It was alive. "Shoot the worm" she thought at it and brought up picture of the worm in her mind. She put her fingers on two triggers on the gun then pulled them. Green flames started to come out of the gun like small balls of fire. They circled the battleground, searching.

She stopped shooting as another grenade detonated. The worm creature shot back out of the ground half burned and half covered in dirt. Whether it was the same one or not, she didn't know. Or care.

It tried to dive back into the ground but the plasma found it while it was in mid air. Bits and pieces fell off everywhere, as the worm virtually dissolved in front of her eyes. Within seconds only the carcass' silver granite bones were left.

The soldiers stopped shooting. The rumblings had stopped.Katheren dropped the plasma gun and walked over to the soldiers. She was happy, the alien troops were all dead or gone and there were no more underground Whale-like creatures left that were going to fight.

She had finally tasted war and it was a taste she liked.

She walked over to a man that was from the Giant squad. " Who's now in charge of your squad ? I have to report to him."

The man looked up to Katheren ." You are the last person of any rank still standing. You're in charge of the squads."

Katheren was quiet. The Medics had come out to treat the wounded. She walked up to one of them." How many people do we have left?" She said.

The medic looked at her.

" Estimated with the injured , we have around 75 people left from the crash and from the troops that were here before the attack."

" Is it possible that the crash site might have any more survivors ?"

The medic became quite silent."There are no more survivors from the ship. And I'll tell yo something else. We have all the supplies that we could of taken out of that can, and with the attack by the Japs and now this attack , we are at minimum. We're limited to thirty shots per man or less."

The medic walked off as someone called for help.

Katheren walked over to the burning worm creature and saw the burning bodies of many alien troops lying around. She saw the bones of them , sticking out of the ground, all covered in black blood and dirt. She sat down and closed her eyes .

" Sergeant?," said a voice.

Katheren turned around . She saw a soldier, partly injured , covered in dirt. He gave off the smell of wet clay every time he breathed.

"What do you want?"

The soldier stepped back, he was a shy one. " We are all waiting for your next command."

Katheren stood up. and tried to ignore him. " I have no commands to give."

" What are you talking about?, Someone has to command us!"

Katheren started to walk away and not listening to what the soldier was saying. "Well, have fun" she said over her shoulder.

Suddenly Katheren tripped .She knelt up and felt that her leg was caught on something. She what it was and laughed out loud..

It was a plasma gun caught under a root and leaning out to the air.

She stood up and grabbed the plasma gun.

" Sergeant! are you all right?" said the soldier .

" Huh?" She said.

" Are you all right?"

"Yes. I am. "

" So are you going to give us a command ?"

"Yes, How many of these do you think are out on this field?"

" Dozens. One for every dead alien.Why?"

Katheren held the object by the two triggers and looked around the battlefield. She looked at the soldier.

" These are going to be our weapons for a while."

The soldier was confused. " These pieces of junk will be our new weapons ?"

"The medic just told me we have almost no ammo. Are you a good shot soldier ?"

"Fair"

"There's a post sticking up behind you - see it ? "

He turned and looked

"Can you hit it without turning around ?"

"No, of course not "

"She turned briefly then looked at the soldier. "See that big tree right behind me ?"

"Yes"

"Watch." Katheren then pointed the Plasma gun at the soldier. She pushed the flashing light and the gun sounded like it was charging up. Suddenly she pulled the two triggers . The soldier ducked, A giant glob the size of a whole fist shot out as fast as a bullet. It went straight up, then curved over her shoulder and hit the tree with full force leaving a giant whole which could hold three men inside.

The soldier was shocked. "You weren't even looking.

Katheren grinned. "Now that's what I call fun."

" I wi- I'll get the scavenge team assembled right away." The soldier ran off .

Katheren looked at the gun . It was small, thin as a spear and covered with veins, spikes, and a sort of warm skin. It was not metal and it was not plastic. This gun was made of a substance she had never seen before. It was grown, not made. It was alive.

" Haul them in!," said a voice in the distance.

Katheren turned around to her left. She saw two

trucks pulling the dead carcasses of the ground whales out of the holes. The cables were cut into the body which made it much harder to get the creature out of the ground. As the truck's wheels dug holes into the ground, the worm body stayed still. They soon gave up on their attempts to pull the creature, it was no use.

Katheren walked back to the medical tent, holding the plasma rifle in her hand. She saw the lights on with many injured men lying on the floor and beds. The medics were running from patient to patient giving them their medicine, antibiotics and new bandages.

Katheren looked at them , thinking about their injuries, their mission and their pain. The survivors of the squadron had been through a lot, they survived a starship, crashing down on them. Survived a sneak attack by Japanese forces and an Alien attack and they still fought like lions. They were tempered now, like fine steel in fire. They knew they could win and with these new inexhaustible plasma guns, and the resolve, they could turn this whole war around.

Katheren walked out . and sat on a stump outside all the tents, near a fire. She looked out to the stars, the moons and the other close planets that shone through the night. She began to think about tomorrow, she was not just going to lead her squad into battle, she was going to lead it into history.

Katheren lay back on the ground and closed her eyes. "What fun that will be" she whispered.

Chapter 16

The last battle in civilized space

Suddenly the message button was flashing. It was in old thought-thrower mode.

"Ah-Jord ?" came the amplified thought. "Are you here ? We've just jumped through."

Ah-Jord smiled, and opened a radio channel on his command chair; " Well Ah-Vink and Ah-nik. I see that you all want a little piece of the action as well ! No need to use that old thought rig. I can barely understand it anymore. Radio is fine. The heums are so confused now that even if they hear us, they won't do anything."

"Are there any humans left. We thought you'd have taken care of all that for us."

"Our fighters put down one of their ships yesterday, but that's all we've been doing. Drake's resistance troops are still causing trouble on the surface in their land-whales, but we haven't dared help them out. We're hiding behind the third moon. We've been madly trying to repair everything. We lost 30 decks in one section and my jump trick squashed 10 more decks all around, so we're pretty lumpy now. Jump over here and see for yourself as soon as you get stabilized."

There was a pause as they both went off-air during their jump, then they appeared, hanging in space beside Frotnerk.

"I have a present for you Ah-Jord" came the voice of Ah-Nik. A scene from space suddenly appeared on one of Frotnerk's monitors. "It's the way that trick looked to the rest of us."

It showed the 5 human ships lined up around that last planet. Suddenly, one by one, they disintegrated with no apparent cause. Thousands of human fighters were left buzzing around. They would eventually run out of fuel and float harmlessly in space or land and try to survive on the primitive planet. In any case they were effectively out of this war.

"What happened to you anyway. We looked all over around planet. We thought you'd been vaporized after that jump-inside-their-ship tactic."

"I programmed the last jump here to Sivil, thinking if I survived, I would be damaged and easy prey for the fighters. Sorry I didn't send out my plan, but I was worried about the humans overhearing the radio too. If one of those ships had moved, I'd be a molecule-thin coating all over that planet."

"What's the situation here, Ah-Jord ?"

"This is the heums last stand. All of their ships are here. We've pushed them back from all over the Galaxy. This is where their wormhole comes out, so if we can squash them here, we can seal it up and the war is over. Then we can go through and smoke their home worlds."

"How many human ships are there ?"

"Thousands."

"And we three are going to attack them all ? Ah-Jord, I know we're good - but there's good and there's suicidal. "

"Ah-Rolik's here. She has a few thousand ships hidden behind the sun. We're waiting on her command, then we'll become part of her attack. So get ready."

" We've already got our fighters out, so we're ready for the action right now." said Ah-nik.

"Roger that" said Ah-Vink

Ah-Jord looked over to one of the crewmen,

" Any signal ?" said Ah-Jord.

"Nothing Sir"

"Ah-Rolik will be dropping on them from the direction of the sun, so let's position ourselves to come at them from the other side. We can get their attention while Ah-Rolik gets here - then she can drop on them when they're not looking. After they turn to fight her, we can close the trap. Blast them from the back and keep any from trying to slip away."

"Sounds good to Skellio" came the voice of Ah-Nik.

"Shent is on-line with that" said Ah-Vink

"Ah-Rolik is on the move. 20 minutes to impact." said the comm officer

"Let's move" Ah-Jord turned to the broadcasting microphone; "Skellio and Shent, we are in play. My crew is ready, are your crews ready ?

" Ah-Jord - we were born ready !"

Ah-Jord smiled. He turned off the broadcaster and faced the view screen.

"Are we close enough ?"

"Affirmative sir, we are in fighting range !"

" Prepare for the assault "he shouted, The ship began to rumble, the plasma cannons started to fire everywhere. "Full impulse, we are going closer !" shouted Ah-Jord.

The crew began to scuffle around,

Ah-Jord looked at the screen. He saw the cold human ships made of metal and wires, all dead and unfeeling. They were big and small, all having different symbols on them. He blasted them all indiscriminately. A few blew up spectacularly. A few just went dead and began spinning slowly. Shent and Skellio were scoring similar hits. It was like target practice.

The humans did not seem to care that Ah-Jord's ships had come in. The humans were not shooting at them or commanding fighters to hit the ships.The human ships were shooting at something else.

" The Humans are attacking themselves, whyever would they want to do that ?" mumbled Ah-Jord.

"Nature of the beast, Sir" said a nearby crewman

Ah-Rolik's huge force fell on them like a pack of sharks fall on a school of minnows. Within minutes the entire human force was almost decimated.

Suddenly Ah-Jord fell to the floor, a giant rumble in the ship started to happen.

" Sir, a human ship has started to fire at us !"

" Keep returning fire at the ship !"

Ah-Jord quickly stood up and sat back on his seat and strapped in.

" Sir, we kakked it. We have minimal damage to the engines !"

Ah-Jord looked at the man," Are any more human ships coming to us ?"

" No sir, but they're starting to fight back. The others are in their own battles" said the man.

Another man came up to him, " Sir, Shent has been destroyed."

Ah-Jord looked at the man; "How many escape pods have been shot out. We'll pick them up ?"

" None sir, it was an intercourse with a human ship. The Heum rammed him. Ah-Vink had no control over the ship."

"Where is the Heum bastard"

"That's it on the far right."

"Bastard. I'll melt you down like slime." Ah-Jord was uncontrollable. His full berserker programming, which he had tried so hard to bring out, was now raging. "You bastard. You killed Ah-Vink. I'll vaporize you. I'll wipe my ass with you."

"Sir ?"

" Pull up along side that bastard. Then tell all of the standing troops to get ready for boarding offense !" shouted Ah-Jord.

"Now - in the middle of ..."

"Now !" roared Ah-Jord

The man nodded and went onto the radio. Ah-Jord went over to the engines monitor, he saw that the engines were at 83%. They were lasting .

" What about Skellio ?" asked Ah-Jord.

" They are in their own dilemma !"

" What dilemma?"

" They got caught in the cross fire between two Heums !"

The ship started to rumble. Ah-Jord looked at the view screen, He saw the other ship in between two human ships fighting,

" Are we close to the human ship that killed Ah-Vink ? Come on. Come on. Let's go. " shouted Ah-Jord.

" We have just locked on to them, the space bridge has been attached to the side of the human ship."

" Good, tell all personnel that we are ready to board"

The man nodded ,

" Is Skellio still afloat ?"

" Barely,"

Ah-Jord looked at the view screen

" Have the troops board the ship." said Ah-Jord.

" They have just connected the plank, the gravity is just about to become operational on the Space-bridge."

" Good, I want to kill our enemies in person. Tell them I'm joining them." said Ah-Jord. He walked to the door and left the room, not waiting for any remarks about his actions.

Ah-Jord walked to the blood lift. The doors opened up and, he walked in. The door closed and the elevator went down to the docking floor. The doors opened and he walked out to find a group of soldiers ready for his command.

One came up to him," Sir, I am Captain Ah-Goldis - one of the transfers from Skellio - we are about to board the enemy ship."

Ah-Jord looked at Ah-Goldis and gave no answer. He walked over to the weapons chest and took out a plasma rifle.

" Will we still have radio contact once we enter the Heum ship?" asked Ah-Jord.

Ah-Goldis said "Yes."

Ah-Jord walked over to the plank door, He looked back at the soldiers then he turned to the door. He put his hand on the handle and pulled it down. Slowly it opened as the door slid downwards into the floor.

Ah-Jord felt cold pressured air shoot into his face, as he looked down the long, glass-walled space bridge.

The soldiers walked onto the bridge behind him. Steam of pressure shot out of the ground in quick flashes, and the door closed behind them.

Ah-Jord walked down the bridge up to the point where the human ship was attached to it. The ending point was this shiny smooth surface, cold and not alive. Ah-Jord touched it. He quickly removed his hands from the human metal." This ship is not alive!, this ship is dead" said Ah-Jord."And all who sail in her."

Ah-Goldis ran up to the metal wall and touched it, then shook his head. "We can't stay here long. As soon as they find we're here, they'll move and break the bridge."

Ah-Jord ignored him and turned around to his troops." We are going to need the wedge birds for this type of skin. Anyone got some ?"

One soldier bent down and took out small bird-like things from his bag and handed three soldiers one each. They walked over to the ships surface and pushed the pointed ends into the surface. Acid flowed out and let the points sink right into the metal.

The living tools began to change shape as they watched. Wings unfolded and began to change into two long sheets of metal. They started to wedge into the crack where the beak was. The wings changed once more, and started to grow claws on the outside surfaces. Suddenly there was a tearing noise .The living tools changed into what was required and tore a giant hole in the side of the Human spaceship. Then the wedgebirds folded themselves up again. The soldiers walked over to the birds and took them off the wall and handed them back to the one who originally carried them.

Gas came out of the human ship. The bridge lost its gravity pressure. The opening of the human ship caused the gravity generators from both ships to cancel each other out. The soldiers and Ah-Jord began to lose their contact with the floor. They were floating around.

" All troops get ready ! We are moving into the ship !" shouted Ah-Goldis, anxious to get out of the bridge.

Ah-Jord held his Plasma gun tightly and floated over to the opening and looked around. He was first to float into the human ship. He saw nothing at first. It was a room with no one in it. The room was large and had strange bird like craft and short stubby craft. There were one hundred or so of them. The whole room was showing neon red all over .

" The coast is clear, everyone come in." whispered Ah-Jord.

The troops one by one moved in.

Ah-Goldis floated over to Ah-Jord." Should we call for back up?"

" How big is this ship?"

" Around one mile long, this ship is a strange one."

" Sure, order some back up and let them know we're inside and moving."

Ah-Goldis nodded and pulled his portable radio down from his helmet.

Ah-Jord floated over to what he thought was a door.Ah-Goldis sent two soldiers to aid him.

" Help me find a door handle on this thing."

Suddenly the door came open. Ah-Jord and the two soldiers quickly floated backwards.

Three humans floated in. They were shocked and pulled out their weapons to shoot at Ah-Jord and the others.But they were too slow. Ah-Jord leveled his Plasma gun and burned two down before they even got their guns clear.The other human pulled the trigger and hit Ah-Jord, nicking a bullet on the side of his hip, then ran for the door.

Ah-Goldis shouted. " Don't let him live !" and pulled out his plasma gun and shot the human that was heading for the door in the back of his head. He dropped and skidded along the floor in his own blood.

One of the humans Ah-Jord had shot struggled to orient himself in the null-gravity. He saw he was surrounded and put his hands up in the air.

The soldiers looked at each other.

" I think this one's a coward, I think he is surrendering to us." said Ah-Goldis.

One of the soldiers floated over to the surrendering human. He pointed the plasma gun at the human's chest .

" @#^^%\$### *?" asked the human.

Suddenly plasma hit the human and his head exploded, spraying nearby soldiers with guck.

" Sergeant Ah-Goldis , did you get through to Frotnerk. Is the back-up force coming ?" asked Ah-Jord, lowering his smoking gun. "Tell them we're killing every human bastard aboard. Including cowardly surrendering human bastards."

Soldiers cleaned the human's brains off their visors.

Ah-Goldis took out a small bottle of fluid. He floated over to Ah-Jord.

"Yes. They should be here soon. Slow down a minute. You might be infected. Humans have all sorts of diseases that we can catch. I need to treat your wound."

Ah-Jord looked at the fluid. " Is that the human virus antibody?" he asked.

" Yes. The antigravity should be able to make your

circulation slow down and give the drug a chance to catch any virus."

Ah-Goldis opened the bottle . The fluid began to float out of the bottle. Ah-Goldis took out a cloth, grabbed the fluid and placed it on the wound, where a thin stream of blood was also floating.

Suddenly the bridge doors opened up. The back up squad came into the human ship. They floated holding their plasma guns in front of them. Ah-Jord floated towards them ,holding his wound tightly."Can the back-up get their chest shields on, We are going into an attack phase and we are taking over the ship, and we will not leave one heum standing! Is that clear?"

The soldiers and Ah-Goldis became suspicious of what his orders were. They looked at each other for a moment.

" Is that clear !" he said once more.

"Yes sir !" said the leader of the soldiers.

Without warning the door opened again and the humans flooded the room, shooting off their guns.

" Shoot them till the last heum falls !" called Ah-Jord, putting his own order into practice and dropping three or four right away.

The soldiers began to shoot off their plasma guns

Ah-Jord floated forward. He picked up an abandoneded gun and started to shoot with that too.

Three humans flew to the wall as they were hit with the acid plasma. The remaining humans started to float forwards. The plasma was not stopping all of them. There were too many.

Ah-Goldis , quickly floated over to Ah-Jord dodging bullets and bodies.

" Ah-Jord, We need to call a retreat !"

Ah-Jord looked at Ah-Goldis." Rubbish. We call no retreat !"

Suddenly a soldier hit the wall right near Ah-Jord and bounced away, dead.

" The humans are killing us!" said Ah-Goldis, "There's too many to fight this way "

Ah-Jord reached for a plasma grenade connected to his chest shield. He held it and was programming it to detonate. "We'll fight the bastards this way then ! "

" Ah-Jord, shut that thing off!, Dammit there is no gravity on this ship ! We can't move out of the way. You are going to kill everyone in the room !" shouted Ah-Goldis.

Ah-Jord quickly grabbed his plasma gun and shot it a centimeter from Ah-Goldis' head. Ah-Goldis was so shocked he dropped his own gun. He quickly turned around and saw a dead human flying to the other side of the room. Ah-Jord had saved his life.

" If we are all going to die, they are going to die here avenging Ah-Vink !" shouted Ah-Jord, totally out of control now. Ah-Jord then threw the grenade to the wall and raised his gun, shooting more humans and going forward.

Ah-Goldis grabbed his gun and flew to the entrance to the plank bridge.

" Retreat!" he shouted.

The grenade gave off a high pitched sound.

Ah-Goldis was pushing soldiers out the door as the humans continued to advance and shoot.

Ah-Jord finally regained his senses and flew to the space bridge. He closed off the outside door on his way through. Human bullets made huge bongs in it.

" All personnel quickly go back to the ship !" shouted Ah-Jord.

Suddenly the inside end of the bridge connecting to the human ship closed up. Ah-Jord and the others fell to the floor . They had gravity again.

" Everyone run to the ship!"shouted Ah-Goldis. "That grenade . . . !"

The grenade exploded. Ah-Jord looked out the window of the space bridge. He saw the explosion start then end in a quarter of a second. The coldness of space had killed everything in that room and in most of the human ship. It was derelict now. Dead pieces of human flesh started to shoot out of the room.

Ah-Goldis grabbed Ah-Jord on the shoulder. " Come on!" he said.

Ah-Jord ran to the ships doors. They opened up and Ah-Jord walked through almost running into a man who had been waiting for him." Sir, we have been ordered by Admiral Ah-Rolik to report to headquarters on Sivel." He said. "We've retaken it. The human force is destroyed. The war is over. Ah-Nik and General Drake will meet you there."

Ah-Jord was silent.

Ah-Goldis walked up to Ah-Jord and the man and spoke; " Ah-Jord is no longer in charge ! I am now in command" Ah-Goldis said.

Ah-Jord looked at Ah-Goldis. " What ?"

" You saved my life back there, but you endangered everyone else's. You almost got us all killed back there with that grenade. I'm worried about you, Sir, and I think Ah-Vinks death has made you temporarily unstable. I want to relieve you of command until we reach Sivel."

Ah-Jord was silent. and held his hands up. " You're absolutely right Ah-Goldis. I am out of control. Lock me up !"

Ah-Goldis turned around." Take him away to the holding cell ." he said

Two soldiers came up to Ah-Jord and grabbed him by his shoulders." This way sir." said one of the soldiers.

Ah-Jord let the soldiers drag him to his cell. The doors opened up as the soldiers took Ah-Jord out of the room. Ah-Jord was becoming confused. He thought his programming was coming undone or perhaps the stress of losing Ah-Vink was breaking through his internal barriers. He did things without the thought of the outcome. He wanted to do violence far beyond what was called for. He wanted revenge and it was personal now.

As Ah-Jord walked with the soldiers, he saw people all over, covered in bandages, cuts and blood-soaked cloths, but still holding their guns proudly to their side, ready at a moment's notice to shoot down the soldiers and free their beloved Ah-Jord.

"Stand down." he told them continuously as he

walked. "It's all right".

The soldiers stopped walking ." Sir this is your holding cell."

The wall in front of Ah-Jord opened up. He gave no answer to the soldiers but just walked into the cell. The door closed.

Ah-Jord sat down on the stool, looking at the blank room, colored in grey with dim lights everywhere. Ah-Jord stood up and went to the bed. He lay down on it and looked up to the ceiling, listening to the faint sounds of shipboard life. Ah-Jord then closed his eyes.

The sound of crewmen running around right outside his doors, preparing to put the ship into orbit around Sivil stopped Ah-Jord from falling asleep. He should have been giving those commands. He should have been in mental contact with the great ship. He should have been . . . no, he realized. He should have been exactly where he was.

Ah-Jord turned around and faced the wall. He closed his eyes and ignored all of the distractions around him. And, for the first time in years, slept without worry.

Chapter 17

The death of Sergeant Ah-Nik

In the Dark control room, all warning systems are in red alert. The Skellio fights dearly for her life. Battered and bruised from the final conflict, the ship is holed, tattered and almost uncontrollable.

Ah-Nik is trying to get her into a stable orbit around Sivil so they can be rescued. But the floor is rumbling.

Plasma shots are heard every now and then, as left-behind human fighters attack madly before running out of fuel. Skellio's gunners fight back, but every blow from these nowhere-to-go fighters, adds to the suffering of the ship. It's brain is barely alive and it's decks are grim places. Some decks are filled with wounded and depressed evacuees, and the survivors of a hundred blasted worlds. Some decks are even worse. They are filled with the coldness of space and dead frozen bodies.

The Control room itself was covered in damaged monitors, sparks and smashed control systems.

" Sergeant , we have lost the radar system!" said a crew man.

" How long till this ship loses it's blood supply ?" asked Ah-Nik, sitting in his command chair. "I can barely feel a pulse."

" Sir, the forty eighth engine just shut down. We have roughly about two hours before the ship dies."

Ah-nik quickly stood up from his seat." I think that it is time for us to evacuate this ship. In two hours we'll never get her across the system and into orbit around Sivil. If the ship dies on us, all systems will shut down. We'll stand a better chance in lifeboats. Send a message that all personnel must report to the cargo bays immediately !"

The crew members were sad at the loss of the only home they'd known for nearly 5 years.

" NOW!" yelled Ah-nik.

The crew members scattered and started to talk into the radios.

" Has the message been sent?" asked Ah-nik.

" Sir, they have already evacuated to the cargo bays."

" How many fighter are left there ?"

" There around four hundred, Sir."

" Four hundred only? What happened to the other hundred?"

" Some were lost when parts of the ship blew open. And some of the passengers took off in others."

"Bastards." Ah-nik walked to the door. " Well quick!, come on !"

The crew members quickly ran to the door. Ah-nik followed them out and went to the blood vessel lifts. He quickly held the door open as the crew ran in.

" Sir, are we going to fight the humans, or are we going to run away?"

Ah-nik quickly jumped into the blood vessel with the crewmembers.

" There are no humans left. All of their big ships have been destroyed !" Said Ah-nik. "So we're going to run away to Sivil. We'll get picked up there."

The blood vessel door closed . "Deck 38" said Ah-nik.

They all began to move inside the vein. Suddenly the floor began to shake and they moved slower and slower..

" What was that?" said Ah-nik.

" The top deck must of been hit . The ship is dying."

They came to a stop. The walls of the vein opened up. Ah-nik stepped off. The deck was filled with people . All of the smaller transports and P.W. ships were being filled to full capacity.

The crew walked up to Ah-nik. "No room for us. What now ?"

" We should be getting to the Shecklak fighters" said Ah-nik. Suddenly the ground was shaking once more. The lights were flickering on and off. All of the passengers were panicking.

"All trained personnel to the Shecklak fighters ! All civilians or non-trained personnel to the P.W. Ships - now !" shouted Ah-Nik. He then ran to the Shecklaks.

The others had already gotten into their vehicles. Ah-nik climbed up the side of the fighter. He reached the cock pit and opened the shaft then jumped into the seat and closed the shaft. " How do I get this thing working ?" said Ah-nik to the brain in the fighter. He strapped on his seat belt and grabbed onto the joy stick.

"Push button" came a thought in his head.

He noticed a green flashing light on the side of the joy stick. He pushed it. Suddenly the computers came on. The engines started to growl. " Computer Co-pilot on !"said the computer, out loud. Ah-nik turned and saw a giant living/mechanical object on the copilot seat right behind him.

"Hello Co-pilot" he said. Then he turned on the radio transmitter. " Are we ready for evacuation?" said Ah-nik.

A voice on the radio responded. " In 5 seconds the cargo doors are going to open. 5,4,3,2,1. The doors have begun to open."

The doors slowly opened.

The fighters engines started up the quick path to getting on-line. Ah-nik started to move his fighter forwards into the door. He misjudged the force of the pressure-wind and his fighter was sucked out before he could get the engines totally online.

He tumbled out into space with no control and punched the "Emergency Power" button until the engines came up to full power. He was surprised the engines weren't damaged by being forced on-line, but they seemed OK although he was now upside down relative to the rest of the Shecklaks.

He looked out the glass shaft. He saw the thousands of P.W. ships to his left. From his unique upside down position, he saw a fleet of human fighters streaking towards the defenseless P.W.'s.

On his right were the four hundred Shecklak fighters he was in charge of.

"Human fighters below All P.W.'s to Sivil orbit. Shecklaks 90 degrees. Straight down. Attack !"

The P.W. Ships began to pull back from the battleground and head away toward the planet.

He flashed across 100,000 miles of space to draw close to Frotnerk, and his three Shecklak wingmen followed him. Ah-nik turned the transmitter into starship mode. "Frotnerk, This is Shecklak #1, Gut leader. Skellio is abandoned. Please pick up my PW's between here and Sivil orbit. we'll see you on Sivel Ah-Jord !"

" We'll be there , don't worry about us!" responded Frotnerk. "Is that you, Ah-Nik ? This is Ah Goldis. We can pick you up now "

Suddenly he felt a vibration. His screen showed the distress beacon of a PW. "No time Frotnerk. They're picking off my PW's. Save them first. I'll go and keep the vultures off."

Ah-nik turned the fighter around. He saw the debris of a Shecklak fighter - one of his wingmen. Ah-nik quickly changed the transmission into fighter contact."Gut leader this is Gut 1 ! We lost a unit ! Are the human birds in stealth ?" Ah-nik looked to the left. A Shecklak flew closer to him. "Where are they ?"

" Sir, some of the heums are dogfighting the main Shecklak force. Some are after the PW's and some of the humans are still attacking the Skellio. There were a couple here but we got them after they blew up Gut 3."

Suddenly a giant flare, like a tidal wave, came flying towards the fighters.

" That's the end of Skellio. Gut 2 ! Pull up!" shouted Ah-nik.

The fighter didn't pull up in time. The flare pushed broken pieces of Skellio before it, like a cosmic cannon blast of grapeshot, the full force of which hit the fighter on the tail bone.

" Gut leader, this is Gut 2 ! My plasma guns have sprung a leak ! The right side is losing gas. The left side is bleeding and the hover engines are off line. I can't hear the brain at all !"

" Don't worry just hang in there ! Get into your pod. I am coming back up to get you. I've got room. Where is Gut 4 ?"

"Lost in the flare. I saw him disintegrate."

Suddenly fourteen human fighters came speeding towards Ah-nik.

" Oh God! Where did they come from ?" Said Ah-nik. He quickly pulled the trigger for the plasma cannons. Three of the human fighters exploded, the rest split up around him and zipped off into space.

Ah-nik quickly turned on the long range transmitter. " Calling all Guts!, In need of assistance immediately!" said Ah-nik.

" No Shecklaks can be recalled ! The P.W.'s are being attacked!"

"DAMN !" said Ah-nik.

Suddenly the damaged Shecklak fighter came to the front of Ah-nik's fighter. "Sir, part of the computer is dead and so is my co-pilot ! I can't pod out." said the radio.

" Don't worry kid, just stay in front of me and we will get to Sivel safely."

"My computer has the damage control pilot working, but navigation is off. Which direction is Sivel ?"

" It's about two hours straight ahead. Just add your brainpower to the Shecklak. Keep it alive and let the computer do all the work ! We are going to have some company - you keep thinking of Sivil. I'll take care of them." Ah-nik responded.

Suddenly another flare-wave shot towards Ah-nik. He turned to the side to protect the damaged Shecklak and, from this new viewpoint saw a human fighter painted black riding the crest of the flarewave.

Ah-nik pulled up." Get off my tail dammit !" he yelled. Suddenly the human fighter took off after the damaged Shecklak. Ah-nik quickly turned the boosters to maximum, aiming a charge bomb at the fighter.

Ah-nik pushed the drop button. The charge bomb hit the fighter directly at the cockpit and blew the fighter into gravel.

Ah-nik pulled to the left side of the damaged fighter as it chugged towards Sivil. "Gut 2. Has anything healed on your ship?" asked Ah-nik .

" Sir, the charge bombs are completely condensed with plasma matter, the computers are roughly working, the bleeding on it's sides has restarted. I still can't make the boost to high speed. The whole disc frame on the top has become swollen, the engine doesn't work very well, but I cannot turn off the damage pilot. So it'll be this speed all the way."

" Just hang in there, we are almost at the gravity well of Sivel."Ah-nik lay back on his chair. He began to sway the fighter from side to side behind the damaged fighter, so he could see any problems coming up in front of them, yet still protect the rear.

Suddenly he saw a giant dark object slowly move between the planet and themselves. As they got closer, he saw the object take form. It was too small to be a starship but too large to be a fighter. It was all covered with strange silver cannons and guns .

" Gut 2, we are going to have to skin the human ship. On the count of three , I'll hit the boosters and shoot anything in our path with everything I've got," Said Ah-nik. "I'll distract him off to the side and you squeak through. 1...2...3..." Ah-nik sat in the damaged fighter punching in his boosters then hit the booster buttons. He leapt ahead of the damaged Shecklak and confronted the the human super-fighter with everything in his arsenal. Plasma flowed. Bombs flew.

The human craft started to shoot back. All the

giant cannons started to fire at him from every angle on the ship. They ignored the damaged Shecklak. The trick was working.

Ah-nik set his charge missiles on the panel in front of him. He looked at the radar and spotted two human fighters coming fast up to him before he could shoot.

"Gut 2, watch it. I count two, no three human fighters coming behind us." Ah-nik got no answer. Gut 2 was deep in mental communication with his craft and had no concentration to spare.

Ah-nik flipped and went faster in the other direction, desperate to head off the human fighters. He shot plasma and hit two, but then lost sight of the third. Suddenly it was behind him and shooting. Steam shot out of the back of the seat as the bullets hit the sides of his fighter.

Ah-nik started to sway from side to side, out of control. He pushed the button sending a heat-seeking charge missile . It shot out the bottom of the Shecklak, hitting the Human fighter at the left wing, causing it to spin out of control and crash into a cannon on the human Super-fighter and ignite a huge explosion.

Ah-nik flew through the explosion and saw nothing for a few seconds. Then he saw another of the long cannons coming fast towards him, He grabbed his joystick and tried to shoot it. Nothing came out of his guns. Ah-nik quickly pulled up but he left it too late. He felt the whack when he hit and bounced off and immediately noticed a change in his engines.

Ah-nik then flew back towards the damaged

Shecklak, still dodging cannon shot from the human superfighter.

He heard beepings and howls everywhere. His hover engines were destroyed beyond regeneration, the tail bone was broken off, the plasma cannons had melted together and the main engines had been smoked by the bullets hitting them. He was running on the sub engines only. The transmitter was in critical damage but it was still working. Ah-nik's only weapons that still worked were the mini-plasma-guns and three charge bombs that were ready to launch.

" Sir, you are damaged. You are shooting sparks from the sides !"said the kid in the damaged fighter.

" I am all right." said Ah-nik.

They were flying over the top of the human super-fighter. The human ships' top finally came to an end. They had made it past the ship, which continued under them and would probably take thousands of kilometers to turn, if it even made the attempt.

" Hey, we made it !" said the pilot of the damaged Shecklak.

"Yes, we are almost in orbit, just keep going and . . .-" Ah-nik's transmitter gave out. Steam came out of it. Suddenly the radar shut off, too. Ah-nik looked at all of the main controls; the navigation was dead, the radar, the radio and the temperature monitors had all failed and the main computer was about to go into cardiac arrest.

" Oh, Gods no!, don't die on me." Ah-nik shouted. Suddenly he was left with only the ammo monitor and the targeting system in a ship where all the automatic systems were dead.

Suddenly he heard gun fire. Ah-nik struggled and turned his fighter around manually. The human super-fighter had managed to turn and was bearing down on them.

" All right you human apes, you wanted to mess, you are now going to mess !"

Ah-nik turned on the boosters and started to race right towards the human craft. Neither would turn aside.

Shots from the human kept hitting Ah-Nik's Shecklak. But he had nothing to respond with, except pure heart and courage. Nothing worked, except the charge bombs.

The bottom hatches were fused together. If he launched the bombs he would just kill himself out here in the middle of space, then the human would go and pick off the damaged Shecklak and proceed on to all the helpless ships on the surface of Sivel.

Ah-nik closed his eyes and hit the boosters to travel even faster towards the human ship. Even if it wanted to, it couldn't turn aside now, but it didn't want to. The humans thought they could easily withstand the impact of a small Shecklak fighter.

Did they have a surprise coming.

As he closed onto the center of the human ship, Ah-nik hit the launch button and crashed into the last human ship of consequence around Sivil.

The explosion was seen over half the planet.

        *   *   *

The damaged fighter made it into orbit. He flew right down to the planet Sivel, thinking that Ah-nik was behind him. He landed in the desert base to a hero's welcome.

Out of the four hundred Shecklaks that had left Skellio, he saw that only one hundred had landed, and most of those were in bad condition.

There was no trace of Ah-nik's fighter.

Ah-nik had died a heroic death to save his young pilot and to save the survivors from all the ships that had been lost. The human super-fighter would have come right down to the planet and destroyed everything. There were no defenses left on the planet's surface. It could have been disastrous.

In the heat of battle Ah-Nik had used his fighter as a missile to stop an enemy battleship from entering the Sivellian territory and had given his one life to save thousands..

The crew of the Skellio mourned his death. When the crew was transferred into another starship, they asked for one request. They asked for all of the Shecklak leader fighters to have one of Ah-Nik's famous quotes engraved inside their cockpits.

" We fight the most dangerous disease in the known galaxy. We fight the Human race."

Chapter **18**

Home

The next day was rainy, dark and muddy. The camp site had been moved away from the crash site and was still on the move. The whole camp was packed away into thirty jeeps running on low cold fusion tanks. The medics drove the jeeps; the soldiers walked.

Katheren led her troops into the deepest part of the forest. It was a shorter way to the base and there was lots of camouflage compared to the bare terrain outside.

" Sergeant Katheren." said a voice.

Katheren stopped walking and turned around. "Yes Private ?"

" Mam, the jeeps have run out of cold fusion water. We could transfer the engine into fossil fuel but that won't last long."

" Private, tell the jeeps to stop and set up camp where they are. If we are going to get to the base undetected by all the Japs out here, we have to walk there.

Leave forty men here to set up camp and guard the supplies. We'll bring a big force out to round them up once we reach the allies in the base."

The private nodded and ran off with the message.

Katheren started to walk again. The mist of the rain in the forest was refreshing but it was very hard to see where she was going. Katheren lit a flare so her troops could follow and continued on the narrow path to the base. The other soldiers caught up with her.

Katheren suddenly heard a noise.

" Sergeant, we are-" said a corporal.

" Shh!" Katheren said. She grabbed her rifle. "Quickly, tell the others that there are soldiers watching us." Katheren whispered. The corporal kept quiet.

"Sergeant, the mist is getting worse! It is jamming our systems in our helmets. are you sure there are soldiers out there ?" the corporal whispered.

The mist started to die down. Suddenly a soldier all covered in weeds and leaves jumped up and began shooting.

The corporal fell over in shock.

Katheren shot off her rifle without seeming to aim. The weed-covered soldier stopped shooting. He dropped his gun and fell to the ground. Katheren quickly stood up and went to the soldier. He was dead.

"That answer your question Corporal ?

" Sorry sergeant, was it a Jap?, a Brit ? "

Katheren wiped off the weeds from the left shoulder of the corpse.

" It was a Martian."

" A Martian ? I thought that they were on our side?"

Katheren sighed." Well it doesn't matter now. We have to keep marching. Are we having fun yet ?" Katheren stood up and walked on as if nothing had happened any more important than killing an insect.

The day quickly turned into night. All of the raining had stopped and the creatures of the night became alive. Katheren was still marching and had not called for one break.

She turned on the night vision goggles in her helmet and stopped suddenly. The soldiers dropped to the ground instantly, respecting her instincts.

" I call a ten minute break !" Katheren shouted, "Since you're lying down already."

The soldiers started to grin and groan. They sat up on the cold mud and started to talk and share food.

Katheren paced ahead, not allowing herself a rest. Suddenly the leaves of plants began to wiggle. The trees began to shake very mildly. Katheren started to get worried. The rumblings began to get more violent. Katheren started to run back to the soldiers.

"Break's over everyone!" She shouted, " Ground whales !"

A giant snout stuck out of the ground. It stood one hundred feet erect from the ground. The soldiers quickly stood up and started to shoot at the creature. Katheren quickly turned around, pointing her rifle at the whale. She started to shoot it, then remembered her earlier trick. Katheren stopped walking and looked for something to hit to cause a spark.

Suddenly a large explosion was heard. The creature howled, then started to fall. Katheren started to run out of it's way.

The creature fell to the ground causing dust and dirt to rise like another explosion.

" Who thought to grenade the whale ?"shouted Katheren. "Good thinking."Katheren looked around.

" I did it. !" said a voice. "They burn if you can get them ignited."

Katheren looked forwards through the leaves. A man walked up to her through the underbrush. He was a tall man, he was dark skinned and was smoking a human cigar. He had no badges or symbols on him.

" Who are you?" asked Katheren.

Other soldiers started to walk out of the bushes and forest.

" I am a Squad Leader. David's my name. We are what's left of the Martian Marines, and you?"

"I am the last Sergeant of the Philadelphia Battalion. Katheren. Where is your Sergeant?" asked Katheren.

" Dead, with the rest of the Martian squads."

" How many of you are left?"

" 300 Martian troops, 100 American troops."

"One of your guys just tried to kill us back there - what's going on ? Was the base attacked?" asked Katheren.

" Yes, The Japs and the Brits took it over. General Nevel betrayed us. All my guys are a bit twitchy. Now the aliens have landed and slagged the base, so there's not much left. The last we heard, they had blasted everything we have out of the sky. The war is over - and we lost it."

Katheren looked at David. "Then there is no mission to complete. No friendly forces to join up with us. No glorious last battle to fight ? Will there be anymore troops that would be searching for us ?"

No, all the starships are gone. The friends are gone and the enemies are gone. The only mission left is to get home, and kill the General."David looked at her troops." How many people in your squad?"

" Around fifty that are soldiers and about the same number of medics. We left 40 more behind setting up a camp."

" Good, your squad will be quite helpful to us."

Katheren looked up to the sky and then at the moon.

" Katheren , are you going to join us , we need to know now. We can't wait."

Katheren gave no answer.

" We need your help."

Katheren walked over to David. " Our goal is to go home ?"

David sternly looked at her." Our goal is to reach home and stay out of the rest of the war."

Katheren smiled and reached her hand out to him. " OK, we'll join you, we have no choice. If we keep going to the base we would probably get killed by the alien troopers -and quite frankly, I've had enough of them. This is not fun anymore."

David reached his hand out and shook Katheren's

hand. He did not let go for a while and she did not pull away.

" Quick, we must get back to the camp."

" Which camp?" said Katheren.

"Your camp. We'll pick up your people and then move on to the British base. They have a cargo ship there. We'll take that home. Does that bother you ?"

" No, a cargo ship is just dandy."

David started to walk into the dark woods. His troops seemed to disappear with him. Katheren looked back to her squad. " Well you heard the man. Let's go home."

The troops stood up but no one walked.

" What is the problem?"

A soldier walked up to Katheren." Mam , permission to speak freely ?"

Katheren became concerned." You may."

" Mam, I don't trust them. If the British and the Japanese took over the base, why wasn't the whole Martian military killed or kept for later persecution ?"

Katheren looked the soldier. "The whole Martian military landed here six months ago. That would be seventeen million soldiers. That amount of soldiers on a single planet are hard to hunt down. It is impossible to eliminate that many Martians in six months. There's sure to be odd squads out in the bush or somewhere - and I trust him. Besides, we need all the help we can get now. Us against a whole alien army is suicide. And if we want to get home, we would stand a better chance with the Martians help. I say we go for it."

" I understand Mam. We'll follow you anywhere."

" Thanks. I appreciate that. Well, we are losing time. Lets move."

The soldiers started to walk into the dark woods. Katheren followed. Within an hour they caught up with the Martian squad. The Martians had stopped walking. Katheren's troops stopped too. Katheren walked up to David." What's the matter ?"

David looked further out into the plains. His night glasses were on at full power." Have you got your night goggles with you ?"asked David." Turn them on,"

Katheren pulled them down from her helmet. "What am I supposed to be looking at ?"

David gave no answer. The fire down in the hollow caught Katheren's eye. She focused further into the fire. " Oh no!" She said.

The flames were coming from the far distance and were hidden by nearby trees and bushes, but there was no mistaking it. What was burning were the supply trucks that she had left behind to set up camp. Around them were three tanks with the Union Jacks printed on their sides circling the burning trucks and gleefully picking off anyone who ran out of the inferno.

Katheren took off her night vision glasses. She faced him." Bastards. What will we do now ?"

" I don't know. It's too risky to try and go around them here and head for the base. And it's too late to try and save your people over there. Besides, if the British are this far out, they've probably split up and abandoned the base by now. Where the hell is the cargo ship ?"

"Wait a minute " she said, flipping her night vision goggles back down. "We had a hell of a time getting those trucks this far into the forest. They could never do it in tanks and be here so soon. They must have flown in. The ship must be right here somewhere. Can you see it ?"

David gave no answer to Katheren and walked towards his squad." All Martian squadrons and surviving American squadrons. We are going straight to plan B. The plan to take the base is now cancelled due to lack of interest. Get prepared for combat !"

His soldiers started taking off their back packs. They spit out their mouth guards and started snapping on their oxygen tanks.They slipped cyclone guns onto their hands and reloaded their rifles.

Katheren was quite puzzled and disturbed. "Plan B ?" she asked.

"Sorry. 'B' for 'Board'. You're right. The cargo ship is here. See it lying along the road you made bringing the trucks in. We'll bypass the tanks and troops and just leave them out there circling your little campsite. We'll head right for the cargo ship and fly off before they notice it's gone."

Katheren was speechless. Could it be so easy. She walked over to her squadron." Listen up guys, their plan is to get to the cargo ship and hijack it. Let's go for it."

The troops willingly followed her orders. They quickly unloaded their tools and started to get ready for their attack.

"Squadron one ready!" cried a voice .

"Squadron two ready!" cried another.

David, all covered in armor and weapons walked to Katheren." Is your squad ready?"

Katheren ignored his comment and snapped on her mouth guard. She turned to her squadron. David walked towards Katheren once more." I said - is your squadron ready ?" he said.

Katheren, tired of his actions, nodded. David walked to his two squadrons and switched on his night glasses. " Martian squadron one, head out first on death trail!"

" Yes sir!" shouted the soldiers. They saluted him and started to run off into the woods. David faced another group , much bigger and more agitated to attack than the other squadron." North California squadron, Head on the north way to the death trail !"

The soldiers quickly stood up and shouted: " Yes sir !" They started to run off at an angle , passing and shoving the other squad out of their way.

David walked over to Katheren's squad." Your squad will be with the Martian squad, it that clear?"

Katheren walked up to him. She gave a stern look at him as she began to talk."David, get one thing clear: we are not under your orders. If push comes to shove, I outrank you, Squad Leader. We'll go wide and come up behind the ship, in case they have any troops waiting there out of sight. You're welcome to bring your squad along."

David grinned. Katheren ignored him and faced her squad. "You heard me guys - MOVE OUT !" she shouted. The soldiers started to run into the woods, and Katheren ran last, seeing that David was going with her squad.

Katheren started to run faster to get to the head of her squadron. The soldiers, fully ready for battle, picked up their pace as they saw her in the lead. The lights of the cargo ship became visible through the forest.

Katheren suddenly stopped running and her squad came to a halt behind her. The other Martian squads had also stopped and were hiding behind trees and bushes.

"Damn" said Katheren dropping to one knee and flipping down her night goggles again. squad slowed down and came to a stop. David, panting franticly, walked up to the front. "What's up" he asked.

"Look. the whole British army is setting up a camp between us and the ship. We're screwed."

" Katheren, come over here, I need to tell you something."

Katheren turned around to David. She walked over to him.

" What ?" asked Katheren.

" Katheren, do you know how whales work ?"

Katheren was puzzled." What ?"

" The transport unit for the Aliens ?"

David grinned.

 "Yes - I know what they are but . . ."

David started to walk backwards." Everyone out of the way !" he shouted.

He silenced his gun then pointed it to the ground

and pulled the trigger over and over again, going through his whole clip. The thumping of the gun shots shook the ground for meters around.

The soldiers walked backwards.

David reloaded and did it again. And then a third time."Be very quiet and don't move. Otherwise it'll send out alien soldiers." he said.

Katheren felt the ground shaking heavily. Suddenly a snout of a ground whale shot out of the ground with thousands of tentacles pushing the creature out further. The huge head circled around, looking for any sound or movement.

David suddenly raised his hands and dropped them. Two soldiers knelt down and dropped dark shells into the barrel of a silent mortar. The shells whizzed over the British camp and landed near the cargo ship, shaking the ground over there.

The creature sunk into the ground and started to spit tons of dirt out of the hole, chasing the vibrations. It headed for the cargo ship. After a few minutes, the dirt stopped shooting out of the hole.

Katheren was stunned.

" The creatures work by sounds?" she asked.

" Shh !" said David.

Suddenly screams and gun shots filled the air in the distance.

"I think it found the ship" said David.

The gun firing had stopped. David walked to the hole." All troops, let's take the subway. We march in the hole !" he shouted.

The Martians quickly pulled on their night glasses and jumped into the hole one by one. Katheren looked at her squad. They were tired and anxious for some action." All troops go into attack formation, we join the Martians in the hole!" said Katheren.

The troops walked to the hole. Katheren went in first, thinking it would be a gradual slope. She suddenly fell thirty feet straight down.

" Ma'am, are you all right?" shouted a soldier from the surface.

There was no reply.

" Ma'am?" he repeated.

Katheren stood up.

The dirt was soft and slimy and smelled like fossil fuel. Katheren looked up. The hole was thirty feet above her. and the Martians had marched further into the tunnel.

" Watch for the first step. It is a thirty foot drop to the bottom !" shouted Katheren.

The troops dropped one by one into the hole and slid down the side, making a better entrance than their leader.

Katheren walked to her squad. " All personnel, This is the tunnel that leads us home. All we have to do is take that ship. I need to know that everyone has functional weapons and grenades. Check them now. You won't get another chance. The Martians have marched on, so we need to catch up with them or we will miss the ship. They won't wait and I won't blame them."

The troops connected their last clips and their

oxygen tanks to them. Katheren connected a cyclone gun
to her hand and kept her captured plasma gun in the
other." All right, lets move!" she said.

The soldiers stood up right and shouted "Yes Sir !"
The soldiers started to run and Katheren led them further into the tunnel. The end of the tunnel came closer
as the sounds of guns and screamings became louder.
Katheren lowered her guns as she came to the surface
and saw the burning bodies of aliens and dead men
scattered all over the ground. She ran up the steep ramp
all covered in blood and rotting gore and started to fire
off her gun. The ship loomed on top of her. She reached
the end of the tunnel and jumped out into the night.Dead
bodies were everywhere. The Martians were nowhere
to be seen. Her troops ran out of the tunnel behind her
and she motioned them to hit the dirt. Katheren quickly
ducked behind a lump of dirt herself. She looked around
carefully. Sparks and shrapnel were flying everywhere.

The British troops ran in from their camp and
started to shoot. She couldn't figure out where the cargo
ship was in the darkness.

Suddenly a hovering sound echoed in the air.
Katheren looked up. She saw that the cargo ship was
right above her and was lowering down with the cargo
doors open widely.

" Troops ! The Martians have the ship ! They
haven't abandoned us. Run for it. "

The cargo ship landed but still had the engines
on.David was at the cargo doors shooting off a machine
gun connected to the ship at the enemy.

" Katheren , get your men aboard, Now!" he shouted. The troops ran to the ship. Katheren jumped up and started to shoot at the enemy, giving them a covering fire as they ran. She then dropped her gun and ran to the cargo ship. Bullets pinged all around her on the metal walls of the ship. She grabbed the handle on the side of the doors and jumped in.

" Close the hatch!" she shouted,

David pushed the close button on the side of the ship. The doors quickly, with a hiss of air ." Door closed!" David said.

The ship began to take off.

Katheren ran to the seats. David walked to the seat next to Katheren and sat down, letting out a big breath. "We made it out alive - most of us !" said David. "Now what ?"

Katheren summed up what everyone was thinking in just one word:

"Home." she said.

Chapter 19

Kill them all

Through out the whole ship, silence was never alive. Noise and plans circled within Frotnerk as it came for a landing on the planet Sivel. All of the crew and soldiers on the ship were working and getting ready for the end of war and the beginning of other things.

" Commander Ah-Goldis. We have landed ." Ah-Goldis stepped off his seat and walked around the command room."Open the cargo doors and passenger doors. Let's get some fresh air and take a look at the area."

"Right sir" said the officer.

Ah-Goldis walked out of the room and onto the deck. It was filled with anxious people hoping to get off the ship, some for the first time in years.

The vessel's mechanical lift opened up and Ah-Goldis got in. It was already cramped inside and filled with people from other decks.

" Heading to boarding deck exo" said the computer.The lift went down.

"Boarding deck exo." said the computer as the lift

stopped and the doors opened up. Ah-Goldis walked out and into the cargo bay where all of the 100 foot doors had been opened up .

Ah-Goldis walked out to the desert landing area on the salvaged base where humans had been in control so recently. The air was hot and the sun was shining brightly. Ah-Goldis looked around and saw thousands of giant ships all landed with thousands of soldiers all unloading and socializing with the other soldiers. The tension of war was gone, like the electricity had been turned off.

" Ah-Goldis, are you enjoying the scenery?" said a familiar voice behind him.

Ah-Goldis turned around and saw Ah-Jord walk up to him." Ah-Jord, I am truly sorry about your demotion but you risked your crew's lives. I'll gladly give you back your command right now if you can assure me you've come back to your senses."

Ah-Jord smiled. " The war is over. I have come back to my senses. You don't need a madman in command any more. Mopping up in the human system is more to my taste. Leading a fighter squadron is where I belong.

Ah-Goldis smiled. "You may be right. There won't be many more places for warriors any more."

" So why have we all been called back?" asked Ah-Jord.

" We are going for the Death Act." said Ah-Goldis

Ah-Jord was stunned.

" That act has never been passed for over 4000 years ! Are they going to make Beasts ?"

" They're replicating them now. It's the human race! It's the only cure. We'll slag their planet and leave it lifeless, like their Mars. Then move a small colony to Venus. It's the last world they have left. It's their last chance to become civilized.

"So what do we want with Basts"

"They'll let them loose on Earth after it's been vaporized. The beasts will kill any survivors - anything that's alive, in fact. So within a few years, Earth will be lifeless."

"Serves them right, the bastards"

"Sergeant Ah-Goldis!" shouted a voice.

Ah-Goldis turned around. He saw a soldier panting and sweating ." We have just gotten news about sergeant Ah-nik!"

"Well pressure it out!" said Ah-Goldis.

" Sir. He's dead" The soldier said.

Ah-Jord walked towards the soldier. "How?" he said.

" He died protecting a pilot in the line of battle. He took down a super-fighter all by himself. Probably saved thousands down here too."

"Damn. I talked with him. I offered to take him aboard, but he wanted to save his people."

"We are honoring his death with an engravement in every squad leader fighter. Something he used to say all the time . . ."

"We fight the most dangerous disease in the galaxy - we fight the human race" said Ah-Jord and Ah-Goldis together, laughing.

Suddenly another soldier came up to Ah-Goldis and Ah-Jord."All sergeants must report to the war room."

Ah-Goldis tapped Ah-Jord on the shoulder."Hey, we have to go to the meeting." Ah-Jord sighed.

" This way" said the soldier.

Ah-Jord and Ah-Goldis followed the soldier into the entrance of the base. Inside the base was cold , dirty and every wall or room was filled with weapons and maps. The soldier stopped in the middle of a room.

" The war room is to your left." he said.

Ah-Goldis and Ah-Jord pushed the handle into the door. The door opened into a room all filled with Sergeants, Generals, and Military Ambassadors. It was a dark room with a few lights but many glowing maps and geographical pictures were printed to the walls all around. Ah-Jord and Ah-Goldis sat down in the nearest seats .

Suddenly the doors opened up and Admiral Ah-Rolik walked into the room. She was very stern looking and had many operations to herself since last they had seen her. Both of her eyes were now artificial, she had a huge scar near her left ear, she had gotten skinny and her left arm was covered in bandages and operation scars. But even these superficial things could not hide her inner beauty and authority. She commanded by force of will, not by appearance.

" All officials have been called for this meeting." she said." As you all know one of our finest - Ah-Nik of the Skellio - has died protecting us from a superfighter.

That was the last hit that the humans are going to get at us out here. They have been completely beaten back to their original system. A human cargo vessel just lifted off and went through the wormhole and that will be the last human travel through that thing. We've sealed it off to human traffic. Only we can go through now.

But the war is not over. In the last 5 years, the humans have destroyed tens of thousands of our worlds or at least scarred them permanently. They have killed your loved ones, relatives and friends, for no reason. And they have effectively destroyed civilization as we know it.

They are back in their stinking lair now, but that is not enough. It is too dangerous to leave them there at their present level of technology. Someone has to go in there and neutralize the threat. Someone has to take care of them once and for all. And that someone is us.

Congress Moon have decided on their fate. Some of you know it already, but for the others, here's the plan in brief:

We will go through the wormhole and mop up all of their remaining spacecraft and military forces. We'll scoop up a few million of the population on Earth and hold them for a while in stasis. We'll Edenize Venus, make it breathable for humans and give it a range of temperatures that humans can tolerate. We'll start a viable plant and animal ecology. We'll create another new, pristine planet for them. In a few years, we'll wake up the humans and release them into the wild in the hopes of getting them to evolve into civilized beings. Fat chance of that, in my opinion, it's been tried before, over and over again with these creatures, without any success. But Congress Moon is full of people who are full of hope."

"Full of something else if you ask me" came a voice.

Everyone laughed.

"In their favor, Congress Moon has passed the Death Act. All heums will be put to death except for the selected few million. So we'll go through the hole and crush their remaining military. Then we'll vaporize their homeworld. Then we will loose the Beasts on that burnt-out relic of a planet. Whatever human and animal life is left alive on Earth at that time, down to the microscopic level, will be hunted down and killed by the Death Act beasts -just as it was done 10,000 years ago on their original homeworld of Mars.

It is our job to enforce this new Death Act. It will not be an easy job. Humans, forced back into their own system, with nothing but burnt-out planets and polluted homelands, will fight like crazy. What have they got to lose - so the worst fighting may actually happen now, after the war is over.

Also, for those of you who don't know, the Death Act Beasts are awesome creatures. Living metal. Indestructible by any means known today. Programmed to kill anything that moves - including us, once they've been activated. Letting loose these Beasts on Earth will be a very dangerous undertaking indeed.

And lastly, there will be a force needed to remain and monitor the last colony of humans. Scientists will

want to study them and this force must keep them from
killing themselves and from developing technology too
soon. It is a thankless job - the only advantage of which
is that you will be given free long-life treatment and
stasis facilities - so you can wink in and out of sleep and
possibly live for thousands of years.

That's all I have to offer you. Battle, pain, fear and
distress. So if any of you have had enough . . . if you just
want to stop now and go home and try to rebuild civilization - I will understand. You are free to go. The fact
that you are here at all means you have already suffered
horrible hardships. There is no shame in leaving now. "

"What will you be doing mam ?"

"I'll be staying - and possibly staying on with the
monitor force. My home world was Komak. I have nothing to go back to."

There was silence at this. Komak, a beautiful world,
had been not only slagged, but actually blown apart by
the humans. It was now an asteroid belt.

"Leave now, if you're leaving" said Ah-Rolik.

No one moved.

The silence stretched out for nearly a minute.

The Admiral smiled."I appreciate your courage.
Now ,the plan for the Death Act to begin- it's seed is
here,"She pointed to a map of Earth."Earth is the planet
completely infested by them. 10,000 years ago we
Edenized this planet for them. Rather than cherish it,
you can see it is now a polluted, scarred wasteland. And
it is about to get even worse, poor planet.

While our battleships will search and destroy the

human forces, we will send 10,000 of the Shecklak fighters to take up different positions, all over this globe. In addition, we'll need 100 super-large cargo ships. This will be the tricky part - as by then, they will know you are there. But whatever cargo ships are positioned over large cities at night will simply enter the atmosphere, use the forbidden mind bombs and put out the entire city. Use the thought throwers to send out commands to the humans to come. Those with rudimentary mental capacities will do so. The others will not respond and they will simply stay there, in a mental fog, and die. In normal circumstances, they would die from starvation and neglect, since they're brain-burned and incapable of independent action anymore, but not this time. We have something else in store for those poor souls.

When the cargo ships have about a million people aboard, they will put their passengers in stasis and head for some safe harbor and wait for further instructions. While they're in stasis, we can likely repair most of the human minds that have been blasted by the mind bomb, so they'll be functional, but most of them will be brain burned permanently and will never remember much of their past lives, which, under the circumstances, will be a blessing.

Now this won't be as easy as it seems. Loading a million zombies will not happen quickly. So the cargo ships may be down for two or three days. Although the entire city will be out, nearby cities will not be and we can expect some attacks during this period. We'll need additional Shecklaks with each cargo ship for tactical support.

Once that has been accomplished, and the cargo ships have all lifted off, at my signal, and all at once, the pre-positioned Shecklaks will all deploy the 10 special vapor bombs connected to each fighter. Usually these bombs give a margin of life up to about 20 feet above ground. But not these babies. These will kill everything on the planet down to a depth of about 10 feet. That's the fate of all humans on Earth who are not picked up by the cargo ships. The winds will be catastrophic. The place will burn for weeks. Within a few decades, with no vegetation to renew it, the atmosphere will break down and start to leak away.

When the vapor bombs have exploded and it is deemed safe to do so, the Shecklaks will land and un-leash a Beast apiece. Then get out of there. Once acti-vated, the beast will shoot anything that moves, includ-ing you, so you may want to drop it from a couple of hundred feet and burn out of area. Don't worry about smashing the beast. Those things are living metal - and virtually indestructible.

By this time - two or three days later - any human forces in the system should be neutralized - and I stress this - there will be no surrender. No prisoners. No mercy. The Death Act is specific about that. We want no mili-tary messiahs stirring up trouble in the new colonies. All must die.

Meanwhile, 1000 cargo ships will be seeding mil-lions of tons of nanotech over Venus. These artificial bacteria and viruses will change the vegetation, the atmosphere and the temperature of the planet in very short order. Maybe 50 years and we will have a new paradise. We'll design an interlocking ecosystem of plants and animals and get that started. Once it is established and all breeds true, we will release the humans at selected spots all over the planet.

Then the monitoring phase begins.

As that process goes on, engineering forces will be working on getting a moon for Venus. We need one for a base for the monitoring force. We'll likely use the Earth moon - which was originally shunted from Mars, but that's not been decided yet.

And there you have it. The next 100 years. Clear about everything ?"

The officials all stood up. They saluted her and one said." Clear Admiral Mam !"

Ah-Rolik smiled." The next 100 years begins in one hour from now ! Be ready for the launch ! You will be given your specific assignments before you leave this room. Remember - head right for your position and concentrate on doing your mission. Don't try to join up on the other side of the wormhole. The humans will be waiting there for anyone who slows down. Burn right towards your assigned position. Good luck to all of you and - dismissed!"

Admiral Ah-Rolik walked out of the room. Aides began passing out pieces of paper to all the commanders.Ah-Goldis got his and stood up. He turned and offered his hand to Ah-Jord and helped him up.

" Frotnerk has drawn guard duty. We'll patrol this

side of the wormhole and make sure only authorized ships go in and out. A bit of relaxation for us. Are you sure you don't want your command back?"

"Nope, I'm going in - and staying for the monitor force. I was created for this stuff and I can't imagine doing anything else."

"Well I guess that this will be the last time I ever see you."

Ah-Jord stood up and said, "Who knows. Maybe you'll eventually come in to paradise - or I'll come out to civilization. "

Ah-Goldis was amused," Well, See you then"

They shook hands. Ah-Jord smiled and walked out the door. He walked down the hall to the fighter landing strip and approached one abandoned shecklak fighter colored grey and red. He touched the side of the fighter. It was cold and dusty, unflown for nearly 5 years while Ah-Jord commanded Frotnerk. It started to come alive under his touch.

" You know that fighter is yours ?" said a voice."Ah-Goldis had it off-loaded from Frotnerk."

Ah-Jord didn't turn around." Well Sergeant Ah-Vessk, how has the war been treating you ?"

Ah-Vessk walked up to him."It cured me of my peaceful tendencies. My betrayal has been forgiven but maybe not forgotten. I have been given my own squad to lead and I've led them through some hairy times. I hear you've had some big adventures too."

Ah-Jord turned around. "Too many, I'm afraid. I may never see you again, so I'd like to say this . . . "

Ah-Vessk prepared herself for a blast.

". . . I'm very glad to have you back on our side. I've always admired you, even though I didn't always agree with you. We launch in thirty minutes, Sergeant. Lead your squad."

Ah-Vessk saluted; "It looks like war has made a pacifist out of you. Your feelings are not so volatile anymore. Thank you for the compliment. I still feel I owe you one. Well then, Ah-Jord I guess that it was nice knowing you." Then she turned sharply and walked down the strip , looking for her fighter.

Suddenly the sirens went off.

The doors opened up, the ceiling rolled back and the walls sank into the ground. Suddenly, they were outside and, as far as the eye could see there were millions of Shecklak fighters, millions of mechanics adding last minute service touches and millions of pilots running to their fighters.

Ah-Jord quickly climbed up the ladder to his fighter. He opened the shaft and climbed into the cockpit. He saw the engravement. "We fight the most dangerous disease in the Galaxy, we battle the Human race..."

Ah-Jord smiled.

"Well Ah-Jord you are back with the lowlifes !" Ah-Jord was startled and turned around.

"Ah-Sarak. I thought you were still with Frotnerk"

" Doing guard duty. Get real. I decided that to be in action was more interesting that flying around the wormhole watching for trespassers."

"What happened to Ah-ztes ?" asked Ah-Jord.

" Hi and his brother weren't ready for peace, either. See the golden Shecklak over there " She pointed off behind him.

"The whole squad's here ?"

"Yep - and we've all voted - we want you in command."

"Didn't you hear about me going nuts when we boarded the human ship. I'm not fit for command."

"Maybe not fit to command sucky walking troops. But Shecklaks ? Hell, crazy is a testimonial."

"You all knew this and voted anyways"

"Yes." said Ah-Sarak. "We were going to spring you on Frotnerk and take over the bloody ship, we were so pissed."

" Well close the hatch. Enough of this idle chit-chat. Let's go and vaporize the heums!"

Ah-Sarak grinned." Yes sir !" she said. She reached for the handle of the hatch and slammed it closed.

"Are we all functional for take off?" said Ah-Jord

" All systems functional."

Ah-Jord grinned. He put his hands on the Joystick and turned on the engines. The count down had started.

" 5, 4, 3,2,1, Lift !" said the computer. All of the fighters took off to the sky at once, like a swarm of killer bees.

Ah-Jord took off with full speed towards space and the wormhole. He looked behind him, seeing millions of fighters and thousands of Starships shooting out into space. It was the grandest thing he had ever seen.

" Ah-Jord , ten seconds till we are out of the atmosphere !"

The color of the sky slowly disappeared Ah-Jord looked around. It was all black now. The Shecklak started to slow as the air ran out and combustion became impossible.

" Ah-Sarak , shut down all engines and put the propellant engines to work now !" said Ah-Jord.

She switched to the solar-powered engines and the Shecklak picked up speed as the engines created gas and blew it out the back.

Ah-Jord felt a rumbling under him. Ah-Jord looked at the radar. A starship was right under them and going full speed.

" Ah-Jord pull up !"

Ah-Jord grabbed the joystick and pulled it towards himself. The fighter went up out of the way. Ah-Jord looked through the canopy. He saw thousands of fighters around him.

"Just a minute ago I was thinking what a grand sight this was - now I see if for what it really is - the biggest traffic jam in the universe."

"Keep that road rage under control, commander. Save it for the heum."

He laughed and increased speed.

" Ah-Jord we have an incoming message!"

Ah-Jord looked back at Ah-Sarak." Well put it on" he said.

Ah-Sarak pushed the flashing button on her left side of the control panel.

"Ah-Jord. This is your former gunner."

"Ah-ztes. You young pup. What are you now - 16 years old or what."

"I'm an old guy, that's for sure." The golden Shecklak pulled up alongside. "What assignment did you pull ?"

"I'm creating a path for the rest, then covering the vapor bomb guys and the cargo ships on earth. I imagine we'll have to blast our way through whatever human forces are waiting on the other side of the wormhole, then we'll zip around and neutralize any other resistance on the way to Earth."said Ah-Jord; "How about you"

"Our assignment sheet had just one word: 'hunt'. And we like to hunt alone, so we'll peel off from the group once we're through the wormhole."

"Good hunting then, young friend."

"You too"

The Golden Shecklak flipped over and got back into position behind Ah-Jord.

"More messages" said Ah-Sarak."You're so popular"

"We've just had word from probes that the humans ar waiting for us in force. Squadrons of Sergeants Ah-Vessk and Ah-Jord go through first and clear us a path. You have about 10 minutes. Then the starships and cargo ships come through. Good luck and we'll see. . ."

The radio quit working and began to squeal when they entered the wormhole . Ah-Jord turned off the radio. It was suddenly silent. He turned to the monitors on his left side and frowned." Ah-Sarak, I can't read the weapons count. How many vapor bombs do we have to launch ?"

Ah-Sarak turned to the weapons count at her side. "Sorry, I dumped them all into my gunners brain. But I'll tell you - we have enough vape- bombs for anything."

Ah-Jord sighed." Ah-Sarak put on your extra belt. we are going to hit the boosters. Here's my thought - we'll go through first, but just before we break out, we'll launch a spread of vapor bombs - sort of a calling card."

Ah-Sarak quickly clipped on the extra belts and held onto the handles at her sides." I'm locked down- hit the booster button !"

Ah-Jord reached for his pocket and took out a pill. He swallowed it , suddenly his eyes became dark. He then reached for the booster button and pushed it. Suddenly the gravity in the fighter began to act on them as the ship started to move even faster.

Ah-Jord saw mist all around him. Suddenly the fighter began to turn red .

" Ah-Jord we should reach the other end in a couple of seconds !" shouted Ah-Sarak.

Ah-Jord became nervous, The fighter began to shake all over. The outside area of the Fighter became engulfed in flames. Ah-Jord kept flying face down. The mist began to disappear. Ah-Jord finally saw the darkness at the end of this tunnel of fire.

" Ah-Sarak!, drop the vapor bombs when I give the command!"

It was getting hotter and hotter inside the Shecklak

" Ah-Jord , Do I deploy now?" shouted Ah-Sarak.

" Not yet!" Ah-Jord said.

The dark hole that was outer space was approaching quickly.

" Now?" shouted Ah-Sarak.

" No !" shouted Ah-Jord.

" Ah-Jord, I can see human battleships outside. The human's targeting systems are locking on us !"

" Ah-Sarak drop the bombs now !"

Ah-Sarak was startled and quickly reached for the launch button." The bombs are away !" shouted Ah-Sarak.

The bombs zipped ahead of them and went out into the dark. Suddenly there was a series of huge flare-waves and the Shecklak whizzed out of the wormhole and into the turbulence of exploding battleships and vaporized bodies.

Ah-Jord pulled up and looked back. Millions of Shecklaks were coming out of the wormhole and attacking the stunned humans. Hundreds of thousands of human fighters buzzed around, trying to pick off the invaders. Many of the big human battleships were moving slowly away, shocked by the sheer number of Shecklaks and the power they packed.

"Wow - look at those fat old battlewagons waddle. They're out of it already after only a couple of minutes - what time is it anyway ?

Ah-Jord grinned as he hit the boosters and sent the Shecklak back towards the battle." It's Heum Hunting time !"

*   *   *

Ah-ztes and Ah-Nawo came through the worm-hole into a firestorm of explosions and flare-waves.

"There's some good hunting" said Ah-Nawo, pointing at a huge battleship which was trying to slip away from the battle"

"Let's go and pay our respects."

They shot away from the wormhole and went after the lumbering human ship. The starship could easily outrun them once it got up to speed, but moving that much mass quickly was impossible. They caught the ship easily and saucily circled it at close range.

"The Victoria. Where have I heard that name before "

"Wasn't it something to do with Sivil ?"

"Probably one of their fights with themselves - say, can you feel that"

"What ?"

"This commander has an ego so big, you can read his thoughts. Like he's got a personal thought-thrower in his brain - unusual in a heum ?"

"What - For them to have thoughts - oh yeah. I see what you mean. It's like a radio broadcast - but in human tongue ?"

"Didn't I hear you could translate that stuff ?"

"Not me - the Recorder can ?"

"You're in touch with the Recorder. What, are you a diplomat or something, little brother ?"

"Before he left for Congress Moon that last day, dad gave me pills to put me in contact with the Recorder. I was supposed to record the Peace celebration. "

"An you're still in contact ?"

"I used to be - I haven't even tried to talk to the Recorder since long before we got together again - let me see " Recorder ?," he thought.

"I am here, Ah-ztes. I will always be here until the day you die. We are spiritual twins, joined at the heart."

"Can you speak to Ah-Nawo as you do to me ?"

"No. He must take the pills. They cause molecular changes that allow you to communicate with me. But you can still share these thoughts with Ah-Nawo. Just establish a thought link with him and he will hear me when you do"

"It's done"

"Wow - is that you Ah-ztes. I can feel the Recorder." Ah-Nawo thought.

"We are all in mesh."

Ha ! Listen to the translation of that human commanders thoughts. He's so crazy, it's like he's telling us his every move in advance. Listen. He's going to talk to us and try to distract us - then zap us"

"At least he doesn't lie to himself - look, they're calling us"

"OK you bug-faced bastards, let's talk . . . just a minute" came the human voice from the radio, automatically translated

"Move up !" yelled Ah-ztes, hearing the human thinking "Shoot - Now !"

The golden Shecklak jumped up 50 feet. A shot sliced the air where they'd been.

"Not even close, human. You're so stupid,we can predict your every move."

Inside the human ship, Nevel was going, if possible, even crazier. He watched the golden alien fighter on his monitor and spoke to his gunners. "They jumped 50 feet straight up. Shoot once where they are and put another shot 50 feet above on my mark - MARK !"

The golden fighter jumped 50 feet down.

"Where they are - 50 feet up and 50 feet down. Mark !"

The fighter jumped 50 feet to the side.

Nevel began shouting. "Bastards ! Bug-Eyed Bastards - they must have a microphone in here. I'll type the commands " He ran to a keyboard and typed furiously, unwilling to let the auto-trackers take over. He wanted this kill himself, not realizing that it was his strong thoughts that allowed to alien craft to evade every attempt.

"Ha ! dance your way out of that, you bastards." The gunners obeyed the typed instructions. The golden fighter jumped out of the way.

"I've heard of you" the General screamed, opening up communications with them again. "Golden fighter, black attitude. Cheeky bastards. You're the Nothing to Lose brothers. Or is it the Nothing-to-speak-of brothers, or the Nothing- but-loser Brothers. It doesn't matter. I'm General Nevel Thomas, bugs. You've messed with the best - now you'll die like the rest. Because the only good alien is a dead alien."

"I've heard that voice before" said Ah-ztes. "I"ve heard that phrase."he shook his head and looked at the monitor, wich showed a raving heum, dressed in bright yellow, ranting and gesturing. "I've seen that human before - Oh Gods. I know. That's the one who killed mom. I'm sure of it."

Nevel Thomas was still spouting nonsense over the radio and Ah-Nawo, reading his translated thoughts and anticipating his actions, was jumping the golden Shecklak out of the way of bullets, bombs and beams.

"It is also the one who killed your father on Congress Moon" came the voice of the Recorder in Ah-ztes' head. The thought passed immediately to Ah-Nawo, too.

The brothers became silent, each lost in thoughts of their loving parents, so senselessly slaughtered.

"I guess the fun's over." said Ah-ztes softly.

The golden Shecklak flipped over and zipped far ahead of the human ship.

"What have we got ?" asked Ah-Nawo

"Vapor bombs. Plasma."

"Definitely vapor - but we have to hit it just right. A miss out here in space won't do any good. There's no air to carry the explosion. We have to get it right inside the ship somehow.

The human ship was a tiny dot of light, approaching them and gathering speed. They could still hear and see Nevel on the radio, although his thoughts were out of range now.

"Had enough, eh, you bug-faced cowards. Stand

and fight you stinking alien bastards."

"How can we lob a bomb right inside. Ah-Jord did a jump right inside a bunch of alien ships ?"

"Yes but his ship was bigger than theirs, so he slit them like a tight skin. We're tiny. We'd just end up like a ball of tinfoil inside a fist. And it's moving."

"We could probably punch a vapor bomb through the skin, but it's a big ship - who knows if we would hit anything vital. And we only have 10 vapor bombs."

"There is a curious thing abut humans " said the Recorder. "In our past encounter I noticed an interesting thing and I've seen it in this outbreak too. Every kind of transport humans build has a face on it. And all are designed in such a way that if you shoot that machine between the eyes, it will die almost instantly."

Ah-ztes punched in a zoom view of the approaching human ship. Sure enough the front of the ship looked remarkably like a human face, with the eyes up on top, viewports for the control room, a nose where the communication equipment sat, pushed out in front, and a mouth with jagged teeth, where two lines of cannons protruded.

"Look at that" he said.

"One vapor bomb, right between the eyes. For mom and dad." said Ah-Nawo, punching in the co-ordinates and sending a strong thought-assist to the vapor bomb.

"For everyone's mom and dad" said Ah-ztes softly and sent the bomb on it's way.

Inside the human ship, Nevel Thomas, in his trademark bright yellow, was pacing the bridge like a madman. Grace had come up to watch the show and stood by the entrance door.

"Look Grace - see that little dot on the central mon - that's lunch."

She laughed and shook her head. They had been together since he betrayed his troops and joined up with her. From a distrusted guest to the ship's commander had become a very quick trip for the General and there were many bodies floating in space who had made that trip possible.

The General stomped to the viewports and spoke to Grace over his shoulder.

"Once we zap that little mosquito, we'll go off out to Saturn and hide around in the rings for a while - see what happens next."

"That'll be nice, Nevel"

"Incoming Sir"

"How many"

"Just one."

"The arrogant little bastard. Thinks he can get us with one shot. Use his own tactics on him. When it gets close, we'll just drift out of the way. Even if it blows up nearly, it won't hurt us."

"Aye, aye, Sir"

"Meanwhile, let's get a little closer and get a better shot at the bastard. Increase speed by half again"

"But Sir - that gives us less chance to avoid the missile"

"Don't argue with me you bastard. Just follow

orders."

"Aye aye Sir"

The human ship speeded up, anxious to meet its fate.

"Missile distance ? " Nevel bellowed.

"200 miles."

"Move left 50 miles."

"Missile changing course, Sir"

"Shoot it down"

"It evaded the shots, Sir"

"Move right"

It's changing course Sir. It's locked on to something. It can't be heat or light. I don't know what it is. "

"Turn sideways and blast it with a broadside."

"It keeps coming around the front - it's locked on the control room.

"Shoot it down" screamed Nevel - running through the control room and heading for the exit door.

"Impact in 5 seconds" said the crewman, watching Nevel try to run away.

Nevel was just trying to shove Grace out of the way when the missile struck. It smashed through, right between the viewports and exploded inside, vaporizing the crewmen and the controls.The ship went dead immediately, all systems including life support were instantly out of commission.

Nevel turned around and had a view of open space and hard vacuum.

For an instant.

*   *   *

" Ah-Sarak, Have you ever done the Burning Arrow maneuver?"

Ah-Sarak became giddy. "What's that, some weird sexual thing like that human wanted me to do back on Degos ?"

" No - it - well no more time to explain. I'll show you. Here it is !"

They were in Earth's atmosphere defending the huge cargo ship below, who was loading hundreds of thousands of human zombies from one of the largest cities. Human fighters from nearby bases were valiantly trying to fight the alien invasion off, but they were out-numbered and out-experienced. They were the few pilots in training or old wounded pilots left on earth. The best had gone through the wormhole. So they never had a chance, really - although they did provide some tense moments for some of the alien crews.

The two human fighters who had been chasing Ah-Jord, pulled up even closer, cutting the conversation short.

" Ah-Jord, they're gaining speed. They're in firing range !" shouted Ah-Sarak.

Ah-Jord quickly turned the Shecklak fighter around.

He now was facing the Human fighters head on."Ah-Sarak, hold on!"

The humans shot their missiles.

Ah-Jord pulled the trigger on his joystick. Giant

plasma globs suddenly shot out of the front of the fighter. Thought-assisted, the plasma hit the missiles and began burning brightly. Ah-Jord pulled up as the burning missiles went off, shooting flaming debris everywhere. Ah-Jord's Shecklak was on fire. The two human fighters were covered in flames and tumbled down toward the planet.

Ah-Jord hit the boosters .The fighter suddenly shot out to space once more. With no air to keep it going, the fire all over the fighter died. There were only burn marks and dents left as a souvenir of that last deadly battle.

Ah-Jord turned to the side until he was in orbit with the planet like a satellite. He shut off the boosters.

Ah-Jord looked to his right. He saw millions of small explosions and thousands of fighters entering the planet's atmosphere followed by even more explosions.

Ah-Jord saw Shecklak fighters returning to space one by one, as they outgunned their desperate human adversaries. They headed for space as soon as their fights were over, for fear of being caught below when the saturation vapor bombing started.

"Burning Arrow, eh ?"

"I just made that up. Could be Smoking Javelin"

"Flaming Insult ?"

"That's good. How about . . . "

Wait, Ah-Jord, we have an incoming message."

" Put it through."

" Ah-Jord it is a message from a human."

Suddenly the translator-voice came on. "To those

who fight me, are the ones who die."

"Do they really talk like that or is it just a funny translation " asked Ah-Sarak.

"Maybe they talk like that. It sounds so familiar. It sounds like . . "

"Like that guy we tortured on Degos ?"

"Yeah."

"What would he be doing back here - it's only the rejects that are left n the homeworld."

"Maybe on mental leave"

"Thought someone was reading his mind ?"

" Ah-Sarak, hold-on."

Suddenly a black Human fighter came soaring head first towards them. Ah-Jord suddenly hit the boosters. He grabbed the Joystick and squeezed it.He pushed all of the triggers for the cannons and guns. The Shecklak spun like a tossed coin, out of the way.

"Ah-Sarak, I want you to lock all the plasma bombs we have on the black fighter."

Suddenly the Black fighter's engines became bright. He was moving faster towards Ah-Jord, shooting his space adapted bullets at him.

Ah-Jord began to sweat.

" Ah-Jord I have a lock on him."

Suddenly a beeping noise echoed. Ah-Sarak became scared. She pushed it." Ah-Jord it is another message from the Heum." I will never die. Suffer like the sub-humans you are !"

Ah-Jord quickly pulled up. The black fighter flew right past him. Ah-Jord became angry. "Ah-Sarak has the planet been -"

Suddenly the Black fighter came out of nowhere and started to fire on Ah-Jord.

" Has the vapor bombing begun yet ?"

" Ah-Jord , -"

" HAS IT STARTED YET ?" Ah-Jord shouted.

" No!" replied Ah-Sarak.

Ah-Jord suddenly hit the boosters once more. He flew the fighter further into space with the black fighter shooting frantically at him.

" Ah-Sarak, The black fighter will try to hit the tail bone of the Shecklak. His best chance of that is from the front, so he will try to get in front of us. I'm going to turn around and head back into the atmosphere. We'll be facing the planet. If they start vapor bombing, we'll be blinded, so watch your eyes. when I say, hit the plasma bomb."

Ah-Sarak put her hand on the launch trigger.

Ah-Jord pulled to the side, flipped over and began flying back to the planet at full speed.

" Ah-Jord the fighter has disappeared."

Ah-Jord smiled. He flew closer to the atmosphere of the planet. "Ah-Sarak fire the bomb now!"

Ah-Sarak pushed the trigger.

Suddenly the Black fighter came charging at Ah-Jord from in front of him. The plasma bomb hit the Black fighter at the cock pit and exploded, knocking holes in the human fighter. The fighter was damaged and it's engines were off line. Suddenly the gravity of the atmosphere pulled the fighter into it like a piece of trash being sucked into a drain.

Ah-Jord pulled up and watched as the fighter flared then burst into flames as it fell faster and faster.

" Ah-Jord we finally killed him!"

Ah-Jord gave no emotions. "Didn't we say that once or twice before. Maybe he's right. He'll never die. He'll always be around to annoy us."

Ah-Sarak smiled and sat back in her seat. Ah-Jord looked at the engravement. He smiled and looked out the side. He saw thousands of fighters going extremely fast and shooting out to space.

Ah-Jord took a deep breath and then hit the boosters.

"We are going to beat this disease." said Ah-Sarak.

" Yes. We'll do it for Ah-nik and Ah-Vink and all the billions who lost their lives to it ! They are the only ones who will ever know the end of war. The rest of us are doomed to fight forever. So it'll be a great victory for the dead." said Ah-Jord. "But what will it do for those of us who are still alive ?"

Chapter 20

Ah-Rolik's final battle

The great starships were the last through the wormhole. Thousands of these city-sized ships suddenly appeared and headed into the human territory. The flagship of the Degosians , MOTHER, was the last of them. It was a two mile ship, a quarter mile thick and armed with millions of plasma cannons and three times the armor of a normal starship. It had been purpose-built for war and had never lost a battle.

" Admiral, we have reached the human territory. The cargo ships have lifted off with their zombie colonists. "

The Admiral walked around the room, looking out the windows and view screens.

" Have the Shecklaks gotten into position yet. The vaporization must be done all at once, all over the globe if the explosions are to build on one another."

"Not yet. There is still some resistance and the fighters are escorting the cargo ships to safety behind the moon."

"Otherwise, what's the status ?

"Most of the other starships are taking up positions around Venus, getting ready to start the Edenization. A couple of hundred are at the Earth Moon, computing how to move it to Venus. The first groups through have cleaned out most of the big opposition, and are off hunting now. We suspect a good number of earth ships are hiding, in the rings of Saturn or in the asteroid belt or other places. We'll flush them out eventually, or they'll just rot there, it doesn't much matter. It's all over except for the victory dance."

"No Earth ships here ? "Asked the Admiral.

" No," said a crew man.

Suddenly the lights went dim. " Admiral -human ship in the vicinity."

"So much for the theory that they were all gone. I guess this is the victory dance ?"

The crewman who had spoken earlier, looked guilty. "The humans have spotted us. Their targeting systems are locking on !" he said

Ah-Rolik became sharp and focused. She looked at the main screen. A giant human battle ship came closer to the screen. Then another appeared by its side.

"How did we miss two of these guys ? " Rolik asked. "Weapons - report" she ordered.

"Shields up."

"Plasma charged."

" Vapor bombs loaded."

"Jump Engines ready ?" she asked

"At speed" came the reply

"Jump engineer ?"

"Yes, Admiral"

"Human ship is turning" came a crewman's report

"Plot me a jump sideways 100 miles, so we end up facing the sun. "

"Plotted"

"Execute"

Mother disappeared and instantly reappeared 100 miles away, pointing at the sides of the two human ships.

"Hold the attack until . . ."

The human ships ignored the move. One human ship turned around and started to attack the other human ship.

Ah-Rolik was stunned. " Change of plans ! Start the attack now, while they're occupied !"

The crew started to run around the room; they were sending messages out to the other parts of the ship and to other weapons groups. Suddenly the starship began to move at maximum speed into the human battlefield. The Admiral picked the closest human ship and levelled her terrible fire at that one. Attacked on two sides, the human ship soon disintegrated into pieces too small to see on the monitor.

" Admiral, the other human ship is coming in our way."

Ah-Rolik quickly ran to her command seat." Give that human ship everything we've got !"

The crew ran to their battle stations and started to program the cannons.The starship all of a sudden moved closer to the human ship, firing off endless rounds.

The Human ship began to fire at Ah-Rolik's ship.

Rolik's plasma shots covered the human ship with holes all over the hull, Gas and small bursts of flames started to shoot out of the holes. Still the human ship fired back at Ah-Rolik's ship. Suddenly Ah-Rolik fell to the floor.

" Admiral, we have lost the shields and the first barrier of armor!" said a man.

Ah-Rolik stood up. " Shoot the Plasma Missiles at the damned humans!"She shouted.

Missiles whooshed out and, assisted by the thoughts of thousands, easily found and hit the human ship.

"Admiral, The human ship is breaking up !"

Ah-Rolik turned to the screen. The human ship still firing at them, was completely damaged. Without warning the doomed ship came apart, thousands of human bodies flew out and froze as soon as they touched space. The ship was destroyed.

" Hold your fire. What are we wasting our cannons on a dead ship for. That'll show the bastards that the humans are the sub -race of the Galaxy !"

The crew started to cheer . Ah-Rolik sat back down on her seat and let out a sigh of relief. She'd taken more damage than she had counted on from these rogue human ships. It was time to rest and repair.

"Get me Admiral Ki, I want to tell him that there are rogue human ships around"

An Admiral appeared on the screen "Everything

going to plan Rolik ?" he asked.

"No, we were just attacked by two human starships. I thought they were all cleaned out."

"These are rat-ships - cowardly survivors, trying to escape. They don't realize the wormhole is closed. Just let them go if you can. They'll go into the sun and, surprise surprise, they won't come out anywhere but hell. Or if they do, they'll just pop out the other side, melted, burning and feeling foolish."

"OK - but be careful Ah-Ki"

I'm always careful Rolik. See you on . . ." His image broke up. The probe's camera image on the monitor immediately pulled back for a long view to compensate for the sudden brightness.It now showed a starship exploding.

"Admiral - Ki is dead"announced a crewman. " The human ship that killed him is heading this way !"

" Where is it ?"

"It's lost in the flare of Admiral Ki's ship exploding."

" Lieutenant, how much armor skin is left on the third layer ?"

" Admiral, it is only 60% functional. Our sensors are down on the front, too. We're blind."

" Go to visual. Send out a probe and point it at us. Use that as eyes. Let's boost inwards. Maybe it's heading for the sun, not for us."

The huge engines began laboring. The giant ship began to move slowly. A probe rocket whooshed out and a picture appeared on one monitor of a huge human ship headed right for Mother.

"See it yet ? Where is it ?"

"Oh Gods. It's here." The human ship filled the monitors. "It's going to ram us. Hang on."

The crew was shocked. everyone froze except Ah-Rolik, who kept her head in any situation.

"Engines to full speed !" Suddenly she felt the ship go forwards a little faster.

The human ship was coming closer.

" Start firing the Plasma cannons!" Ah-Rolik shouted."Maybe we can break it up"

The cannons started on, but it was too late. The human ship was now only a 100 meters away.

" Roll up - try to hit on the side of the ship!" shouted Ah-Rolik.

Mother turned a bit just as the human ship crashed into her. Sparks and cables shot out everywhere, the lights changed to red. Mother's sharp side and thick armor cut through the human ship like a knife, splitting it open. Suddenly the human ship exploded. But the momentum kept the two ships on their course, one cutting the other from stem to stern.The cut now went along the entire side of the human ship. Pieces of the human ship along with thousands of frozen bodies shot into space.

Ah-Rolik fell to the floor once more, but did not hit it hard. Instead she bounced off and suddenly began to float .

" GRAVITY GENERATOR IS DAMAGED BE-YOND REPAIR !" screamed the computer.

" Lieutenant, Are we safe ?" shouted Ah-Rolik.

" Admiral, That has to be the last of them. We're safe now"

"Thank the Gods - that was a close one. Damage control ?" she shouted

Everyone in the control room began laughing and talking. Those who had not belted down were floating around the room.

"The jump engines were sheared right off. The gravity generator too. Everything on the outside hull is gone ?"

"Main engines, auxiliary engines ?

"All gone, Admiral, everything but the attitude jets. we're dead in the water, Mam. "

"That's all right. I'll call Moonbase and get some-one to come out and give us a tow. Meanwhile, have a little rest people. We're not going anywhere."

"Yes you are. You're going straight to hell you bug-eyed alien bastards" came a human voice from the communicator. Ah-Rolik looked at the screen. Suddenly a giant human ship came into range.

"Oh no."

" Admiral , the humans have ranged us. We can feel their targeting system locking on !"

" Admiral, the human ship is closing in on us!"

The crew , floating and scared waited for her orders.

" Kill it!"she shouted."We can't move, but by the Gods' I'll not sit here meekly and wait for incoming. "

"Only the plasma works - the vapor bomb tubes

were cut away during the collision. We can only drop them off behind us."

"Plasma the bastard then. Think dead humans "

The crew bounced back to battle stations and soon comforting plasma blasts were heard throughout the ship. Incoming bullets and cannon rounds shook Mother, but didn't hurt her badly.

Ah-Rolik saw the ship through the screen, It was partly damaged but three times the size of her ship. in both width and length.

The human ship kept up an almost constant fire.

" Shoot the plasma missiles at the front of the heumship !" Two thirty foot missiles shot out of the front of the alien ship.The missiles exploded at contact.Flames shot everywhere, Pieces of shrapnel rattled on Mother's skin.

The flames disappeared, snuffed out by the lack of air. The human ship was still there. There were dents and holes in her, but the ship was still intact.It kept kept firing. Mother quivered at every hit, but was still solid.

Ah-Rolik floated in the air. Sparks and pieces of hot metal were flying all around her, killing many crew members, but it didn't bother her. Ah-Rolik quickly called out ; "Secure for All Weapons Kill !"

As the crew grabbed onto anything solid, she quickly moved the blob of blood floating on top of the weapons control, then she pushed all the buttons.

Mother shuddered as every weapon remaining went off and hit the human ship. It disappeared in smoke and explosions, but when the smoke cleared, it was still there.

The Human ship closed in and fired off it's weapons in a similar all-at-once blast.

Mother, unable to move, shuddered and shook. This time she was badly hit.

Ah-Rolik responded with another All Weapons Kill and nearly blew the human ship in half. It responded with it's own broadside, and Mother started to break up.

Ah-Rolik looked around. Everyone in the control room was dead except for the lieutenant and one crewwoman. Smoke filled the cabin. She set off another All Weapons Kill onto the Human ship. Both ships hung in space, damaged badly , yet they continued to kill each other. One couldn't move. The other wouldn't.

Ah-Rolik, looked around, the smell of vomit and blood replaced the smell of fresh leather. She saw a flashing button on the message receiver. She floated over to it and pushed it.

" Admiral Ah-Rolik!, This is sergeant Ah-Jord. Are you in trouble ?".

"Where are you Ah-Jord ?"

"About two hours away, close to Earth."

"Anyone closer ?"

"No, we're all in position for the vapor bombs"

"Then we are in very serious trouble."

"I'll despatch starships. We can . . ."

"No. Relay my order. Go ahead with the Vapor bombs. Tell Ah-Goldis on Frotnerk , that I now put him in charge, Ki and I are both dead. His guard duty is over.

His mission now is to finish up the plan. "

"Admiral . . "Ah-Rolik turned off the message receiver and quickly floated over to the pilot system pads.

"We're not going to make it, Lieutenant."

"Admiral, you've led us all across the universe and we've followed you - and never regretted it. Now lead us straight into hell - let's kick some ass there too !"

"And Admiral - do it without weapons. That was our last shot. Everything else is stuck in the tubes."said the crew-woman, grinning.

"If we're out of bullets, we'll become the bullet." said Ah-Rolik. "I'm damned if I'm just going to sit here meekly and die"

"Tell us what to do"

"Roll the vapor bombs out the back and detonate them in descending 10, 9, 8 second intervals. The reaction should get us going and ram us right into those bastards. Then well set off whatever's in the chute. And be in hell shortly thereafter."

"We'll be right behind you, Admiral"

The first bomb detonated and the ship jumped and began to move. 10 seconds later, the second bomb went off. 9 seconds later, the third. The ship began to move faster and accelerated with each new blast.

Ah-Rolik floated over and fastened herself to the command chair. She looked out the fractured viewscreen.

" Beware the wrath of a patient woman !" she shouted .

The range closed. The human ship fired mightily

at Mother, but nothing could stop her now. She then crashed into the side of the human ship at hundreds of thousands of miles per hour.

Flames and pieces of metal shot into Ah-Rolik's grinning face. Flames and black space engulfed the entire command room. The ship turned into a two-mile-long butcher knife, cutting up the human flagship, Mayflower, into May petals.

Ah-Rolik's ship exploded and dissolved into millions of pieces of shrieking shrapnel before reaching the end of the human ship.

The human ship exploded within a fraction of a second later - two huge spurts of fire shooting out into the coldness of space.

Then disappearing.

Chapter 21

In Hell's domain: Earth

The vapor bombs went off on the precise schedule required for total vaporization.

The firestorm built, bomb upon bomb until it covered the entire globe, pole to pole and lasted for hours. It fed on itself and scorched the dirt and water down to ten feet deep, everywhere. Anything it touched, died.

The thousands of fighters who had dropped the bombs and the others who had been there to protect them, were suddenly lost in the mile-high flames. All headed immediately for space, sailing fearlessly through the sea of hot light particles.

" Ah-Sarak, we 've lost contact with the other ships!" shouted Ah-Jord.

Suddenly the fighter became extremely hot.

" Ah-Jord, everything went off line!"

Ah-Jord looked at the controls, they were all off.

" Ah-Sarak, don't worry "

Suddenly the flame-light disappeared as they broke out of the atmosphere and into space. The other ships suddenly reappeared too and they were all in perfect condition. The controls in Ah-Jords fighter came on.

"It must have caused some kind of electronic pulse - remember that vapor bomb Ah-Vessk tried to kill us with on Degos - the same thing happened."

"Yes. I should have remembered that. I hope nobody got caught going down when the controls went off."

"That would be a pity, now that the war is over. Although dying now might be a blessing in disguise. I wonder how we'll adapt to peace. I was just a kid when this started."

"Don't feel bad - I was in a test-tube."

" Ah-Jord we have a message coming from A-Drake." Ah-Sarak pushed the transmission button." Ah-Jord, I have to go out and relieve Ah-Goldis outside the wormhole. He can't come in until I'm out there, so I'd like you to supervise laying down the Beast Creatures. Remember what Ah-Rolik said - 'drop 'em well, then run like hell'. The Avenger squadron will plant the beast weapons. Your squad's job is to protect the Avenger squad. The other squads will be on the other side of the Earth doing the same thing."

Ah-Jord turned off the radio.

" Avenger squad? Who are they?" asked Ah-Jord.

" Ah-Vessk's squadron. Ah-Jord, we are down to three vapor bombs and the mini plasma guns have burned out."

Ah-Jord looked at Ah-Sarak," That makes the war more exciting !" he said,

Ah-Jord looked down at the planet Earth. Burning. It was all so sad. And so unnecessary. He let out a sigh, thinking this would be the beginning of his comfortable life. No more combat except in memories and finally, he was ready for that new relaxing life.

Suddenly thousands of human fighters shot out of the burning atmosphere of Earth.

" Ah-Sarak, lock all weapons to rapid fire. We have to protect the Avengers."

The message button came on. Ah-Sarak pushed it.

" Ah-Jord, this is Ah-Vessk, the flames give a measure of safety for us -we are starting the beast run now ! See you on . . . " The message was cut short.

Ah-Jord grabbed the Joystick as he saw the Avenger squadrons drop towards the flaming planet. They couldn't see the human fighters from their position, but the humans saw them and swerved to follow them down.

Ah-Jord started to dive into the atmosphere, and his squadrons followed him without the need to talk about it. All knew their jobs.

Ah-Jord was hoping to catch the human fighters from behind before they could ambush the Avengers, so he went to boosters, straight down. The fighter caught on fire, from the flames or the fast re-entry he couldn't tell. The gravity was far greater than home, too at this speed. Moving around was difficult.

Ah-Jord and his squadrons shot right through the human horde and all split up, drawing groups of human fighters away from the Avengers.

" Ah-Jord, there are eight fighters on our tail!"

Ah-Jord pulled up quickly and the g-forces nearly made him black out. This low, the smoke was beginning to disappear and the scorched earth was visible as far as he could see.

This view effected the human fighters more than it did him, obviously, because they suddenly lost focus. possibly flying through tears, some of them. But he had no pity for them and their lost world. He looked upon it as a good opportunity. Ah-Jord started to shoot all the plasma bombs he had. He took out all eight of his attackers before they got off a single shot.

"Bring them down to the surface" he instructed his squad. "Let them see the results of their actions. Break their hearts first. Then kill them" he said.

The rest of his squad started to dart in and out of the clouds, seducing human fighters into following them down then shooting all the stunned humans they could.

Suddenly one hundred grey Shecklak fighters dived down into the atmosphere all covered in flames.

Ah-Jord turned on the message sender. " Attention all grey pilots, we need to protect the Avenger squadrons ! Take half your squad and go high - watch for humans coming down. The other half - go right down and cover the Avengers from any attacks."Ah-Jord looked out the cockpit shaft and saw the grey squad splitting neatly into two columns to follow his orders. He saw hordes of human fighters rising from the surface of the planet.

Ah-Sarak started to program the vapor bombs.

"How can that be ?" he asked. Ah-Jord dived and circled the squadron again to make sure.

"Maybe underground bases ?" said Ah-Sarak.

"Ah-Jord - this is Wingman One - the stun-em and gun-em plan isn't working anymore. The Humans are right behind us and they're really mad now !"

"Wingman One - put on your dancing shoes. Lead them upstairs then tippy-toe away. Grey squad high, we'll be leading some humans up to you. Smoke them please."

"Our pleasure" the grey squad leader replied.

"Jeez - this peace is really boring. Forgive me if I fall asleep here" said Ah-Sarak.

Ah-Jord ignored her comment and sent the Shecklak straight up to the ambush zone at the edge of the atmosphere. Suddenly a missile flew to a nearby shecklak fighter and blew it up. A swarm of humans zipped out of the clouds chasing a few Shecklaks, who quickly flipped and dived back down into the cloud cover. Ah-Jord pulled to the side to prevent any damage from other stray shots.

The grey fighters shot off their missiles and the human force ran into a solid wall of death and just disintegrated. Only a few escaped back down into the clouds.

"The Beasts have been set loose !" shouted the radio.

Ah-Jord spoke into the message sender. " All fighters, the Avengers are coming back up - cover them. This is your last chance to show your anger and have some fun ! Remember the three words of victory: ' KILL THEM ALL"

The grey squad gleefully dove into the clouds, looking for human prey.

Ah-Jord quickly pulled the trigger and sent a stream of plasma at a human fighter who had cautiously poked his nose out of the clouds. More and more human survivors were visible now in the thin clouds near the edge of space.

" Ah-Sarak, shoot the vapor bombs at the enemy there. Vaporize those sneaky bastards !" Ah-Sarak grabbed her missile trigger.

Suddenly a message came into the fighter." Ah-Jord - this is Ah-Vessk, I am taking my squad out to space !"

" Ah-Vessk, take my guys with you. I'll stay a minute and cover your ass - we'll drop our last vapor bombs into the soup and see if we can cause an electronic pulse up here and drop the bastards like metal hail !"

" OK - Everybody's out of range. My guys, your guys are all out. The greys have left already ! Anybody left in the fog is a bad guy. It's all yours to waste !"

Ah-Jord left the radio on. There was no more talk. " Ah-Sarak drop the vapor bombs now!"

Ah-Sarak squeezed the trigger. The bombs shot out of the Shecklak and into the clouds." Ah-Jord we have ten secs to get out or we'll drop like a rock too !"

Ah-Jord quickly pulled up. The mist turned into space.

The bombs exploded. They could see the shadowy earth fighters in the clouds, suddenly go out of control and arc in toward the planet as their electronics were stunned.

" Ah-Jord, you made it out !" said the radio.

Ah-Jord looked out the cockpit glass. He saw the Shecklaks all around him, He saw Ah-Vessk's fighter in the far distance.

" Ah-Vessk, we have won the war!"

" Indeed we did!" the radio responded.

Suddenly one lone human fighter appeared above them, like a hawk, dropping silently on the unsuspecting Shecklaks.

"Above you !" came Ah-Vessk's voice.

The human fighter began to shoot and three nearby Shecklak fighters blew to pieces.

Ah-Jord hit the boosters and held down the trigger on the joystick. Nothing shot out. No plasma. No nothing. He was furious. Everywhere he looked , he saw fighters exploding, unable to get out of the way of the lone human kamikaze fighter.

" Ah-Jord , the fighter is closing on us!"

Ah-Jord pulled up to face it." The damned human wants to fight, we got one for him !" shouted Ah-Jord. He boosted and flew up at around one thousand miles an hour .

" Ah-Sarak, do we have a last bomb?"

Ah-Sarak grinned.

" Armed and ready. I'm way ahead of you !"

"Might be a good time to shoot it"

Ah-Sarak pushed the launch trigger. Nothing happened."Ah-Jord, the missile is jammed. And so are the controls."

A missile lazily shot towards Ah-Jord's fighter. Ah-Jord was locked, He couldn't move. Only watch.

Suddenly a Shecklak crashed into the missile. The Shecklak spun around in a circle and took out the last human fighter in a spectacular explosion .

" Ah-Jord , There is a message in memory."

" Put it through !"

Ah-Sarak pushed the play button.

" Well I guess I don't owe you one anymore !"came the voice of Ah-Vessk, probably recorded seconds before she rammed the missile.

Ah-Jord started braking with retro rockets and finally stopped, his Shecklak's controls still frozen. He looked down at the remains of the Shecklak and the human fighter, tangled in a last hug. They continued to burn brightly as they drifted away into earth orbit.

" She gave her life for me," Ah-Jord said. "and we didn't even like each other very much. I always thought she was selfish and deceitful"

"You can't tell a hero from its cover, I guess."

Chapter 22

The ending of the One War

The war was finally over. They'd said it so many times and been attacked immediately afterwards, that it became almost a superstition not to say "The war is over", but this time it really was.

Ah-Jord and the rest of the fleet returned to Moonbase on the farside of the Earth's moon. Around the Earth, there were many thousands of floating human ships all empty and destroyed. Bodies and shrapnel were everywhere. G- forces gathered them all in one common orbit and they had become almost a visible ring around the dead planet.

Ah-Jord , partly injured and tired from the battle, turned on the radio for the last time .

" Moon base, are we clear to land ?" Ah-Jord said.

" You are clear to land."responded the radio.

Ah-Jord turned off the radio ." Well, we survived this war, what do you think will happen to the human race?" asked Ah-Sarak.

Ah-Jord smiled. "I think, in a few thousand years our great grandchildren will have to do it all again." he said.

Ah-Jord slowly lowered his Shecklak onto the vast plain on the moon that would be the alien monitoring base for the next few thousand years - even during and after they moved the moon to Venus orbit.

The hover engines moved the fighter safely into the landing strip blowing up huge clouds of moondust. Ah-Jord turned on the landing engines. The Hover engines turned off. The fighter had landed. The landing engines engaged and Ah-Jord drove the Shecklak down a ramp and through a giant airlock and then into a huge underground parking lot which had been recently been rediscovered. It was 10,000 years old and had been built as an alien base the last time.

Ah-Sarak quickly opened the shaft and jumped out. Ah-Jord slowly climbed out behind her. The air was cool and fresh. All around him were the ships and fighters and tools of war.

Ah-Jord walked to the doors and pushed them open. Ah-Sarak followed. The room was filled with soldiers and pilots. Everyone, everywhere in the base was celebrating and happy.

They had killed off the humans -the most dangerous disease known to the galaxy and the 5-year long war of pain and suffering was finally over.

Until next time.

Chapter **23**

Life goes on

The months of after-war re-organization and re-living of war-stories passed quickly. It was time for laundry to be done. It was time to worry about the future and fix the roof. It was time for the government to take form once again.

A few months after the vaporization of Earth, just off Degos, on Congress Moon, a group of officials from the surviving tens of thousands of civilized worlds had arrived and communication had been taking place all under the able leadership of Chairman Xentos.

Old friends met for the first time in peace. Ah-Goldis and Ah-Drake. Ah-Jord and Ah-Sarak. Ah-ztes and his brother Ah-Nawo.

Of the thousands of bright-eyed children who had been playing together with toys only a few short years ago, this small group were all that were left. They had all been summoned for new assignments.

The congress building was now an ex-military base since the original had been destroyed in war.

Inside, in the new congress, the new jobs and the new laws were being made hourly and veterans and civilians were constantly being given new assignments and new responsibilities.

Ah-Drake and Ah-Goldis became officials in the congress. They took their new positions very seriously. Within the first hour, Ah-Drake stood in Congress and said " It is time to add new laws to make the government stronger and the people safer. For starters all human survivors seen on any of the habitable planets should be exterminated with no questions or regret. We cannot afford to have such a danger anywhere but in a carefully controlled quarantine area." said Congressman Ah-Drake. His suggestion was approved and instantly became law.

" Now, as to the subject of the Humans that we have contained on planet Venus," said Congressman Ah-Goldis, " a previous resolution says that we must keep a colony of these things and try to evolve them into civilized beings again. Some of you believe that this is our burden as intelligent creatures. I disagree with that, but I submit to your views on this matter. What I do suggest is that you put someone in charge who has fought them, who understands them and who will not be swayed by any sentimental feeling towards them. I strongly recommend, as War Leader, that you give that job to Ah-Jord Trey "

The motion was passed in seconds.

Ah-Jord walked out the door. He looked for Ah-Sarak, to say good bye but didn't see her.

He walked to the cargo bay to board his ship for Venus. He would be in orbit around the planet until it was Edenized and would later take over the base on the moon, once it had been moved into Venus orbit.

The loss of Mercury would keep all the planets unstable for a while until an equilibrium was reached, and he would have to be making minute-to-minute decisions on Venus, so he would stay in the ship.

He found Ah-Sarak along with Ah-ztes and Ah-Nawo waiting for him in the boarding area. He walked up to them and looked at them both fondly.

" Well, I guess that this is good bye." he said.

Ah-Sarak did not want to say anything at first. "I'll miss you" she finally whispered.

Ah-ztes walked up to him." I 'll never forget you." he said and gave him a two-handed hand shake and a big smile.

Ah-Jord then walked to Ah-Sarak once more. He hugged her tightly. " Not a day will go by that I will not be thinking of you." Ah-Jord said.

Suddenly the doors opened up on the ship. Ah-Sarak walked back. Ah-Jord walked into the ship, thinking of only of his friends.

Within seconds, the doors closed up, the engines started up and the ship rolled through the air-lock and shot off into the sky.

Ah-Sarak and Ah-ztes looked off to the sunset.

They missed him already.

* * *

Years passed. The humans were awakened and released into the newly cleaned up world, so Ah-Jord was kept busy. Ah-Sarak became a member in congress and a leading advocate of total destruction of all humans. Ah-ztes and his brother went back to Degos as civilians and lived happily back in their home town, helping to rebuild their planet, with the silent help of the Recorder.

Life went on, but it was not the same.

No one thought much anymore. Everyone spoke aloud. Machines, which used to be all living things, more and more became dead metal tools, like the humans had used.

The news always reported mobs finding and killing small bands of humans and also killing those who were thought to be hiding humans. It became the favorite hobby of many.

Riots began often, and often turned violent as people objected to those with different colored skins or different heights or different cultures. Violent crime and murders, which had never existed before, started to grow almost common.

All the civilized races now had characteristics that they had never had before. They were no longer peaceful. At the slightest provocation, they became angry, they became aggressive and they became violent.

. . . they just became Human.

THE END

Neil Lee Thompsett

Neil came to America from Hong Kong when he wa
10. At 11 and 12, he won consecutive Science Fairs i
his school and, at the age of 13, he wrote this book.

Impressive under any circumstances, this is all th
more remarkable because Neil suffers from a seriou
learning disability - he is a Gifted Visual-Spatial Learne
- which, according to Neil, is a great excuse to contin
to think you're smart, even while getting bad grades.

Neil is a Lego-Warrior, a great storyteller and a
average student at Beverly Hills High. He prefers to la
around in his room listening to Jolt Music, real loud.